ALL THE TREES CRYING

Craig Robertson Brown

For my grandchildren and nieces
With love and pride

By the same author:

Monaco Grand Prix-Portrait of a Pageant (Non-Fiction)
An Air That Kills (Fiction)

British Library Cataloguing In Publication Data
A Record of this Publication is available
from the British Library

ISBN 1846853990
978-1-84685-399-9

First Published 2006 by

Exposure Publishing, an imprint of Diggory Press,
Three Rivers, Minions, Liskeard, Cornwall, PL14 5LE, UK
WWW.DIGGORYPRESS.COM

*Thank you...to Valerie, for being there, which matters most of all
to Tea, for the poem
and, with apologies for the deliberate descriptive licence,
to the people of Tobermory, for the closing scenes' inspiration*

When we met
My life changed
But I wasn't to know it
There was a small spark
But only on my part

As time grew on
The closer we became
Our friendship blossoming
Like a rose in bloom

The closer we got
The deeper the feeling
My friend became my lover
Entwined in lust
But not love it seems

Although it was brief
Our illicit passion
I managed to push you away
What have I done?

I want you so badly
I never realised
Now you're gone
No longer able to feel your touch
You're now with her
It breaks my heart

I want to hold you again
To feel you caress my body
To have you take me in your arms
Tell me everything's going to be fine

But that won't happen
Not now
I've lost the fight
It's too late
It breaks my heart

Teresa Fisher

1

Winter

HIS flattened hand felt warm and slightly moist in the small of her back. Yes, he would remember that, though for no obvious reason. It wasn't important, yet somehow it worried him. The thin silk of her blouse felt sealed against his palm as he guided her about the floor, the music thudding in his ears, the vanilla-musk scent of her surging somewhere between his eyes like sweet smoke. She leaned into him, loosening his left hand, and then the music swung into a slower tempo and she eased herself back again, so he had to support her spine, and he was sure she would feel his nervous dampness there, crumpling the fabric, discolouring it.

Someone standing by the window was watching them, a small, dark-suited man with oiled, sweptback hair, a broad forehead and piercing dark eyes, glinting behind horn-rimmed spectacles. A thin smile played about the man's lips, but his eyes were cold and slightly querulous.

He nodded at the stranger. "Is that your husband?"

She shook her head, in confusion rather than reply. Lifting her chin, she moved towards him until her lips brushed his ear. "I can't hear you, Gavin. Too much noise."

The brief intimacy, however trivial, excited him, for it seemed to invite some manner of reciprocation, and he bent over, nuzzling her ear, the silver droplet of her earring touching his lip, his cheek carelessly against hers. "I said, is - "

The music stopped. They broke apart, laughing quietly.

"Now, what was that?" she asked, squeezing his arm.

"Man with glasses behind you. No, don't look. I wondered if he was your husband."

She pulled a sour expression, making no attempt to turn round. Even wearing this grimace, she looked attractive to him, her vaguely sallow face suggesting a kind of classic confidence. "I should hope not," she said, a touch imperiously.

"You haven't seen him."

"You told me not to!"

"Right. Well, he's still there, sort of leering at you."

"Really? Then I absolutely don't intend to look at him."

The DJ gabbled something unintelligible, and the hall exploded once again, distorted rock music ricocheting from the walls amid careening green and red waves of strobic light.

He shook his head, reaching out for her hand, wanting to retain some small physical claim on her, though the beat was too frantic now for dancing close together as they had before. She seemed to dangle loosely from his arm, less a partner than an ornament, and when he tried to spin her round, she screwed up her face again and he felt a resistance, a reserve he read as embarrassment.

"You all right?" He mouthed the words, knowing she wouldn't be able to hear them.

She nodded, but he saw the light go out of her eyes. He began to panic then, afraid that he was losing contact with her. Suddenly the music was a nuisance, no longer an accompaniment but an obstruction, preventing communication. He squeezed her hand, but she didn't respond. Her dancing had become half-hearted, uninvolved, politely mechanical. Instead of moving in rhythmic unison with her, he found himself reduced to a state of perfunctory imitation that perfectly mimicked her aimless robotism.

He studied the floor, willing the music to stop.

Her hand reached out and gently lifted his chin. In her eyes he saw a glint of concern, an interrogative appeal. He shook his head, tight-lipped, dazed by uncertainty.

"Gavin?"

He saw the word form on her lips, though he couldn't hear it, and on the second syllable her front teeth showed in the gloom, with a trace of her lipstick staining the enamel, pink as gum-blood.

The music crashed into silence, leaving a thin ringing in his ears, a wire pinging in his brain. "You look tired," he said, his voice nervously unsteady. "Can I get you a drink?"

She blew air from the corners of her lips, lifting strands of dangling hair. "Some water, perhaps."

When he came back, she was standing by an open window, her face turned towards the darkness outside. On the stage, someone was making an announcement, his voice crackling through an inadequate microphone.

"Here. It's ice-cold."

"Thanks."

"Do you want to stay? Or is it too warm in here?"

She turned and looked at him, offering the briefest of smiles. "Let's just wait till they do a slow one. I want you to hold me."

His eyes widened, and he dipped his head, hoping to hide the reflex that came from a constriction in his throat.

"I'm sorry, Gavin. Have I shocked you?"

"Mmm? No, of course not."

She smiled, coolly regretful. "Oh dear. That was a silly thing to say."

"No. It was a wonderful thing to say." He glanced towards the stage and the dark clutter of sound equipment. "I could ask him to put on something - you know, for us."

8

She arched her eyebrows in a knowing smile. "I see. Are we an item now?"

"No. I mean, I don't know." He shook his head, as if to jolt himself back to reality. "How can we be, Vivienne? You're married."

She took a long drink, peering at him critically over the raised rim of the glass. "Right. I quite forgot." When she lowered her hand, a bead of water slid slowly down her chin like a tear.

"You're funny, you," he said. "So what now?"

"How d'you mean?"

"Shall I ask for something smoochy?"

She stared at him for a moment, then shrugged. "Okay. If you want."

A raucous noise blared out as the DJ went back to work. She watched him threading his way through the dancers, twisting his narrow, boyish shoulders to left and right, stumbling slightly as he stepped on a rolling bottle.

The man behind the sound desk responded almost at once, and Gavin was still foraging back through the milling throng as Celine Dion's voice swelled around them. Vivienne stepped across the floor, squinting for his face amid the swirl of coloured lights. As he drew near, she held out her arms, almost involuntarily, and let him fold her into him.

"This do?" he asked, his lips brushing her ear.

She nodded. The light was back in her eyes again, tiny flickering candles of pleasure. A moment later she freed her arms and draped them over his shoulders, locking her hands behind his neck. Slowly, she pulled him towards her, until he felt her breasts pressing his chest.

He looked at her lips, wondering if it would be safe to kiss them. He let his hands rest on her back beneath the rigid crosspiece of her bra. If he kissed her now, he decided, it would be as a pebble dropped into this still pool, disturbing the reflective calm. There would be other times, perhaps better places. There would be a sweet hunger in the waiting.

For now, he reminded himself how little he knew about this woman. Apart from her name, Vivienne Drexler, and the fact that, at thirty-nine, she was twelve years older than him, he had little by which to judge the wisdom of a relationship. A relationship? Well, she was married, of course, and he understood there were children. She spoke of the family sometimes, but these references were oblique and did not seem to infuse her reflections with any genuine warmth. Indeed, she appeared oddly alone, and he realised that it was this very isolation that attracted him. There was about Vivienne Drexler an engaging aura of cool vulnerability.

He glanced at the clock on the wall. It was five past eleven. "Stay or go?" he asked her, speaking quickly. Celine Dion had faded away, and there would be but a few seconds' pause before a new cacophony.

Waiting for her glass of water, he had scooped up some peanuts from the bar. Now he wondered, in sudden alarm, if they had made his breath smell. He ran his tongue around his teeth, tasting his saliva. It had been right not to kiss her.

She was nodding her head ambiguously, offering up that thin, uncertain smile again. "It's work in the morning," she said.

"I'll walk you home," he offered, and then instantly realised his stupidity, for he had no idea where she lived.

"That's very kind of you," she said, patting his forearm, "but it's not necessary, really."

"I just th-"

"I know." She sighed. "He'll be back now." She glanced over her shoulder and back at him. "I don't want a scene. It's been such a nice night."

"It has, it has," he agreed, absently. These were redundant words, but he was stalling for time while he speculated on the true reason for her rejection. 'I don't want a scene.' What did she mean? Why should there be a 'scene'?

"I've got to get my coat, Gavin. Don't come out. I'll see you in the morning."

"At least let me come to the cloakroom with you."

A storm of rock music raged into the hall, brain-tearing, stomach-wrenching. Vivienne spread her hands helplessly. He read her lips. "I can't hear you."

"I said, I'll come - "

She was waving one hand dismissively in front of his face. He frowned. When she turned towards the exit door, he followed her, head down, bumping against reeling, swerving dancers without seeing them.

The corridor felt cool and vaguely damp, the air permeated by a faint smell of lavatories and wet clothing. Vivienne shifted impatiently from one foot to the other, smoothing down her hair, while the attendant searched for her coat. In a nearby alcove, a door clicked open, and a man emerged, tugging at his fly. Gavin recognised the little man in the dark suit who had stared at them on the dance floor.

The man winked at Gavin, inclining his head towards Vivienne's back. "I think she is very beautiful, your wife."

Gavin tried to identify the foreign accent. It could have been middle-eastern, or maybe Moroccan. "Thanks," he said, curtly, turning aside, only slightly ashamed of his dishonesty.

Ignoring her huffy embarrassment, he helped her on with her coat. They walked to the door. "That chap thought you were my wife," he told her.

"What chap?" She sounded tired and irritable.

"Back there. We saw him inside, gawping."

"I never looked - remember?"

"Well, anyway."

He reached round her and pulled open the door, admitting a steely draught of night air and the brackish smell of coming rain. When they were outside, she stopped and turned to face him. A lamp above the doorway bleached the colour from her face, making her look fragile and anxious. He wondered again about kissing her.

"Thanks, Gavin. I enjoyed myself. It was good."

Somehow this sounded to him like a recitation. The emotions she hinted at didn't show in her eyes.

"I could walk with you," he said.

"No!" she insisted, a little too loudly. Then, more quietly, she added, "I mean, like I said, it's not necessary. It's not worth it." She turned up the collar of her coat. "You wouldn't understand."

He shrugged. "I could try."

Once more, she touched his arm. "It's been a nice evening. Don't let's spoil it."

It was starting to rain. In the cold lamplight, a single bead rolled down her cheek, and silently he asked himself if this was a raindrop or a tear.

"It's late, Gavin. I have to go."

"Goodnight then."

Without reply, she turned and walked slowly away. He watched for a moment, then blew her a kiss. For now, it was the best he could do.

2

RAJ KUMARI fiddled thoughtfully with the thick folds at the front of his turban. "Why do you want to know?" he asked.

"Curiosity," Gavin replied.

Kumari thumped the desk with the side of his fist. "Oh, come on! You'll have to do better than that. You're asking me to divulge confidential information."

"I know. I realise it's difficult."

"Difficult? It's not difficult at all. It's unethical and it's a gross breach of company regulations. I could get the sack."

"I know." His voice trailed away. "That's why I don't like asking you."

"So why are you asking me? Is this important? Do you have a problem?"

"No," Gavin said, wearily, "I don't have a problem. I think she may have one."

"So what's it to you?"

"I danced with her at the Christmas party. She said things."

Kumari manipulated his beard irritably with both hands. "She said things? What things? What does she want?"

"It's not what she wants."

The young sikh rose to his feet and spread his hands wide. "Gavin, you'll have to come clean. You're asking me to give you information from an employee's personal file. You have no authority to request these details and, apparently, no reason for wanting them."

"I know."

"Don't bloody keep saying 'I know'. The fact is, we could both be dismissed."

"I - " He shook his head in frustration. "Yes. It's all right, Raj. I shouldn't have asked. I'll find another way."

"This woman. Have you got something going? Is that it?"

"No, of course not. I hardly know her."

"Which is why you want the information."

"Sort of."

"Gavin, Gavin." Raj Kumari sighed and sat down again. "What happened to your powers of communication? If you really want to know about Mrs Drexler, the person to approach is Mrs Drexler. You don't come asking for her personnel file."

"I know."

"Gavin, shut up!" He nibbled nervously at the side of his thumbnail, his narrowed eyes roaming over the doodles on his desk blotter. Then, with an air of reluctant finality, he pushed back his chair and strode to a row of metal filing cabinets along the wall. Pulling open a drawer, he flicked through the marker tabs and withdrew a bulky file.

Gavin waited, arms folded, watching him. He knew Raj would help him, or he wouldn't have asked.

Raj dropped the file on his desk and opened it at the first page. He pulled a handkerchief from his pocket and blew his nose extravagantly, as though this act might clear his mind for what he was about to say. "I'm busting for a pee, Gavin. I'm leaving this on the desk."

"Right."

"You've come to see me. I'm trusting you to behave professionally while I'm gone for a few minutes. Otherwise it's not my look-out. Okay?"

"I understand. I appreciate this, Raj."

"I've done nothing. Just remember that."

"Sure. Thanks for the help."

Raj went to the door, yanked it open and looked back into the room. "Gavin."

"Yes?"

"Shut up!"

Gavin waited for a few seconds before sidling up to the back of Raj's chair. No-one came in, and the corridor outside was quiet. He leaned over the chair and peered at the printed details on the first page of the document. It would not do to be caught copying anything, so he hoped to rely on his memory.

The first part was easy. Name, address and date of birth: Vivienne Anne Drexler; 72 Launceston Road - just around the corner; born 5th May, 1966. He whispered the date. He would remember her birthday, send a card up to her office, or perhaps a bunch of flowers. Flicking the page over, he found a neatly-typed CV with some copy certificates clipped to the back. As he traced a finger lightly over the text, he felt a swelling underneath, and he lifted the A4 sheets and saw a handwritten letter, several pages long, set out in blue fountain pen in a neat hand, the leaves apparently taken from a watermarked pad.

He glanced at the door. He would rather not be doing this when Raj Kumari came back. If anyone else came in...well, he would not allow himself to think about that. His mouth was dry now, his fingers fluttering over the paper, and he tried to snatch quick visual bites from the long screed of the letter, to get some vague idea of its content and significance without stopping to read each page. She had signed it 'Vivienne A. Drexler', with the determined flourish of a looping underline. It was a good, strong signature, stylishly feminine. As his eyes danced madly over the script above, random, emotive words spat back in his face: 'painful'; 'Jack wouldn't stand for it'; 'he twisted my arm' (did she mean literally?); 'might as well give up'; 'talk to someone'; and, ominously submissive, 'not while the children are young'.

It didn't tell him much, it lacked detail as a largely unread document, but for now it was enough. He closed the file and stepped back, leaning against the wall with a slightly ridiculous air of contrived nonchalance. If someone came in and saw him loitering there, gazing vacuously into inner space, he reflected, they would surely find his presence as suspicious as if he were caught extracting classified information from the files. His guilt could hardly be disguised.

The door opened and he held his breath, only to release it in relief when he saw Raj Kumari. Without looking at Gavin, Raj scooped up the file and hurriedly replaced it in the filing cabinet.

"Thanks," Gavin said.

Raj sat down with his back to Gavin. "Got things to do. Busy time."

"Yes. Of course. I'll be off then." He walked to the door. "I - uh - appreciate your - "

"Nothing happened, remember. I haven't even seen you."

There was nothing more to be said. Gavin crept through the door, clicked it quietly shut behind him and almost glided along the corridor, hoping to make the most of his invisibility.

His office was a half-glassed rectangle partitioned off from the main administrative suite, and Gavin sat down heavily in his executive chair and gazed dreamily at his secretary, Carolyn Vickers, as she squinted myopically ahead of her, trying to start up her computer. After a minute, he screwed a sheet of paper into a tight ball and threw it against the glass. Carolyn turned and stared at him.

"Any chance of a cup of coffee, Carolyn?"

"Well, good morning, Gavin," she said, rather labouring the tone. "Why, yes, I'm quite well, thank you. And yourself?"

"Oh, are we in a strop this morning?" he asked, arching his eyebrows.

"You might be. I'm fine."

"Right. I just thought - "

"Maybe if you tried going out and coming in again." She spun round and carried on tapping the keyboard. Gavin saw the screen flicker into multi-coloured life. He sat quietly watching the curve of her back, the white suspension bridge outline of her bra through the thin pink cotton of her blouse. His mind drifted back to last night, to the dance, the brain-crunching music, the reek of spilt beer on the floor, Vivienne Drexler folded so comfortably into his arms.

Emerging from his reverie, he found her standing in front of him. "Let's try again, shall we? Good morning, Gavin."

"Good morning, Carolyn," he responded, a touch nervously.

"Right, that's better. Would you like a coffee?"

"Thank you."

"What for? I haven't brought it yet. You're supposed to say 'please'. Then I go out and come back with the coffee. That's the bit when you say 'thank you'."

"Hmm. You're in a funny mood this morning," he observed, shaking his head. He looked at her legs. She had on a short, dark blue pleated skirt. Her knees were a little thick, but she had finely sculpted ankles and her thighs were - inviting. "Do I get a biscuit?"

14

"So far, you don't get anything."

He sighed deeply, leaning back in the chair. "Carolyn, please may I have a cup of coffee? Don't bother with the biscuit, I think I've run out of time."

She laughed, turned and went out, shaking the dark bob of her hair. He watched her go to the outer door, take a tray from the shelf above the photocopier and pause to stroke the back of her hair with a free hand.

"Carolyn!"

Waving the tray in front of her like a fan, she turned back, her faint smile tolerantly imperious.

"Do you know Vivienne Drexler?" he asked.

She knitted her brow for a moment, thinking. "A little. She works in Marketing. Always seems a bit snooty."

"Do you think so?"

"Well, you did ask."

He was surprised to find that her judgment offended him. Already he felt vaguely protective of Mrs Drexler, though he couldn't properly understand why. His own unease intrigued him. How well did he know himself, never mind Vivienne Drexler?

Carolyn was staring at him, her mouth falling open. "What's this about then? Here, you and her, you're not - ?"

His reaction was probably too hasty, but the impulse overtook him. "Course not! Anyway, she's married."

"Doesn't make much difference these days," she said, with a smirk. "So long as you don't get found out."

"There's nothing to find out. I told you, I just - "

"All right, all right." She waved one hand in a placating gesture, her face mobile with suppressed amusement. "Don't get cranky. I'll fetch your coffee."

Gavin leaned his elbows on the desk to make a shadowed tent of his arms and hands, and rested his head inside, fingers gently massaging his temples. He gazed at the doodles on his blotter. Next to a childish picture of the sun, he wrote her name: 'Vivienne Anne Drexler'. Then he crossed it out and waited for the coffee.

As she always did, she brought his morning coffee in a white china cup and saucer with a silver spoon and, angled in the saucer, two digestive biscuits.

"Thanks, Carolyn."

"Okay," she said, a softness in her voice that slightly surprised him.

"I - er - I didn't see you at the dance."

"Probably because I wasn't there."

He nodded absently. "It would have been nice."

"How do you mean?"

"I'd have bought you a drink. We could have had a dance. We could have talked."

"We talk every day," she said, tossing her head. "Ah, I think you're going soft, mama's boy."

15

The taunt hurt him, because it came from someone he liked. He drank some of the coffee, swilling it round his mouth, feeling the sting. His eyes were on the blotter again, as he heard the door click shut.

Mama's boy. Why did she think that? The words seared something deep inside him, like an inflammation. Yet, how absurd to feel slighted by a girl he hardly knew, five years his junior. He wished, pointlessly of course, that he'd never confided in her now, never told her anything of his private life. He knew next to nothing of hers.

From a framed photograph hanging on the wall behind his head, his parents' faces, benignly protective, gazed down at him. They were pictured sitting in the sun on folding canvas chairs against a low box hedge, their feet quaintly splayed on the daisy-speckled lawn. Gavin recalled the day, the sun's hot stain on his back as he set up the photograph, the thin cat's pee reek of the box irritating his nostrils as he tried, with minimal success, to tease a smile from either pale mask. His father clutched an upright walking stick between his thighs, while his mother, hands cupped in front of her, held a glass dish of fruit cocktail with a glinting silver spoon. It was the well-manicured garden of his sister's cottage in Dorset, and they were celebrating his mother's sixtieth birthday.

That, if not directly addressed, was Carolyn's point, he realised. In her sixtieth year, his mother was still burdened with her son's presence in the house. With a generation between them, Mrs Lake still washed his underpants, made his bed and put a hot meal on the table for him when he returned from work. She was as much his housekeeper as she was his mother. Sometimes, in a self-consoling moment which he nonetheless suspected might be merely selfish, he told himself that she liked having him there, for his father's death from cancer at the age of sixty-five had robbed her of the male companionship she had enjoyed for almost forty years.

"I take it you don't sleep with her," Carolyn had said, acidly, when he had rashly disclosed his domestic arrangements.

Curiously, this barbed remark had offended him rather less than he might have expected. He found his indignation mitigated, or perhaps thinly overlaid, by the merest patina of excitement that she had offered him a vaguely sexual reference. It was a perversely pleasurable insult.

Launceston Road. He knew where that was. It ran steeply uphill, across the main road bordering the waste ground behind the office block. Some of the residents' cars were parked at the kerb with their front wheels turned inwards to prevent them from running away if the brakes failed. He thought of strolling up there after work, just to stretch his legs; but then, of course, it would surely be more a stretch of his imagination that motivated him. If he waited, loitering suspiciously, at the foot of the hill, he might see her coming along on her way home. She wouldn't walk with him, though, for fear of her husband seeing them together. He recalled her misgivings at the dance. There was something going on there. 'Jack wouldn't stand for it'. That was what she had written. Now he had to find out what she meant, what it was he wouldn't stand for. He needed to find out what she was afraid of. She had leaned against him and then drawn back into herself. That made her seem available but unattainable, willing but reluctant, open yet enigmatic.

Carolyn was back, shuffling papers in the doorway. "Here!" She held out a fan of A4 sheets.

"What's this?"

"I told you last week. They're sending me on a course. It's the timetable and programme."

He took the pages. "I'll look at them later."

"Right. Do you want a temp?"

"No, they're useless, expensive and intimidating. I'll manage."

"Get it sorted, Gavin, your insecurities are showing."

"Yes. Blame my mother."

"Oh, I do, believe me." She drew back, then leaned forward, fixing him with a steely glare. "That woman. That Mrs Drexler."

"What about her?"

"Just be careful. Her old man - he's a nutter."

"Oh. And why is that something I should beware of?"

"Apparently he shot someone."

"What, with a gun?"

She blinked in exasperation. "With a water-pistol. Of course, with a gun!"

"I see. Did they die?"

"I don't think so. Does it matter? I mean, if someone's going round shooting people."

"To them it does. It makes a difference."

"Gavin." She lowered her head to gaze levelly into his eyes. "Don't even go there, all right?"

"As a matter of fact, I haven't - been there."

"No, but you'd like to, right? Well, I suggest you curb your curiosity. Remember, it killed the cat."

"Why are you giving me advice, all of a sudden?"

"Because I'm your P.A. I'm paid to look after you."

He turned away, scratching the thick hair at the back of his neck. He needed a haircut, he thought. "Carolyn."

"What?"

"Why do you need to go on a course? You know it all already."

"That supposed to be sarcastic?"

"No, not at all. It's just an observation."

"Hmm. Like I said, you need to be careful who you observe."

That was her parting gift of youthful wisdom. He abandoned his concentration to the capricious currents of his idle reverie, though he allowed himself a further brief study of Carolyn's back, seen through fingermarked glass, as she bent over her desk, her blouse too tight, her skirt too short - her knees too plump for unqualified admiration.

Someone, or something, bumped on the floor above, a dull percussion on the ceiling over his head. That, he reflected, was the office where she worked: Vivienne Anne Drexler, born 5th May, 1966. Lipstick runny on her teeth as pink as guava juice. The hot poultice of his fevered hand in the small of her back. Hints of cinnamon in her hair.

Her old man - he's a nutter.

He could simply walk up there. Some pretext would have to be invented, but that would be easy enough. The girls in the office would stare, exchange glances, maybe snigger behind their hands. Then, when he had left, she would have to wave away their idiotic challenges. Working women were like that; they thrived on the tantalizing possibility of scandal. Still, she would hardly warm to him for exposing her to speculation. It would not do to pitch her into a defensive state, encouraging her to set up barriers.

There was a way. Occasionally he lunched at *The Eagle*. It was only five minutes' walk along the road. He had taken Carolyn there the day she started. They had installed themselves snugly in a sunless corner booth, all darkly polished wood and leatherette seats, the faintest drifting aroma of chips and tobacco. The food was hot, cheap and sensible. They had no music, so you could hear yourselves speak. Pensioners in caps sat by the window and coughed softly to one another. A tabby cat, rotund on patrons' generosity, stalked the tables, meekly expectant.

Almost as if it responded to some unbidden instinct of its own, he saw his hand reach for the phone and dial her extension. He waited, his mind racing for control.

"Good morning, Viv Drexler."

That, at least, came as a relief. He hadn't had to ask for her and risk being challenged for his identity. It was a small convenience, but in that instant it somehow seemed important.

"Good morning, Vivienne. It's Gavin."

"Hello," she said, flatly.

"I was wondering if you got home all right."

"Of course. Why shouldn't I?"

"No reason," he said, feeling slightly stupid. "It - it was all right then, when you got in?"

"What do you mean?"

"I just - oh, it doesn't matter." He drew a deep breath. "It was good to see you, anyway. I enjoyed the evening."

"Yes. Me too."

"I hope you didn't get wet walking."

"No. Actually Gavin, I am quite busy."

"Sure. Only I wanted to ask you something."

There was a silence, just the sound of her breathing.

"What is it, Gavin?"

The mercurial interaction of sensors and stimuli in his brain told him in a millisecond that he must at once blurt out his appeal, or lose it among the smouldering detritus of disintegrated confidence.

18

"I had an idea," he said, and he sensed the edginess of a tremor in his voice.

He heard her sigh, further unnerving him. "I really think you should get to the point."

"Yes. Vivienne, can I buy you lunch? We could go to *The Eagle*. The food's not bad."

"I see. Well, I'm glad you think enough of me to offer me a meal that's not bad."

Absurdly, he heard his heart pounding, and there was a sudden dryness in his mouth. "Well, what I mean is - "

Her unexpected laughter interrupted him, and for a fleeting moment he was left to deduce from its timbre whether her response was sympathetic or scornful.

"Did I say something funny?" he asked, cautiously.

He heard her clear her throat and then exhale with a soft mewling sound, as though her mirth had soothed her. "Dear Gavin," she murmured.

"It's up to you," he said, feeling the opportunity slipping from his grasp.

"How can it be up to me?" The laughter still hung in her voice. "You phoned me, remember. It's your invitation. No use being faint-hearted, Gavin."

"I know. I really would like you to say 'yes'."

"Hmm. Why don't you try fixing a day and time?"

His throat locked up. In that breathless interval, trying to speak was as futile as struggling to extract money from a time-delay safe.

"Talk to me, Gavin. Make me an offer I can't refuse."

"Tomorrow. Meet me in Reception at twelve-thirty."

"Gavin, you're so bold!"

He ignored the sarcasm, preferring to pursue a victory. The receiver was shaking in his hand, the plastic slippery with sweat.

He took a deep breath. "Is that all right then?"

She was laughing again, this time a high, girlish squeal that jarred his ear. "For God's sake go away! I'll see you tomorrow."

Gavin sat back in his chair, carefully replacing the receiver in the handset. His hand was trembling, and he bunched it tightly into a fist. He sat there staring at the telephone, as though it had made the call itself. A slow, bemused smile crept over his face.

3

VIVIENNE DREXLER, eyes downcast, listlessly stirred a glistening mound of lasagne with her fork.

"Penny for them," Gavin offered.

Slowly, she looked up and raised her eyebrows. "That's a strangely old-fashioned remark."

"You're calling me old-fashioned?"

"No. I didn't actually say that."

"Perhaps you thought it."

She was prodding her food again. "No, I was thinking something quite different."

"Like, 'Why did I choose the lasagne?'"

She smiled. "No, it's fine, honestly." Shaking her head, she switched the fork to her other hand. "I suppose I was wondering why I'm here."

"Because I asked you."

"You know what I mean."

"Okay. Because you're an attractive lady, whom I find rather fascinating."

"Hmm. I see. You obviously don't know me."

"Exactly. That's why we're both here."

"Right. So this isn't just a casual lunch invitation. You have a hidden agenda."

He shrugged. "If you like. At the dance - you seemed sort of friendly."

"You seemed attentive."

A sudden flash of sunlight from the opening door distracted him. "Don't you know those girls?"

She peered cautiously over her shoulder. "My boss's P.A. and some of her mates. I tolerate them but I wouldn't say I knew them."

The haughty response reminded him of Carolyn's remark: 'Always seems a bit snooty.' He would wonder about the judgment, or misjudgment, for a long time afterwards, like someone repeatedly picking at a sore. If this were a blemish in Mrs Drexler's character profile, he wanted it to go away. He didn't want to have to measure it or justify it.

She was bending down, reaching for something under the table. Her blouse gaped open at the top, briefly revealing a dark slot of cleavage, the glossy fullness of her right breast. "You might like to see these." She held out a thin plastic wallet, open to display two photographs.

He took the wallet. In one photograph, a slender, dark-haired girl, whom he judged to be about seventeen, smiled generously at the camera from her perch astride a mountain bike, one sun-tanned thigh angled upwards by the raised pedal.

"That's Lizzie," Vivienne told him. "My darling daughter."

He nodded appreciatively. "Attractive girl."

"Yes, I think so. But then I'm prejudiced."

"And the other one's your son?"

She leaned towards him, elbows on the table either side of her plate, her hands cupping her face as she gazed proudly at the pictures. "Yes. His name is James, after my father. James is sixteen. He loves cricket, and he plays chess for the club at school. That was taken at a friend's barbecue. Don't you just love the chef's hat and the Donald Duck apron?"

He grinned, handing back the wallet. "He looks like a boy with a sense of humour."

"Yes." She bent over again to replace the photos in her bag, allowing him a second glimpse of the tops of her breasts, and the lacy edge of a white bra. "It's difficult sometimes."

He bit into his hot beef baguette, feeling the brittle bread score his gums. "How do you mean?"

"Oh well, you know. There's not too much laughter in our house." She picked up her fork again. "Anyway, you don't want to hear all that stuff."

Surprising himself, he reached across the table and traced a finger lightly over her wrist. "Perhaps I do. Try me."

"How's your baguette?"

For a moment, he stared at her in silence. He could feel the meat sticking to his teeth. "Please, Vivienne."

"What?"

"I care about you. If you're not happy, at least I can - "

"That's ridiculous. You don't know anything about me."

"Like I said, that's why we're here. To find out about each other."

"Oh. I'm not altogether sure about this 'each other'."

"Er - right. Do I seem to threaten you?"

"Threaten me? No, of course not." She waved the fork at him dismissively. "Eat your lunch."

He wondered about the photographs. Had she introduced them to ease the flow of conversation - in which case, the ploy had been less than successful - or to underline the point that she was fully committed elsewhere? This could be her way of saying, 'Nice of you to ask, but you can see that I'm settled. I don't need your intervention in my life.'

Or did she? A house starved of laughter, she had admitted. What did that mean? The letter troubled him again. *Jack wouldn't stand for it...might as well give up.* What had she thought of giving up? Her home? Her marriage? Her life, for God's sake? When he had offered her a sympathetic ear, all she could say was, 'Eat your lunch.'

So, very well, he ate his lunch. Now, instead of chewing carefully at the stick of bread, he forced it into his mouth, tearing at the unyielding mass, punishing his gums and palate until he felt they might bleed at any moment. Hunger had nothing to do with it. The more his appetite diminished, the faster he crushed and pulped his painful meal.

Vivienne watched him, leaning back in her chair. Half her lasagne lay uneaten on the plate, congealing around the discarded fork. Neither of them spoke. Gavin returned her gaze with a concentration that bordered on defiance. It was as though, rather than eating the baguette, he raced to dispose of it in a machine-like process engendered by trance. What he consumed with relish was Vivienne's face; her eyes improbably blue against that lightly-tanned, vaguely olive skin; the soft pink bow of her lips enhanced by the palest tint of lipstick, a thin daub of meat sauce clinging engagingly to the corner of her mouth; the faintest suggestion of freckles he had not noticed before, scattered on her upper cheeks and around her eyes.

"You're staring at me," she said.

"I'm sorry. I didn't mean to."

"You had that far-away look. Like something was on your mind."

"I was just thinking..."

"What?"

"Those photographs. You didn't show me one of Jack."

"How do you know his name's Jack?"

"Well - you told me, didn't you?"

"I don't think so," she said, guardedly. "I don't remember telling you anything about him."

"No. So is there a reason for that?"

"What do you mean - a reason?"

"Is he someone you don't like to talk about? I mean, you seem proud of your children."

"I am."

"But not of him?"

She sighed. "Okay, so I don't carry his face about with me. Gavin, where is all this going?"

"I - look, it's none of my business - "

"You're absolutely right. So can we just leave it, please?"

With a paper napkin, he wiped the crumbs from the corners of his mouth. "I've gone and loused it up now. I've upset you."

She turned out her lower lip, showing the wetness inside. "No. It's okay. So long as we understand each other."

"I'm not sure we do," he said quietly, as if to himself.

She pushed her plate aside and took a last long draught from her lager. "You're a kind man, Gavin. It was good of you to buy me lunch."

"So that's it. We're done."

"Don't say it like that. There'll be other times."

"Will there? How will we manage that?"

She laughed. "Sounds like you want us to engineer something."

"No," he replied, seriously, "I just hope we can be friends. I'd like to make you happy."

"Maybe that's rather presumptuous of you," she said, pulling a face.

"Hmm. You mean, I'm getting above myself."

"Gavin, it was intended as an observation, not an insult." She reached for her bag again, dropped it in her lap and took out a compact mirror, which she unfolded to study her face. "Can I borrow your napkin?"

"Shall I get you a clean one?"

"No. You didn't tell me I had crap all over my face. I look like a commando."

Now it was his turn to laugh. "You have a gift for exaggeration."

That feeling he'd had at the party returned, and he found himself wanting to kiss her again, holding back the urge to lunge forward and kiss her on the side of the lips so he could taste the smear of mince deposited there, maybe lick it away with the point of his tongue.

"You're doing it again," she said.

"What?"

"Staring at me. Is my mouth okay now?"

"It looks lovely to me."

"Gavin!"

Sometimes, he thought, you have to go for broke. "He doesn't hit you, does he? I'd hate it if he hit you."

She slumped back in her chair, as if to give herself space to consider a response. "Don't do this, please. You know I don't want to discuss it."

"Why? Because it's painful? How is it painful?"

She put her bag on the table and snapped it shut. "I have to go back. Thank you for lunch." Her tone was brisk and taut, the way she clipped her handbag.

"I'll walk with you, if you're not ashamed to be seen with me."

"Now you're being ridiculous."

After the sombre light of the pub, the sudden wash of steely winter sunshine at the opened door dazzled and surprised him, and he reached for the sunglasses he kept in his shirt pocket.

"Looks like you're travelling incognito," Vivienne said. "At least they aren't those dreadful mirror things."

"The only advantage with them is, people can't see where you're looking."

"I know. They're sinister. Murderer's glasses."

He shook his head, sniggering. "I think I said something about exaggeration."

"Jack's got a p- . No, it doesn't matter."

"Your husband wears them?"

"I said, it doesn't matter."

A team of builders had moved on to the open ground behind the offices. Green and white cabins were already arranged in an L-shape just inside newly-erected steel gates giving access from the road. Opposite the first cabin, a large wooden sign bore details of the proposed development, and underneath it a smaller notice urged those entering the site to wear hard hats. Whether, now that the land had been requisitioned, it would be considered trespass to cross it, Gavin was uncertain; but he had regularly used this route to the main road and decided that they should press on regardless.

Next to a cement-mixer, a huddle of workmen, some wearing yellow helmets, sat on folding chairs, eating their lunches from plastic boxes. A few drank from cans of lager, others smoked, gazing listlessly into the distance. A man in a blue woollen hat, pulled down tightly so that he appeared to have no ears, pored over a newspaper crossword, tapping a ballpoint pensively against his teeth.

As though sensing some vague threat from the group, Gavin placed a hand protectively in the small of Vivienne's back as they walked past. She glanced at him but made no comment.

"Fancy a drink, darlin'?" One of the men, grinning broadly, held out a can.

Instinctively, Gavin applied a gentle pressure to his companion's back.

A man standing in the cabin doorway whistled shrilly and winked.

Gavin shook his head and chuckled softly. Instead of cursing the workmen, he found himself infused with a quiet, private pride, for he suspected that although the men naturally ignored him, he was nonetheless the subject of their envy, just as surely as Vivienne Drexler, poised and disdainful of their attention, had attracted their lascivious speculation. He knew, of course, that this woman was not his possession, in itself suggesting a pride absurdly misplaced; but still the brief warmth of the incident succoured him, and he stepped ahead with a self-satisfied smile upon his face.

In the back door vestibule, she unbuttoned her coat, sighed and ran both hands back through her hair to the nape of her neck.

"You okay?" he asked her.

She nodded.

It was quiet there, little more than an undecorated fire exit, and he thought once again about kissing her, not on the lips, not yet, but perhaps on the side of the cheek in a gesture of uncomplicated friendship. He caught the sweet tang of her perfume, released by the building's warmth, and he surprised himself with the sudden awareness of wanting her, longing to put his arms around her and hold her for a moment, fleeting and yet timeless.

"I'll see you around then," he said.

A light, ambiguous laugh, an almost girlish toss of the head. "I hope so. Thank you for inviting me."

"My pleasure. Maybe we can - "

"Do it again?"

"Yes. I'd like that."

She stood staring at him, unblinking. Slowly, she wetted her lips with the tip of her tongue. "I ought to get back."

"Yes. Look, I'm sorry if I - "

"No, don't!" She put out a hand, touching him briefly on the shoulder. "Just - don't spoil it."

He nodded submissively. "You're a very private person, aren't you?"

"Until I really know someone, yes."

"Perhaps trust doesn't come easily."

"Hmm. Perhaps you shouldn't try to psycho-analyse me."

He wondered at the defensiveness of this woman. Was this a form of aggression or self-assertion or simple insecurity? How could he get close enough to her to find out? Was she warning him off, or testing his determination?

"I'll let you go," he said, and there was a weariness in his tone that was almost deliberate.

"Right." She waited. "Haven't you forgotten something?"

"I don't think so."

Without moving from the spot where she stood, Vivienne craned quickly forward and planted a feather-light kiss on Gavin's cheek. "There, I've done it for you," she murmured.

Gazing at her, his eyes mirroring disbelief, he touched the place with his fingertips.

She saw the flush of surprise on his face. "Don't say a word," she said.

4

JANET LAKE brandished the phone at arm's length, as though the instrument repelled her. "A woman for you," she said gruffly.

Gavin took the phone and weighed it in his hand for a moment. "Gavin Lake," he said, finally.

Her voice sounded quiet and far away, but there was no mistaking it. "Hello, stranger. Not heard from you."

The feeling was like a fluttering, a small bird trapped in his chest. "Hello. This is a surprise."

"And do you like surprises?"

"Sometimes. I mean, yes. How did you get my number?"

"That'd be telling. Is it not all right to call you?"

He glanced over his shoulder, and immediately felt foolish for his attempt at secrecy, for even thinking of it. "No, it's fine, honestly."

"Right. Only I was thinking about lunch. We did say we might do it again."

"I remember." His heart was racing, sending acidic saliva slapping into his mouth. "I - what had you in mind?"

"Well..." She carried on speaking, but the rest of what she had to say was lost when a movement at his shoulder distracted him, and his mother stood, hawk-like, staring down at him.

Pointlessly, he covered the receiver with his hand. "What is it, Mum?" He tried to keep the irritation out of his voice.

"Who is it? Who are you talking to?"

"No-one if you interrupt me."

Her face subsided into an injured scowl. "I was only asking."

A dismissive wave with the back of his hand turned her away, and he hunched his shoulders over the phone. "I'm sorry, Vivienne. I missed that."

"Who's there with you?"

He wondered: could she possibly be jealous? "It's only my mother."

"Oh. Is she visiting?"

"What? No, she - don't worry about it."

"I'm not worried," she said, with a brief snort of laughter. "Why should I be worried?"

"No reason." He knew he hadn't got the measure of this woman; perhaps he never would. There was something *spiky* about her, something that almost scared him, but in a nice kind of way. "Say what it was you wanted to say."

"I was going to invite you for lunch."

"Oh, right. When did you - ?"

"Wednesday. I'll cook."

"You'll what?"

"Are you a bit deaf, Gavin? I said I'll cook. I'm off that day for the double-glazing people. I can do us something in the morning."

"You mean, come round to you?"

He heard her sigh. "No, Gavin, I'll get a trolley and wheel a big pot of beef casserole round to the park and we can sit under a tree and - of course, come round to the house. I'm making you lunch, okay?"

"Uh - yes. Great."

"Try sounding like you mean it, Gavin."

"Sorry. And - what about your - you know?"

"He doesn't control my lunch-times. He'll be at work. That's why I have to be there."

"Okay. What time?"

"Come at twelve-thirty. Bring some red wine. Be happy."

That was it; he wanted desperately to be happy. That was the only response that made any sense. For days he had turned Mrs Drexler's ethereal image over and over in his mind, struggling to construct some machinery to facilitate another, more meaningful, more - he hardly dared formulate the word in his brain - *intimate* meeting with this enigmatic woman; and now, out of the blue, she was building the opportunity for him, inviting him to her home, inching open a door in her private life. Yet, in anticipating this modest apocalypse, Gavin found himself mired in a curious amalgam of elation and apprehension. As he imagined the door swinging open, so he recognised not merely the welcoming face of Vivienne Drexler, but also the previously undisclosed layers of his own *persona*; for he had already confided to his conscience that he viewed lunch and a glass of wine with this vaguely spectral friend as simple instruments to unlock a veritable catacomb of interwoven ambitions and emotions. The vital question was: did he seek a friendship or a relationship? How much of Vivienne Drexler did he want? How much of her attention could he afford to engage?

There was a certain haughtiness in Janet Lake's tone as she informed him, "That's a rather good wine."

He was standing diffidently at the dusty wine-rack in the scullery, drawing the stacked bottles towards him, one by one, angling his neck to read the labels. A South African red with an eye-catching gold sheath over the cork dangled from his left hand.

"Are you saying that to impress me or to reprimand me?" He didn't turn to face her, but spoke to the hovering dark blur in the corner of his eye.

"What an odd question!" She fiddled nervously with her hair. "What do you want it for?"

"Now who's asking odd questions? To drink, of course."

She sighed. "I mean, is it for a special occasion?"

"Lunch with a friend, that's all."

"I see. I don't know what your father would think."

He straightened up and turned to stare at her. "He's dead, Mum. It doesn't matter what he might think. Anyway, wine's for drinking, not storing." He waved a languid hand over the rack. "They're not ornaments. Cars are for driving. Money's for spending. Wine's for drinking."

Tight-lipped, with glassy eyes, she gave him a cynical smile. "Very well. I don't need your philosophy of life, Gavin. So who's your friend?"

"Oh, just someone at work."

"Why don't you just go to the pub?"

"We have. Now she's inviting me to lunch."

"She?" The word was charged with emphasis.

"Is that a problem?"

A short, derisive laugh. "Not to me it's not. Is it anyone I know?"

"Since you don't know anyone I work with, I should hardly think so."

"Right. Does this girl have a name?"

"She's a woman, not a girl. And she does have a name."

Mrs Lake waited, peering at him critically, until sufficient time had passed for the hiatus to become pointless. "That's it then," she said.

"It's only a bottle of wine, Mum."

"Oh well, if you don't want to talk about it." She flapped her hands in front of her face, as if swatting away a fly. "Enjoy your lunch."

He took this instruction to mean that the conversation was at an end. There could be no more suitable outcome, he reflected, for his mother's predictably conventional attitude to relationships would ensure that she disapproved of his burgeoning friendship with Vivienne Drexler and would make a nuisance of herself in regularly reminding him of her opinion.

He appreciated, of course, that it was his own fault for being there at all. Demonstrably, he was in the wrong place at the wrong time. A kind of comfortable inertia had settled over him like a warm, if sometimes itchy, blanket. His mother's love for him was deep and doubtless, but she was worried by his shiftlessness and by his social isolation.

"About time you had a girl-friend," he recalled her saying, in an accusatory tone.

That was two years ago, on the afternoon of his twenty-fifth birthday. He smiled to himself, remembering the moment, a little sadly, for his father was there, urging him, in a gaseous voice reduced to a muffled croak by the throat cancer that would shortly kill him, to make a wish as he blew out the massed candles on the cake Janet Lake had baked for the occasion. The wish, quietly articulated to the fates on Gavin's quivering lips, was for his dad to live a few years longer; but it had not been granted, and within six weeks Roland Lake was gone, snuffed out as surely as the candles had been.

Cheap, spindly things, those candles. They bent in the ferocious heat of his accumulated age, dripping tears of blue wax on to the cake's snowy icing. Everyone got a slice of speckled wax, a plastic pox, to munch with dutiful grins once the acrid smoke had dispersed.

"Plenty time," he told his mother. "There'll be someone. I'm not worried."

28

"Really? You're not - ? You know."

"Not what?" He knew perfectly well what she meant, but he derived a grim pleasure from pretending otherwise.

She raised her eyebrows despairingly. "A quarter of a century's gone by, Gavin. You'll be left behind in the rush."

"It's not a race, Mum. Okay, so I'm running late."

"That's just it; you're not running at all. You're completely and utterly stationary."

So the bottle of wine he clutched in his hand was oddly symbolic, something to split upon the gleaming bow of the mist-shrouded vessel that was Vivienne Drexler. To launch a dream, perhaps? *I name this improbable prospect...Foolhardiness.   Immaturity.   Emotional Blindness.*

He imagined he would feel uneasy carrying the naked bottle along the road, so he secreted it in a Tesco bag, which had the unfortunate effect of seeming to devalue the entire gesture. Perhaps, he thought, he should tell her that he had not bought the wine at Tesco; but surely that would simply sound like an unnecessary over-compensation. Far better to let matters and events speak for themselves, allow the occasion to find its own level of social intercourse. After all, as he had aptly remarked to his mother, it was only a bottle of wine.

There was a skip at the kerb when he reached the house, and a man in jeans and a tattered pullover standing inside it, breaking up what looked like a wooden window-frame. The man glanced over and bade him good morning in a cultured accent which he found mildly surprising.

Vivienne was standing at the open door. Beside the doorway, the bay window was a ragged hole, nakedly glassless. A red can of Coke glinted on the ravaged brickwork.

"You're right on time!" she called out.

"I always try to be," he said, and then promptly regretted the admission, in case it made him sound like a control freak.

She walked close behind him, guiding him to the kitchen, humid with the smell, the heady hum, of something simmering in the oven. Pulling out a chair at a pine table in the centre of the room, she swished a tea towel playfully over the seat and nodded to him to sit down.

"What's that, your sandwiches?" She cocked her head at the bag.

"Sorry. Here." He produced the wine with a self-conscious flourish.

Peering down her nose with a studied air of mock superiority, Vivienne read the label while Gavin settled himself at the table.   A sudden burst of music reverberated from the front room as a workman fiddled with his radio, and Vivienne winced and butted the door shut with her bottom, a somehow uncharacteristic gesture which Gavin would remember for a long time afterwards.

"Food in five minutes," she said, sitting down opposite him. There were wine glasses on the table, and she reached behind her for a corkscrew. "Let's get drunk."

His eyes widened. "Do you mean that?"

"I don't have to go back to work," she said with a shrug.

"Unfortunately I do."

"Of course," and she nodded gravely at the table top, so that Gavin was unable to determine whether she found the realisation disappointing or merely tedious.

She poured the wine and lifted her full glass to eye level, her bunched fingers gripping the stem, twirling it around thoughtfully with the light from the window daubing a red streak on her face, a shimmering glaze like a sudden blush. In the dancing luminescence, the freckles under her eyes appeared as specks of golden dust.

Tipping back her head, she emptied her glass, refilled it and took another mouthful. Gavin watched her. She didn't mention the food, but he wasn't hungry. He was content just to sit there quietly, gazing at her, studying every line and contour of her face. She wore no ear-rings, but he noticed the tiny grey puncture at the soft centre of each lobe, a microscopic blind eye, sweetly redundant. Freed from the constraints of the office, she had put on a high-necked pink T-shirt and a pair of weathered jeans. That he could not see any flesh below her neckline somehow made the unmistakable swell of the cotton, tightly enclosing her breasts, all the more enticing, and his eyes fell from her face to lie firmly embedded in her chest like two blobs of putty thrown at a wall.

"You're doing it again," she said, glaring at him over the rim of the glass.

"Sorry. Doing what?"

"Staring at me. You're always staring at me."

He shook his head, as though this might make her meaning clearer. "I'm not staring at you. I'm - uh - admiring you."

"Really? I'm not sure I want to be admired. You make me sound like an artifact in a museum."

"Unintended. It was meant as a compliment."

She drained her glass, reached for the bottle and filled it again. He watched her. Any nearer the top, he thought, and there'd be a meniscus.

"I take it you approve my choice of wine," he said.

"Very palatable." She raised her glass. "Cheers!"

"Perhaps we should leave some to go with the meal."

Her eyebrows arched. "Are you saying I drink too much?"

"Of course not. In your own home you - "

"Precisely." She pushed his glass towards him with her fingertips. "Drink up, Gavin. Relax."

He did as he was told, and then, when his hand slowly settled on the table again, he felt a light, swift gift of pleasurable surprise, as Vivienne unexpectedly wiped a forefinger across his wrist in what he dared to interpret as a sign of affection.

"What was that for?" he asked her, less because he needed to know than to prolong the moment.

She was toying with her glass again, two outstretched fingers on the flat base, shunting it back and forth beside her knife. Her eyes were downcast, clouded with uncertainty.

"Vivienne? Are you all right?"

"Just thinking," she said, in a small, tense voice. "I suppose - " - she paused to clear her throat - "well, I haven't been fair to you, have I?"

"In what way?"

"Oh, you know. I mean, I haven't told you any lies, but I haven't really opened up."

"So? You don't have to. You don't owe me anything."

"Don't I? Perhaps I do." She took another sip from her drink. "Perhaps I owe you an explanation for my evasiveness. Perhaps I owe you some small gratitude for your concern, for offering to help me. Maybe it's time I stopped being a mean bitch."

He waited, not exactly embarrassed, but unsure of his timing, for tears were brimming in her eyes and the bow of her lips was drawn tight in a quivering slit. Slowly, he slid out a hand to cover hers.

"Don't," she said, her voice strangled by emotion.

He squeezed her hand, then let it go. "We could just talk - instead of eating," he said.

She forced a laugh through her tears. "You mean, 'This woman is getting pissed in front of me, drinking my wine, while I starve.'"

With some small mutterings of half-hearted protest, she let him help her with the heavy crock of casserole and the oven-warmed bread. Soon the room was awash with the thick aroma of meat and garlic, a cloying miasma that almost tangibly overlaid the false detachment in the atmosphere. They ate silently at first, their wordless thoughts punctuated by the clicking of cutlery and the brittle snap of fresh bread. Every so often he glanced up at her, checking her face, watching for an inexorable tide of tears. The food didn't matter to him, he thought, so long as he could sit there and watch her face.

When her eyes flickered and met his, he stopped eating and shook his head. "I'm sorry, I'm doing it again."

She waved her fork carelessly in the air. "It's all right, really. It doesn't matter."

"Okay. This is very good."

"Do you mean the casserole or our situation?"

He stared at her, blank-faced. "Do we have a situation?"

"I don't know," she said, pursing her lips doubtfully.

"We can talk if you want. You talk and I'll listen."

She sighed. "Not enough time, Gavin."

"You could make a start. You could find out how good a listener I am."

"Hmm. Is that what you want from me - my life story?"

"You make it sound like an accusation. As though I'm probing."

She was stirring her food again, as she had done in the pub. "I suppose - to you I'm like a character in a child's picture book. You're just trying to colour me in. Sorry, I didn't mean you were a child."

"Maybe I am. I still live at home." Hardly had the words left his mouth, when he questioned the wisdom of the disclosure. This was not an admission to enhance his credibility. "I suppose you didn't know that," he said, unhappily.

He had expected her to gape in surprise, but her face showed little reaction. "How would I know? I really don't know you."

"The feeling is mutual," he said.

"I bet you know more about me than I know about you."

"Now you're trying to turn the conversation around."

She smiled, though there was still a wetness in her eyes. "You mean, I'm trying to divert attention from myself."

"The possibility had crossed my mind."

"I think I've had enough of that." She let her knife and fork drop with a clatter into the plate, and pushed it away from her. "We're calling it a day, by the way."

"Pardon?"

"That's what you wanted to know, isn't it? Jack and me. You did ask."

"Oh. I see." The suddenness of the announcement disorientated him. For some disturbing reason, he felt more relieved than concerned. "Is this - something you're both agreed on?"

"Not exactly. I want out. I've told him."

"What will you do?"

"How do you mean?"

He spread his hands in the air. "This place. The children."

"Lizzie and James are unhappy. With the relationship, that is. The house - well, it's just a house, isn't it?"

"But you're having the windows done."

She shrugged quickly. "Old ones were practically falling out. Got to protect our investment."

"I see."

"But you don't, do you? How can you? You don't even know me. It's none of your concern."

"Then why did you tell me?"

She drank the rest of her wine and grabbed the bottle again. "I don't know. Sometimes it helps - to confide things."

Gavin put down his knife and fork, rested his elbows on the table and held his head in his hands. Streaks of congealing grease glistened in his food. Over the noise from the radio in the front room, he heard someone sawing, urgent, high-pitched strokes, like a revving engine.

"Glad you brought the wine," she said. "It's defera-definitely helping me get my head together." She nodded at his plate. "Don't have to finish that."

He poured himself more wine, emptying the bottle. "I wish I could say something constructive."

"You're here. That's constructive. It's good to talk."

There was a knock at the kitchen door. Vivienne stood up, opened the door a few inches and spoke in a low undertone to one of the workmen. Gavin pushed both plates to the side of the table.

She curled her lips distastefully as she sat down. "That man could use a deodorant," she said.

"Ah, you're looking for a fragrant workman," Gavin said, surreptitiously angling his head to sniff his left armpit.

"I have to sit in that room. I have to inhale his sour beans. I have to immerse myself in his stale soup."

"But if there's a big hole in the window..."

"Shut up, Gavin!"

He helped her clear away. Doing this in his shirt and tie, he felt stiff and uncomfortable. His fingers seemed not to work properly. Not knowing where anything belonged made the task still more awkward. Every few seconds they would bump softly against each other, an arm brushing an arm, a hip touching something yielding, vaguely unseen, and after a while it seemed to Gavin that Vivienne was carelessly permitting these collisions, whether through calculated deliberation or because the wine had unsteadied her. Though it increased the risk of his dropping a glass or plate, he could not find it in himself to dislike the contact.

Standing up, he realised how nervousness was distending his bladder. He asked her where the toilet was.

"Top of the stairs, first left."

The bolt on the door was out of alignment. He fiddled with it briefly, then gave up. It hardly mattered, he thought. He emptied himself gratefully into the bowl and, as he was finishing, he heard a sound on the landing behind him. In the next instant, she pushed open the door.

"I should have said, the bolt doesn't work."

"No." He glanced anxiously over his shoulder. "Something wrong?"

"Not really. Well, yes, actually everything's wrong."

Gavin struggled to conceal himself. He wanted to wash his hands, but Vivienne was standing against the wash-basin. As he turned towards her, she slid round him, slammed down the lavatory lid and sat on it.

"I haven't flushed it," he said.

"Doesn't matter." She pointed at the rim of the bath. "Sit down."

"What?"

"Sit there. This won't take a minute."

He perched precariously on the edge of Vivienne Drexler's bath, feeling faintly ridiculous and both emotionally and physically vulnerable. Though they sat at right-angles to each other, their knees almost touched. He wondered how he had arrived at this absurd situation. He tried leaning forwards, for safer balance, with his forearms resting on his thighs; but that way they came close to bumping heads, and he had to lean back and support himself by gripping the cold rim of the bath either side of his body.

"It's Jack," she said.

He threw an instinctive glance at the door, then felt foolish. "What? What about him?"

"I just want you to know - okay? I don't love Jack and he doesn't care for me, except perhaps as a possession. He doesn't feel anything for the children, and they certainly don't love him. I doubt they even like him. We don't sleep together. I think he goes to prostitutes sometimes, but I don't ask about it. That's up to him. Anyway, it's his money he's squandering. Financially, we aren't in each other's pockets. I work directly for Ross Glaister, as you know, and he pays me very well. He does that because I'm good at what I do, and because we were together on the Dublin training course and I slept with him both nights. I'm not proud of it, but it doesn't trouble me, either. If you're a - a, dare I say it, an attractive woman - then work is a form of prostitution, you're liable to be compromised somewhere along the line, then you have to decide what to do."

Gavin opened his mouth to interrupt, to reassure her that this was more than he expected, but she put up a hand to silence him.

"Hear me out. I want to do this. I'm not in love with Ross, by the way, never have been. Let's just say, we used each other. I don't know what you think about that, don't want to know. I'm not immoral, just practical. Being - how I am, well, that's a personal quality, a quantifiable attribute, like any other. If you've got it, you can cash it in for self-betterment whenever you need to. Maybe you think that debases me. Well, like I said, I really don't care. No-one's been harmed. Now that I've made my decision about Jack, I feel a whole lot better about myself, I'm getting back my self-esteem. I'm going for security for myself and my children. I'm going for happiness and freedom. And that's not a crime. So please, don't think badly of me. And for Christ's sake don't fall in the bath; you look like you're about to collapse."

He passed a hand slowly over his eyes. "I feel as if I've been mugged," he said.

"Well, that wasn't my intention, Gavin." She reached back and flushed the toilet. "I thought you wanted to know."

"Yes."

"Is that all you have to say?"

"For the present, yes."

She grabbed his wrist to look at his watch. "You ought to be getting back."

"Yes."

"I'm sorry it didn't work out - the lunch, I mean."

"It doesn't matter."

"Call it food for thought, eh?"

"Yes."

"Thanks for the wine. I couldn't have managed it without."

He followed her downstairs to the hall where, unceremoniously, she held open the door as if pointedly expecting him to leave at once.

"My jacket. It's on the kitchen chair."

She fetched the jacket, holding it out to him on the peg of one finger.

"Vivienne, I really - "

"You don't want to be late," she urged him.

"No. Look, what you told me...it'll go no further."

"I'd appreciate that," she said, curtly.

"Right then. And I - well, it was good."

She threw back her head in a mocking laugh. "Come on, Gavin, it was pathetic! Neither of us can possibly have enjoyed a minute of it. If we're going to be friends, at least let's try to be honest with each other."

Gavin buttoned his jacket against the cold billowing in from the street.

"Do you want your plastic bag back?" she asked him.

He peered at her through narrowed eyes. "Of course not."

"I guess that's it then," she said.

He leaned slightly towards her, seeking a place on the side of her cheek, but she put out a hand and pushed below his throat. "Please don't. It'd be like you were doing it in sympathy."

He stepped down without turning round, and heard the door click shut behind him. Tears were starting in his eyes, but he told himself that these were produced by the cold wind in his face. He walked briskly, with his hands shoved deep into his pockets. A dull ache of sullen anger lay like a lead ball in the pit of his stomach; but there was nothing objective or outward-focused in this simmering rage, for Gavin knew that at the root of his anger festered nothing more than the severest knowledge of himself. Vivienne Drexler's invitation had presented him - had *appeared* to present him - with a perfect opportunity to communicate with this reticent, elusive woman. He could crack the protective shell she wore with that curious, depressing confidence. He could gain her trust and convince her of his integrity. His despair was the wellspring of his failure. He was not the man he had hoped to be, but he was indeed the man he feared he was, imperfectly constructed by an interlinked framework of limitations.

Yet, in some small part of himself, he believed he could take heart from what Vivienne had told him, or from the way she had said it, for there were inconsistencies in her account of herself. She spoke of regaining her self-esteem, but he found nothing in her manner, in her self-awareness, to reflect either pride or contentment. If she truly felt she was on the road to recovery, why those brief, frustrated tears? As for confessing her dalliance with Glaister, her claim that she didn't care what he thought about it, as if his opinion did not interest her, quietly collapsed when she asked him not to think badly of her.

He forced a smile, then, for he believed that he, Gavin Alexander Lake, was valuable enough to her that she cared what he thought about her and wanted his approval. She would deny it, of course, but she had offered the evidence out of her own mouth. In her rejection there was also an appeal. So he held this ray of hope bravely within himself, lifting it peacefully before his senses, breathing it like a small, bright flower, inhaling the sweet scent of it.

5

AMANDA FINCH, long, slim legs extended before her, supported her slippered feet on a leather-inlaid footstool, ankles neatly crossed. "So, what's new in your world, mate?" she asked her brother.

Gavin put down his wine glass on the tiled hearth and gazed at her vacantly. "Not a lot," he said. "Nothing to get excited about."

Amanda took a thoughtful sip of Chardonnay and nodded her head. She had no cause to challenge this disclaimer, for her brother, to the best of her recollection, had never done anything exciting since the day he rolled out from his mother's tented thighs and made a startling mess on her feet.

"How's Mum?" she asked.

"Coping," he replied.

"With what? With you?"

Gavin felt mildly affronted. Though she seldom alluded directly to the situation, Amanda's particular style of reticence had long ago appraised her brother of her disapproval in the matter of his domestic arrangements. He reasoned intuitively that her economical discourse on the subject was tantamount to reprimand.

"I meant, she's coming to terms with - Dad."

Amanda's soft chuckle was almost a scoff. "Two years, Gavin. It's a long time."

"To us, maybe. But when you've lived with someone, breathed the same air, day in, day out, felt them all around you..."

She sighed heavily. "Right. So where does that leave you?"

"Meaning?"

"Meaning, we're at the stage in the game where they send on a substitute." She rocked her head charmlessly from side to side. "It's all right, you can use Dad's boots."

"Hmm. Maybe we should talk about something else."

"If you want." She puffed out her cheeks, staring into the hearth. "Mum said you'd got a girl-friend."

"Did she?"

"Well, have you?"

"Actually, no. It's - she's just someone at work. We had lunch, that's all."

"Mum said you were reticent about her."

He shrugged. "What's there to say? It's not a romantic thing. Anyway, Mum probably wouldn't like her."

"She doesn't have to, does she? Is she black?"

"What?"

"Gavin!"

"No, no, she's not black," he said, testily.

"Okay. Is she a Jehovah's Witness?"

"I don't know. I don't think so."

"Is she deformed or of peasant stock?"

"Now you're being ridiculous."

"Very well, I shall take that as a 'no'. In which case, according to my initial assessment, you can safely take her home to mother."

"The thing is, she's married."

"Well now, there's a surprise." She lifted her glass as though offering him a toast. "Is that an insurmountable problem?"

"Not at the moment. Why should it be? There's nothing serious in it."

"And would you like there to be?"

"It would only complicate matters," he said, shaking his head slowly.

"Matters? What matters? In your life, Gavin, there are no matters to speak of."

That, he reflected ruefully, was how his sister perceived him. What he had artlessly fashioned for himself was less a life than a routine, more a schedule than an adventure. Her brother was a man who revelled quietly in the satisfactory. He viewed the world from the outside, looking in, like a visitor to an art gallery, pausing at each painting before nodding appreciatively and moving on.

"The garden looks beautiful," Gavin said, tilting his head at the window.

Amanda smiled and sucked in her cheeks knowingly. "Here's another issue to be ducked," she said.

"You're always trying to put me on a spot, aren't you? Anyway" - he stood up and brushed irritably at his clothes - "I ought to be taking my bag upstairs and hanging up my things."

She waved a hand languidly over her shoulder. "Usual room," she said. "I left the window open an inch. Shut it if it's too cold."

The small spare room, which looked out over the back garden, smelled musty and slightly damp. Gavin dropped his bag on the bed and closed the window. The roughly painted sill was stippled with puddles of condensing water. In one dim corner, a tawny-yellow patch of dampness stained the ceiling.

There was another empty room across the landing, just a tiny box room with a folding bed, a wooden chair and no other furniture. The emergency room, his mother called it. Sitting solemnly in a row along the bed, backs to the wall, were five teddy bears, rescued from the random carnage of Amanda's childhood. Gavin remembered the bears, could even remember their names, but he didn't like to look at them now. When he opened the door, they stared reproachfully at him like dead animals.

His sister was clattering dishes downstairs. Even in this routine act, he somehow read a gesture, the edginess of a rebuke. Now that he had invited himself to the cottage, she would have to cook for him and hope that he would help with the washing-up. This was how it was with her brother. Wherever he went, he fastened himself on to someone, invading their domain, laying waste their privacy. For the individual, freedom and independence meant an imposition for other people. A free-spirited lifestyle was only sustainable by a degree of parasitism.

Stripped to the waist, a towel flung round his neck, he went to the head of the stairs. "Don't cook for me!" he called down. "We can go out. My treat."

"What did you say?" She was squinting up through the banisters, and Gavin could not be sure whether she had simply not heard him, or if she was affecting incredulity at the offer.

"I said, I'll buy us dinner. You must know a chic little restaurant somewhere nearby."

"You being sarcastic? This is wildest Dorset. Nothing *chic* around here."

"Oh. Well, a pub then."

She nodded sternly. "I'll think about it."

Gavin, returning to his room, silently accepted the undertaking, though he wondered, in some small pique, what there was to think about. Somehow he found her indecision intimidating, because it might deny him the chance to make a token gesture of self-redemption. He suspected that Amanda had no need to ponder his proposal, but took a grim pleasure in deliberately stalling him.

He had brought clothes enough for three days. From the bag he produced socks, underpants, handkerchiefs, shirts, trousers and a spare pair of shoes. It would be enough. The cottage was warm downstairs, and if he went out he could wear his coat or the fleece that fitted snugly underneath it. Rummaging deeper, he realised he had forgotten to pack any pyjamas. That meant he would have to sleep in a shirt and pants, the ones left over from the day before. He smiled ruefully. The sense of economy pleased him.

Amanda was in the doorway. "Where did you get that towel?" she asked.

"It's mine. I brought it."

"On the chair on the landing. I've put you one out. Men usually forget."

"Thanks." He decided not to mention the pyjamas. "I try to be systematic."

"Hmm. Proper little robot, aren't we?"

"Do you really think that?" he asked her, averting his eyes to hide the injury.

"I wouldn't say it, otherwise."

"Of course. You always were one for speaking your mind."

"I'm not complicated, Gavin. I don't mask my feelings."

She started shaking her head then, and slowly moved towards him, stepping almost nervously round the end of the bed, until she was standing at his shoulder. Without touching him, she dipped her head forward, like a bird, and kissed him on the cheek."

He peered at her, anxiously. "What's that for?"

"I don't know. Reassurance, I suppose. Since the moment you arrived, I've hardly said a kind word to you."

He laughed, and it came out as a snort, something worse than amusement or sympathy but less than bitterness. "Correction: you haven't said a single kind word. There's no 'hardly' about it."

"Okay, okay. Now you're sounding sorry for yourself. Still, maybe that's my fault. Me and my plain speaking."

He could smell her perfume, a thin, steely waft of lemon and herbs that he inhaled and held suspended in his throat. A pity it hadn't worked out for her with Michael, he thought. She was still an attractive woman, poised, self-confident, almost infinitely capable. Everyone had a weakness, but he struggled to identify it in his sister.

"I'd better get on with this," he said, feeling uncomfortable with her sudden closeness.

She ran the back of her hand lightly across his chest, just below the collarbone. "You've got a bit of a tan there," she said.

"Probably a trick of the light," he said, with a shrug.

"Whatever. About your suggestion."

"What?"

You buy the meal, I'll get the drinks. The Black Lion. It's five minutes in the car."

"Is it good?"

"Oh Gavin." She punched him playfully on the arm. "This is Amanda Finch. Remember me? I don't go to places that aren't good. I certainly don't take other people there. There's my reputation to think of."

"Of course. Mandy, I'm going for a shower."

"Please don't call me that. You know how I hate it."

"All right, all right," he said meekly. "It's only an abbreviation."

"Thank you, I have no wish to be abbreviated. I like myself as I am. Do you want to be called Gav?"

"Point taken. I was just being friendly."

"Gavin, you're my brother. I take your friendship for granted."

"Yes, that can be misconstrued," he said, acidly.

"Oh well, if you're going to be like that." She turned away, gazing vacantly round the room. "Come down when you're ready. Maybe we can talk sensibly."

A sensible conversation with Amanda, he reflected ruefully, all too often meant conceding her point of view. Her self-belief was unshakeable, allowing no shadings of opinion. Michael Finch, whom she had married less than a year ago after the briefest of engagements, had quickly discovered this characteristic, to his cost. Michael, an executive in the Probation service, had honed his career with the delicate instruments of tact, diplomacy and judicious compromise; but such measured craftsmanship inevitably proved painfully ineffectual in constructing a harmonious relationship with Amanda. Their separation after eight weeks of subdued turmoil had conferred upon her an air of icy freedom, while Michael somehow managed to appear as much relieved as regretful.

His sister never spoke of the departed Michael. With ruthless efficiency, she had dismissed him from her memory. Though he had always respected the privacy of this contrivance, Gavin was prepared, over dinner, to break silence in the matter if Amanda were to tackle him afresh about his friendship with Mrs Drexler.

It was with her, with Vivienne, that he had last eaten in a pub, and he hoped, as he settled into the uncompromising wooden booth, that this meal would pass more successfully. A young waitress in a red gingham frock, steel braces on her teeth, came to take their order, and Gavin smiled at her sympathetically, trying not to look at her mouth.

"Why are you doing that?" Amanda asked him, when the waitress had gone.

"Eh? Doing what?"

"I was watching you. That's your famous 'There-there' smile."

"What on earth are you talking about?"

"What on earth were you smiling about?"

"For goodness' sake, Amanda," he hissed through his teeth, "I smiled politely at a waitress, that's all. Does that have to be explained?"

"Not really, not to me. I just find it a bit irritating, that's all. Okay, so the poor girl's got braces on her teeth, which unfortunately compromises her attractiveness, so you, dear brother, weighed down with your emotional overload, have to grin soppily at her to tell her she'll get better, she hasn't blown her chances."

Gavin fiddled testily with his tablemat. "Sometimes I can't believe you, Amanda. That's about the silliest thing I ever heard."

"Well, yes, it was silly all right."

"I mean, what you said was silly. It's almost like you're trying to pick a fight. We've only just sat down, for God's sake."

"There, there!" she said, exaggerating the words, but Gavin saw her pawing hand reaching out, and snatched his arm away.

Still, she was right about the food. She had the house venison pie, a musky-fragranced golden dome that took up half the plate, served with a bright scatter of vegetables just moister than *al dente,* while Gavin settled for the Aberdeen Angus sirloin grilled as he liked it, so under the pressure of the fork the steak wept a thin, teak-coloured gravy of pearled blood.

"How long can you stay?" she asked.

"I thought maybe three days."

He liked the way she had worded the question. Not 'How long are you staying?' or 'How long do you want to stay?' She had asked how long he *could* stay, which somehow seemed more accommodating, more passive.

"If that's okay by you," he added.

"Yes. I'm not going anywhere."

"How's work?"

"I've finished for Christmas. I don't go back until January." She speared a baby potato on her fork, popped it in her mouth and carried on talking around it. "Hey, that room's not damp, is it? The bed could be damp. It smells kind of musty in there, even though I've kept the door open to air it."

"Don't worry about it, Amanda. It's not important."

"It is if you catch your death."

"How come you're so concerned for my welfare, all of a sudden?"

"It's not all of a sudden. I'd always look out for you." She put down her knife and stroked the back of his hand with her bunched fingertips. "I know I 'm a cow sometimes, but I do love you, Gavin. And I worry about you."

"You worry about me? Why?"

"Oh, you know. On your own and stuff."

"I'm not on my own. There's your mother."

"Come on, Gavin. You know what I mean. That's not companionship; it just emphasizes your - your aloneness."

Gavin paused, tugging at his earlobe, lost for an adequate response. He gazed around at the other diners, couples mostly, smiling at each other, casually well-dressed, the Christmas lights and multi-coloured baubles sparking reflections in their eyes. The audio system was pumping out carols, not loudly but to lend a perfunctorily seasonal ambience, the music fusing effortlessly with the bright chatter of conversation and the clink of glasses and cutlery to create a softly enveloping cushion of soporific sound. He rode the warm, lilting wash of it now, his attention carried lazily round the half-dark, low-beamed room on a shifting tide, his eyes bumping gently against the lanterns of floating faces fanned by the ferns of flickering firelight from the splintered logs slung in the hearth. Probably she was right, he thought, all these people, they were here together, this whole place was about togetherness, about warmth and friendship, the security of someone to lean on, to love and be loved.

"So what's her name?"

Her question jolted him back from his reverie. "What? Who?"

She jabbed her fork at him, a baby onion impaled on the prongs. It looked vaguely clinical, he thought. "This woman. Has she got a name?"

"Of course she's got a name."

"Do you want me to guess it?"

"Okay, okay," he murmured, sighing. "Vivienne Drexler."

"Vivienne Drexler," Amanda repeated, rolling the syllables slowly across her tongue. "Posh name. Is she foreign?"

"I don't think so."

"Don't you know?"

"I'm not going to ask her, am I? 'Excuse me, but are you by any chance foreign?'"

She clicked her tongue impatiently. "Normally you can tell. Does she have an accent?"

"No she doesn't," he replied, his voice rising to a register where it sounded strained and breathless. "She's well-spoken but I wouldn't say there was anything unusual about her accent."

"I see. And she's married, this Vivienne?"

"I told you. Do we have to have this conversation? I came here to enjoy my meal."

"Are you not enjoying it? Shall I bring the waitress back so you can simper at her again?"

"Amanda, the food is fine. My steak is done exactly as I like it, the fries are crisp, the mushrooms are beautifully nutty, this is a nice pub, so I would like to relax and forget about people at work, if you don't mind."

"Hmm. The point is, you see, well - is she *happily* married, or just accounted for? Does she have kids?"

Gavin stared grimly at a knot in the wood panelling above her head. "Yes, she has two children."

"And are they all happy together? Because, you see, there's no family to disrupt if they're just going through the motions, living under the same roof in misery. There's no such thing as an unhappy family, Gavin. Either there's a happy family, or there's people with the same name tolerating one another and wishing they didn't have to, but not being a family any more."

He dropped his knife and fork in the plate, spreading his hands in disbelief. "Wait a minute! What's this about disruption? Are you suggesting I just wade in there and - "

"If that's what you want, Gavin. If she's what you want."

He propped one elbow on the table, cradling his head in his hand. "I don't know," he said, "I don't know what I want."

His sister studied him with an intensity suggesting as much pity as concern. "No, that always was your problem."

"*My* problem?" Gavin saw a chink of light, an opportunity for diversion. "Well, if you're such an expert in relationships, how come...?"

Amanda's face seemed to go into spasm, the bulge of a potato distending her cheek like a boil. Finally she bobbed her head and swallowed. "I might have known we'd come to that. You mean Michael."

"In the circumstances, it's a reasonable line of enquiry."

"Yes. I saw him the other day. We exchanged feeble waves."

"Do you miss him?"

"No. Why should I? Anyway, it was all over nine months ago." She picked up her napkin and dabbed thoughtfully at the corners of her mouth. "Okay, sometimes at night, you know. About the only thing he was any good at."

"I see," he said, awkwardly, and in the next instant, foolish and dismayed, he felt himself blushing, hoping she wouldn't notice in the subdued light. Too much information. She was his sister, for God's sake.

"There's no-one else, no-one new?" he persevered.

"No. What do I want a man for? Well, for that, obviously. Otherwise they're an impractical adornment. You carry them about, mewling pathetically out of their mother complexes, their self-doubts and indecisiveness." She shook her head and shuddered. "I can't be doing with it."

Gavin offered her a wry smile. "Which neatly brings us back to me, I suppose."

"You said it, brother of mine, not me."

Perhaps Amanda sensed that this was a moment for him to work something out for himself, and for several minutes she left her brother in peace, while they quietly finished their dinners. Occasionally she looked up at him and smiled, more openly than she had done before, and once she lifted her wine glass and chinked it against his as he drank, a gesture he found warmly comforting.

"Thank you for taking me out," she said later, as she licked clean her dessert spoon.

"My pleasure. What'll we do tomorrow?"

"For food? Ah, I've got a new Indian recipe book. I feel a creative mood coming on. You can be my first victim - my guinea pig."

"Mmm. Guinea pig biriani - my favourite."

She laughed, touching his hand again, and he thought perhaps the wine had diluted the acid that so often seemed to flow freely in her bloodstream.

He slid some pound coins under a plate. "For the waitress," he said.

"Good idea, Gavin. Help to defray her orthodontic expenses."

Outside, she insisted on helping him scrape a ragged window in the frost-hazed windscreen. "After all," she said chirpily, "it is my car."

"And I'm a gentleman," he added, flexing his numbed fingers.

"Hmm, I think that could make you an outmoded commodity. You know, like a chamber pot or one of those wooden toadstool thingies Mum used when she was darning socks. A redundant accessory." She opened the door and peered through the screen from the inside. "It's okay, I can see now. Let's go."

The Aga in the kitchen streamed a steady, reassuring warmth into the room, a presence at once welcoming, constant and dependable. Amanda made mugs of hot chocolate. Gavin's nose ran until it bubbled fruitily. Pearled cobwebs of condensation bloomed across the window panes.

"That's it," he declared, pushing his mug away, "I'm tired, I'm going up."

"Of course. You've had a long journey today." She pecked him quickly on the cheek. "Sleep well. Don't hurry in the morning."

Well, he thought, the sheets did feel slightly damp, but he reckoned the chill would soon be dissipated by his body heat. He was simply too tired to care. In his shirt and underpants, he slid down and dragged the thick duvet over him. He had forgotten how inky-dark it was in the country at night, and he waited for a while, his eyes flicking around the walls, until he could make out the outline of the curtained window, the chest of drawers, the old marble mantelpiece bearing the antique clock that hadn't tick-tocked in a generation.

Just before he submerged effortlessly into the limpid waters of sleep, a fleeting, wraith-like vision of Vivienne Drexler swam in the mists before his eyes, and he smiled to himself in the darkness. His sister clearly believed that he should be guided in this affair - his smile deepened, then, as the word *affair* crossed his mind - not by his innate sense of propriety, which brought to his machinations more of constraint than of guidance, but by an instinctive identification of a need he and Vivienne shared and had the right to develop and consummate.

Then he was sinking into sleep, nibbled by the warm animals of dreams, darkly cocooned in his own humidity, until a dull sound, a sensation of peripheral movement, disturbed him. He opened his eyes and saw the door swinging ajar, a thin orange light fanning in from the landing. A dark figure loomed in the doorway.

"Are you asleep?" she whispered.

"Mmm? Well, I was, until now."

"Sorry. I shouldn't be waking you."

"What time is it?"

"I don't know. One o'clock, I think."

"Something the matter?"

"Not really." She came and sat at the foot of the bed. "It seems a bit - ridiculous, that's all."

"What? What does?"

"Oh, you know. Us rattling around here in the cold and the dark. Like this."

"Like what?"

"Gavin, are you looking forward to Christmas?"

"Amanda, I don't - "

"Just answer."

"Yeah, I think so. Why?"

"Do you remember when we were little? When we were home in Chalfont and it was Christmas Eve, getting late, and we were waiting in case we saw Santa? Do you remember, Gavin? All that quiet, whispery excitement?"

"Yes. It's never the same when you stop believing in an old man with a white beard and a team of reindeer pulling a sled loaded with bulging sacks."

"I know. And - and I used to come in to your room, didn't I? I used to snuggle up beside you in the dark, sort of curl up against you, and we'd whisper so no-one could hear us, and then we'd fall asleep, waiting for the jingling. We were always fast asleep when he came. We never did get to hear the jingling."

"That's right. I remember, Amanda. Nice times, eh?"

"Nice times, Gavin." He heard her sigh deeply, a small cry in the shadows. "Do you think those times will ever come back?"

He chuckled softly. "In our dreams, maybe."

Amanda stood up, and he heard the bedsprings creak as her weight lifted from the mattress. "I suppose we can live a dream, can't we?" She whisked her nightdress over her head, and Gavin saw her small breasts, slightly pointed, in faint silhouette against the greyness of the window. "We can make things possible."

She moved towards him, reaching out to touch his face.

"Amanda, what are you doing?"

"Shove over, Gavin. It's cold out here."

"Amanda, what on earth - ?"

"Don't talk, move."

She squeezed in next to him, sighing in the sudden warmth. "That's better," she murmured.

He turned his head away from her. "This is crazy," he whispered.

"Oh, don't worry, Gavin. I'm perfectly sane." She reached down and pinched his thigh. "We don't have to do anything."

"What is it you want, Amanda?" He turned to face her once more. "Why are you doing this?"

"What do I want? What do I want?" She rested one curled fist in the hairs on his chest, a small, nesting bird. "Hold me, that's all. I just want you to fucking hold me."

6

SHE looked rather smart today, he thought, in a black trouser suit with a very fine grey pinstripe in it and, beneath the jacket, a crisp white blouse showing two unfastened buttons below her throat. A small gold cross on a delicate chain glinted against the pale flesh below her collar.

She fussed with the papers on the corner of his desk, making room for the cup and saucer. "Here you are. Don't spill it on all this stuff."

"Thanks, Carolyn," he said, staring at the saucer.

" There's no biscuits," she said.

"Well, I can see that."

"It's Christmas Eve tomorrow. There weren't any biscuits."

Gavin frowned, struggling to reconcile two apparently unconnected statements. "I don't follow you," he said, meekly.

"I'm glad about that. I don't like men following me."

"I meant the biscuits."

"Right, you see, it's like this." She paused for a short, sharp intake of breath. "It's Christmas, so that shop - and I'm not walking all up to the supermarket - that shop is full of putty-faced women in track suit bottoms, stocking up, with tattoos and their fat bellies sticking out, driving pushchairs nine foot wide, and they've had all the damned biscuits, because that's what they eat. This is not Chelsea, mate."

Gavin sniggered behind his hand. "Point taken. Though I don't think your explanation is satisfactory from the standpoint of political correctness."

"Sod that." She turned to go, then hesitated. "Oh, nearly forgot. That woman phoned."

"What woman?"

"You know, the one you like. Mrs Whatserface."

"Um, you mean Mrs Drexler?"

"That's her. You're to ring her back. Sounded urgent."

"Thanks," he said, biting his lip, "I'll ring her in a minute."

"Better do it now. Seemed like she was telling you to ring her, not asking you."

She closed the door, and Gavin picked up the phone. An unfamiliar voice sounded down the line.

"Is Mrs Drexler available, please?"

"Yeah." An acoustic rattle, then: "Vivienne - for you. I think it's that bloke."

He waited, biting his lip again.

"Vivienne Drexler."

"Good morning. This is that bloke."

"Hello, that bloke. What're you doing lunch-time?"

"Today?"

"Yes, today."

"Yesterday?"

"Pay attention. Look, I've got the chance of a flat, first floor, ground and basement. I need to see it before everything shuts up for Christmas. Would you come with me this lunch-time?"

"Well, I - uh..."

"I'd really value your opinion. Please."

"How far is this flat?"

"It's...wait a minute." He heard her unfolding a piece of paper. "It's number ninety, Stalbridge Road. I think it's about ten minutes in the car."

"And you'd really like me to come with you?"

"Don't make me say it again, Gavin. Why else would I be asking?"

"No, that's fine, really. Meet you when?"

"Can you do twelve?"

"It's Christmas," he said, "the time of miracles. I can do anything."

Though undeniably less than miraculous, how strange it felt to be sitting in the passenger seat of Vivienne Drexler's Volkswagen. Soon the passing traffic and the preoccupied jaywalking pedestrians, which he had initially regarded with the vaguest of interest, ceased to engage him at all, and he turned his attention inwards, his eyes catching the glint of Vivienne's gold wedding ring as her fingers curled around the rim of the steering wheel, the way the slanting sun inflamed the loose strands of hair above her temples, the slow upward glide of her skirt hem as she worked the pedals so the smooth curve of her left thigh was a pale flash of enticement at the corner of his vision, while the herbal fragrance of her perfume, mingling with the warm plastic odour of the car interior, wafted to his nostrils on the breeze from the open window.

They pushed open the weather-scarred wooden gate to number ninety and stood staring idly at the big uncurtained window, streaked with dirt and bird-lime from an overhanging tree.

"Don't worry. They're going to cut the branches back," she said, anticipating his disapproval.

"Who's they?"

She slotted the key in the lock and leaned on the door. "Tangvale Housing Association. They're pretty good."

Standing in the hallway, they inhaled the cheerless smells of an unoccupied, unloved house.

"So you'll be paying rent?"

"If I decide to take it, yes."

"Unfurnished?"

She nodded. "Apparently there's a kitchen table and nothing else."

He followed her dutifully from room to room, feeling redundant, trying to think of something useful to say. Every so often Vivienne would pause and, in a voice carrying just the edge of an echo, make some practical observation - questioning the quality of a painted cornice, the security of a window-frame or a floorboard - which Gavin sensed he was expected to endorse or challenge. Seldom did he initiate an assessment himself, preferring to wait for her to speak, so that he might then be seen as someone acting in a supporting, sympathetic role, someone discreetly capable of offering a complementary or alternative view, but having no axe to grind in the matter.

That he constantly moved behind her was neither laziness nor etiquette. Rather, it enabled him the better to relish, for the short time it would last, the secret *frisson* of being alone in an empty house with Vivienne Drexler. Though he recalled his lunch at her home a few days ago, they had eaten amid the workmen's noise and interruption, destroying all sense of intimacy. Now he could shadow her in quiet admiration, knowing they would not be disturbed, and as she stood to consider the aspect of a room, imagining how it might contain the components of her life, her concentration momentarily elsewhere, he gazed at her in wonder and with a fondness not far removed from yearning, as he absorbed the touch of the window-light on the delicate H behind her knees, the pale sketch of it in the near-translucent skin, the swell of her breasts as she lingered in profile against a cream-coloured wall with her jacket unbuttoned, the way she occasionally licked both her lips in a circular motion, top to bottom, first in one direction, then the other, as she hesitated thoughtfully over the angle of an alcove or the run of a skirting board. The feel of this moment thrilled him.

"So what do you think?" She was standing in the front room with her back to the window, arms spread out before her.

"I - uh - well, it's very spacious. Downstairs feels a bit damp, perhaps."

"Yes. But it's been empty for six weeks. It needs living in."

"And the rent? You'd be paying for three bedrooms. Do you need three bedrooms?"

"I don't know," she said pensively. "I can't tell what Jack's likely to do, you see."

"About what?"

"Well, Lizzie and James intend to stay with him, for the time being, at least. But if he gets mad and throws them out - they could come and live here. They'd have a room each."

"What does Jack think about all this? It's a bit final, isn't it - if you desert the family home?"

She stared at him for a few seconds, working her tongue around her teeth. "Gavin, this is Vivienne Drexler you're talking to. I'm an independent woman, I don't carry passengers. I love my kids to pieces, believe me, but they don't dictate the terms."

"That doesn't answer my question," he said boldly.

"Jack? Jack can't live with me, Gavin, he doesn't know how. All I'm asking of him is a few sticks of furniture, for Christ's sake. He's got the house and the children, and he's got shot of me, a thorn in his side. There's really nothing for him to complain about."

"You make it all sound very simple."

"These things are as complicated as you make them, Gavin." She turned and leaned on the window sill, gazing into the front garden. "Do you know how old I am?"

"No," he lied.

"I'm nearly forty. If I'm to make a fresh start, I need to get on with it."

"Would you - would you hope to meet someone else?"

She sighed, and her breath misted the glass. "I don't know," she said, over her shoulder. "That's not something I've thought about."

"You're still an attractive lady," he said quietly.

She turned to face him, her eyes mirthful but mocking. "Spare me the platitudes, there's a good chap."

"It wasn't - I'm just saying."

"I know. I heard you." She was looking through the window again. "This paving's a bit of a mess, don't you think? Someone could break their neck."

"What's the deal on the gardens?"

"The front's communal, the back's mine. Well, that's if I take it."

"Hmm. The back needs work, too. It's quite overgrown."

"They use a man called Lorne Mowler, which I think is hilarious. I'll get him round before I move in. Lorne Mowler with his lawn mower."

She shook her head in amusement, regarding him from lowered eyes, and Gavin knew that he was expected to reciprocate, perhaps offer some facile comment on the comical aptness of the groundsman's name; but only the thinnest of smiles creased his lips, leaving his eyes brimming with sad disappointment, for he could tell that another opportunity to draw closer to this lady was about to be lost, squandered through a kind of emotional inertia. He had the will, but not the confidence. Vivienne's preoccupation with the house eclipsed all other considerations, and she was using Gavin as a sounding-board by which to measure the quality of her judgment. Here, now, today, she had no perception of him as a person in his own right, merely as an accessory to the task in hand.

She beckoned him to the glass-panelled back door. "What do you think? Grass right up to the door. I could ask Lorne to do me a paved patio, maybe even a crazy paving path up the lawn."

"I don't know. Would they mind?"

"Who?"

"The housing people. It's their property."

"Oh, I can get round them. I'd pay, and it would enhance their asset. Why should they object?"

"Right. This Lorne - is he expensive?"

"Possibly. If he knows I've got the money." She traced a finger thoughtfully round her lips. "Of course, I could always offer to sleep with him."

Gavin allowed himself a nervous laugh, his eyes dancing uncertainly from side to side. Would he ever get the true measure of this woman? She was checking him out now, fixing him with that calculating, artful smile he had seen many times before, that haunting self-awareness barring the route to the real, human, unashamed Vivienne Drexler whose private, intimate inner self he sought with quiet desperation, a secret world filled with the smells and sounds of her, the soft gloss of the light on her, a place he imagined with a fervour that gnawed at him like a physical pain.

She read his confusion, placing a steadying hand on his shoulder. "It was a joke, Gavin. All right?"

"I see. Maybe that's as well."

"You mean, maybe my life is complicated enough as it is?"

"Like you said, things are as complicated as you make them."

"Well, if you're quoting my words now, I shall take that as a form of flattery."

"I could flatter you in better ways," he said, and then he looked away, avoiding her eyes, unsure of his composure.

Vivienne was walking back to the front window, where her bag lay on the floor. "Best not to bother," she advised. "I'd only think you were being pat- Shit!"

He wheeled towards her. "What is it?"

"Shit shit shit!"

"Vivienne?"

She stood pointing out to the road. "Look! Parked behind me!"

He moved to her shoulder. "What are you looking at?"

"It's him - Jack! He's only bloody followed me!"

Gavin stood back, tasting bile in his mouth. "Is that going to be a problem?"

"I don't know yet. We're about to find out."

Studying his shoes, he speculated silently on the implications of the 'we' in Vivienne's statement. She was muttering under her breath, fussing with the clasp of her bag. Gavin breathed deeply, working to contain his anxiety. To assess the gravity of the situation required knowledge and experience he simply did not have, but the mere fact of Vivienne's discomfort was enough to convince him that he was right to feel threatened.

Pulling her mobile phone from the bag, she pressed it to the window.

"What are you doing?" he asked, hoping his voice would not falter.

"Photographing him. Evidence. He might try to lie his way out of it."

"I see. So - what next?"

"Well, I'm ready to go. But you" - she prodded his chest with a rigid finger - "I think you should stay here. I'll go out and confront him, tell him to piss off and leave me alone. Then I'll signal you to come out."

"Is this subterfuge really necessary?"

"You don't know Jack. He's not reliable."

"Reliable?"

"Never mind. I don't want this going wrong."

"Supposing he won't go away. Supposing he just sits there and watches you drive off."

"Why would he do that? Watching an empty house."

"But it isn't empty, is it? I'm here - and if he followed you, he most likely saw two people cross the road."

"You'd be surprised. His eyesight's not what it was. I'm always telling him he shouldn't be driving."

They wandered into the hall and stood quietly by the door. Gavin looked at her face in the stark light and wondered if he was in love with her. How could he even tell?

"If he's suspicious," he said, "he won't go away that easily."

"Oh, he's suspicious all right. The most suspicious character I've ever met."

"What I mean is, if - "

"Gavin, I know what you mean. Please." She hoisted her bag on to her shoulder. "I'm going to drive off, lose him and come back for you. Wait here. Give me at least five minutes." She squeezed his arm. "Don't worry, it'll be all right."

"Vivienne, I don't think you should come back. That'll only increase the risk."

"So how are you going to get back?"

"I can walk down to the main road. There'll be a bus."

"Oh Gavin, why should you? This is ridiculous. Why should he dictate what we do?"

"But he is, isn't he? He's making us change our plans. He's making us scared."

"You may be scared, Gavin. I'm not. Angry I may be, but not scared."

He grabbed her shoulder, kneading the muscle. "Vivienne, I - "

"What's the matter?"

He shook his head miserably. "Nothing. Here, you could ring him, tell him to go."

"No, that might alert him. He might come over."

"Does it make any difference? It's not as if we have anything to hide."

"From ourselves, no. But from him...the pair of us alone together in an empty house..."

"It's just - I don't see why we have to hide from him. Why I have to hide from him. After all, he doesn't know me from Adam. I could be anyone, the agent, anyone at all."

When she punched his shoulder, he nearly fell backwards in surprise. "Of course, you're right! Here's me, so concerned about his discovering you, I never thought - you don't have to be *you*, at all. You can be anybody we want."

That acid taste flooded his mouth again, a mingling of fear, relief and excitement. He could walk out bold and innocent, cloaked in the perfect disguise of anonymity.

Suddenly her eyes shone with renewed confidence. She unlatched the door and peeped out.

"Is he still there," Gavin asked.

51

"Yes. Look, I think we'll have to give you a name, otherwise it won't sound believable."

"A name?"

"Yes. You can be - you're Michael Lord from the agency. We don't have to say which one, and he'll be too dim to ask. You were just showing me round. Only don't say more than you have to."

"Well, I wasn't about to engage him in conversation."

"Jack doesn't do conversation. Grunts and accusations are his specialty." She drew the door open wide. "Come on then, miracle man. We need you now. You ready?"

He nodded. "I'd better go first. Make it look convincing."

"Gavin," she said, with a smile, "you're much too pale to look convincing."

He led her slowly across the road to the car, wishing he'd had the foresight to bring some spurious paperwork with him, or a clipboard, perhaps. They walked slowly but deliberately, and neither of them looked at the blue Vauxhall parked behind Vivienne's VW, although Gavin could not resist a fleeting glance from the corner of his eye. Vivienne unlocked the car and told him to wait for her inside.

"We could just drive off," he suggested.

"Not a good idea. If he thinks we're anxious to avoid him..."

Adjusting the interior mirror, he saw her walk back and tap on the passenger window of Jack's car. The driver leaned across, steadying himself with one hand on the steering wheel.

As he had no ignition key to power open the front window, Gavin could only hold his breath, one ear to the glass, to hear what was said. Vivienne's face looked taut and pale in the harsh winter sunlight, while her husband, dark-bearded and bespectacled, strained towards her, his greyish skin mottled by reflections in the windscreen.

"What the fuck do you think you're playing at?" he heard her demand.

There was an instant reply, but he couldn't catch the words.

"It's no business of yours," she insisted. "Mr Lord is just showing me the flat. What's it to you?"

She yanked open the door and seemed almost to spit her next words in his face. Gavin listened to his heart beating. He gazed into his lap, and then the car shook as the driver's door opened and Vivienne bounced into her seat.

"Done and sorted!" She started the engine. "We're out of here!"

Gavin realigned the mirror. "What if he follows us to the office? Then he'll know I'm not Mr Lord."

"Trust me. He won't follow us."

"If you say so."

She turned in the road and drove past Jack's car, still parked at the kerb. Neither of them looked at him.

"Well done!" Gavin said.

She was staring grimly ahead, her jaw set rigid. Her knuckles stood out white as they gripped the wheel. The car bucked and weaved as she swung through the traffic.

"I'm sorry I got you into this," she said. "You probably won't want me in your hair after this." She glanced at him quickly. "I'll understand."

Gavin let out a deep sigh, and he slid his right hand over Vivienne's thigh above the hem of her skirt, letting go when she moved her leg inwards. His heart fluttered at the feel of her.

"Traffic's crazy," she cursed. She glanced in the mirror. "He's gone."

"Vivienne, I - well, I don't want to stop seeing you," he said, and there was a quaver in his voice.

"Seeing me? You make it sound like an affair."

He swallowed and licked his lips. "The point is - I think I'm in love with you."

She snicked into another gear and accelerated hard over an amber light. "Don't be ridiculous!" she said.

7

NOTHING from her all Christmas. Still, he thought, maybe that was as well. Whatever she meant to him, at this family time she was a distraction he could do without. Despite her brusque dismissal of the pledge he had made to her in the car, he felt glad that he had revealed his affections. About his confession there was a sense of relief, a conviction that, by this simple statement, he had turned a corner in their precarious relationship. From now on, everything they did or discussed would be based upon a different understanding.

Of course, he acknowledged that the clumsy declaration he had offered her was not without risk. He had exposed his perception of her while her view of him remained shrouded in mystery. His honesty made him vulnerable. That she had made no attempt to contact him since their last meeting could well be an eloquent silence, a means of conveying dismay or apprehension at his disclosure. *I never asked for this. I never wanted you to be in love with me. I don't want to be possessed; I am uncomfortable with the presumption.*

On the first working day of a new year, he turned these reflections over in his head as the tube clattered into London, walled in by the trembling darkness of soot-caked pipes and conduits that seemed to writhe, snake-like, against the carriage windows. When the girl sitting opposite turned aside, he could see himself mirrored in the glass behind her, head down, pale, hollow-eyed, worried.

When he rose from the canyons of warm wind into the monochrome daylight of a January morning, the rain was splattering the streets, sending commuters into a robotic frenzy. Gavin tucked his chin into his coat and barged ahead, shielding his face with a newspaper he had picked up on the train. Scurrying in and out of the cover of shop awnings, heedless of everyone around him, it was inevitable that he should bump shoulders in the eddying throng, and be jostled in return, not caring, not feeling or seeing those with whom he shared the slicked and puddled pavement. When the collision occurred, it seemed almost too predictable, in that first bruising instant of contact, for him to register more than mild surprise; but the person now clinging to his coat-sleeves was not about to let the moment pass without protest.

"Christ! Why don't you watch where you're going!" She was crushed so hard against his chest, he smelled her perfume. "Get off me!"

"I'm sorry! I didn't mean it!"

"Well, I know that, don't I?" She lunged backwards, clutching a magazine and a paper cup of coffee sealed with a plastic cap. "Lucky you didn't get this all over you!"

"There's a lid on it."

"Yeah, that's hardly the point."

"Okay, I've apologised." He took in her face, contorted with petulant anger - rather pretty, he thought, dark hair tumbling loosely out of a red wool hat, reddish copper lipstick on full lips. "Really, there's no harm done."

She stuffed the magazine under her arm and stepped round him. "Pillock!"

He flinched as her explosive 'P' sent a fine spray of spit into his face. A second later she was gone, mingling with the crowd, her hat bobbing like a red light in the gloom. In a state of flustered pique, Gavin marched on, hardly noticing the driving rain, finally slamming through the glass doors of Hain Maybury with glazed, unfocused eyes, dropping the folded newspaper in the nearest bin. Going up in the lift, he stood steaming inside his clothes, teeth gritted, averting his gaze from his fellow passengers.

The office was deserted when he arrived. He hung his rain-splashed coat on a hanger, combed his hair and wiped his face with his handkerchief. Walking to the water cooler for a drink, less to slake his thirst than to rinse the bad taste from his mouth, he heard the windblown rain peppering the window, the city lights glimmering through the glass in mobile streaks of red, yellow and amber.

How dare she call him a pillock! He swished the water round his tongue and gulped it down, tapping the empty cup crossly against his teeth.

Five minutes later, the outer door burst open and Carolyn swept in, coat flying. She shook herself angrily and glared at Gavin as if the wild weather was his responsibility.

"Good morning, Carolyn!" he said, dredging up a smile.

"No it bloody isn't!" She peeled off her soaked coat and threw it over her chair. "It's coming down like stair-rods out there. I am absolutely *effin'* drenched!"

He pulled a face. "Thought you had an umbrella."

"I have," she said, sighing, "only I left it behind. It was dry when I left home."

"Okay, well, get yourself sorted out and hang up your coat."

"Gavin, I am *drowned*! I am soaked through to my underwear!"

"So what do you expect me to do about it? Couldn't you have sheltered?"

"I'm late as it is." She stood beside her desk, flapping her arms in frustration. "Oh, what am I going to do?"

He studied her face - hair sticking up in slicked spikes, make-up smudged, the tip of her nose pinked by the raw wind. She was never pretty, he thought, but she had a kind of disdainful attractiveness, now cruelly moulded into vulnerability by the elements.

"What are you going to do?" he repeated slowly. He slumped back in his chair and regarded her over tented fingers. "The way I see it, you have three options."

"Which are?"

"Carolyn," he said, frowning, "can you move away from my door? You're dripping all over the floor."

"What, is that one of the options?"

"No. Sorry. I mean - look, you can sit steaming in your wet clothes and hope you don't catch pneumonia. Or you can go home and change." He waved his hands in the air in mock triumph. "Or you can take off the wet stuff and hang it over the radiator."

She stared at him solemnly, unblinking. "Right. And that's it?"

"Yep. That's it."

The way the wet blouse clung to her body, he could see the lace outline of her bra cups through the fabric. There was water in his shoes and it was nine-thirty in the morning. Some girl he'd never met had just insulted him. He gazed at Carolyn's chest, but nothing happened, everything was wrong, he didn't feel remotely aroused.

"Well, I can't go prancing about like I'm in a wet T-shirt contest. And the second option's completely impractical." She collapsed heavily into her chair. "And you can stuff the third one!"

"Sure. Only you did ask."

She nodded at the window. "Stopped raining now, look. Bloody weather!"

Lying bundled in the chair, legs splayed, she looked like a scarecrow, he thought, with her mussed-up hair, her blotchy face and dishevelled clothes. He couldn't help wondering if her knickers were wet as well. Probably not. That didn't seem likely, somehow.

An idea edged its way into his mind. He'd found himself thinking of Vivienne again, and that was how the thought came to him. It was a long shot, but it was worth a try.

He stood up and spoke to Carolyn from the doorway. "There is another way," he said.

She sat there, immobile, her chin sunk below her throat. "There is another system," she growled tonelessly.

"What?"

"It was a film. Did you see it? It was called 'The Forbin Project'. It was really good."

He laughed nervously. "What are you on about?"

"This film - it was about when the Americans built this amazing super-computer. It could do anything - well, almost. It was housed in this huge building, and all the scientists and media people arrived on the day they were going to start it up." She winced, tugging the wet blouse away from her skin. "Anyway, whatever the computer wanted to say, it all came up written on this massive screen, it couldn't actually talk."

"That's a relief."

"Yes. Well, anyway, so they start up the machine to give it its first instructions, and then, on the screen, it says: 'There is another system'. You see. And what that means is - what they don't know - the Russians have built a super-computer of their own, and what happens next is, these two computers start communicating with each other and completely ignoring what their designers want them to do, until they get to plan world domination. It's really brilliant."

"Right. Sort of electronic anarchy."

"I suppose, yes." She puffed out her cheeks, making a popping noise, and gazed at him thoughtfully. "It's just - that's what it reminded me of, when you said there w-"

"Yeah, I get the message, Carolyn."

"Sorry. Am I rambling on?"

"Sort of. I mean, it's not going to get your clothes dry, is it?"

"No. I think I've made the chair all wet."

"Right, okay, I think we have to see if we can get you some fresh clothes."

"What, you mean buy some?"

"Course not. But maybe we could borrow some."

"Borrow some?" She pulled herself upright, laughing. "Who from, for God's sake?"

"Trust me," he said, backing away from the door. "I know the location, it's just a matter of access."

"Gavin, what are you talking about? I'll have got dry by the time you start making sense."

He turned, pivoting round the end of his desk, and sat down. They stared at each other without speaking. A babble of voices sounded in the corridor as people arrived to start work. Carolyn's rain-spiked hair and streaked face gave her a punkish appearance, he thought, like an anaemic teenager.

"Carolyn, is there any make-up in your bag?"

"Why, yours need touching up?"

"Don't be cheeky, or I won't help you."

"I think I'm beyond help. I'm ruined, destroyed." She grinned, plucked a toffee from a pot on the desk and threw it at him. "Here, breakfast!"

He bent down and picked up the sweet. The carpet was mottled with water. Someone opened the outer door, looked in and ducked out again.

"I think you should go and do your hair," he said. "Clean your face up. You look - unusual."

She shrugged, dragging herself to her feet. "Spare me the euphemism," she said, coldly. "And I'm not taking any clothes off, right?"

"Of course. Let's keep this entirely professional."

Once she had left the room, he dialled Marketing and asked for Mrs Drexler. Even as he pressed the buttons, he wondered whether he was doing this for Carolyn or for himself. There was a sense of giving in to something, of not wanting the silence to last any longer. If he claimed a reason for the call, he recognised an excuse.

Someone went to find her. In the background he heard her saying, "Who is it?" and the clang of a filing cabinet drawer sliding shut. Then there were footsteps, a mumbled remark to a colleague, a sharp intake of breath.

"This is Vivienne Drexler."

"I know. I've missed you."

"Oh, hello."

"Good Christmas?"

Why did he half expect her to say, 'Sorry I haven't been in touch'? Even for allowing the thought to cross his mind, he cursed himself, for in a chilling instant of self-analysis he realised that only a deeply ingrained and utterly absurd measure of faint-hearted reserve had prevented him from attempting to contact her while he sat meekly waiting for her to take the initiative. He was smothered by a kind of emotional decorum, a creeping miasma of self-doubt.

"It was all right," she said. "We stayed at home. Peaceful."

He took the last word to mean that Jack had not hassled her about the flat or been abusive. By now he knew her well enough to understand that she needed her space.

Though he gave her a second or two, she didn't ask about him or what he had done during the holiday. He told himself it didn't matter. It didn't affect anything.

"Vivienne, I rang - uh - actually we've got a slight problem here."

"What sort of a problem? Where?" Her voice sounded taut, strained.

"Well, you know my assistant, Carolyn Vickers..."

"I think so. I've seen her around, I don't know her."

"Right. The thing is, she got soaked to the skin coming in this morning, I don't want her to sit around in wet clothes and - well, I just wondered if - God, this is going to sound really strange, but - er - is there any way you could let me - let her have a change of just what she needs till tomorrow? Like, I don't know, maybe if your daughter had something, you know, which might fit her, I know it's an imposition and all that, but I feel I ought to, to at least..."

Gavin felt his throat constricting, and he let the words peter out, until there was just a pregnant silence hanging on the line.

"I think I should know," she said at length, "what the essential facts of the matter are. I mean, 'something which might fit her' - so what does that amount to? What exactly do you want, Gavin?"

"Um - I'm not quite sure. She prob-"

"Is she there, Gavin? Can you put her on the line? You're obviously not her wardrobe manager."

"No. She's gone to tidy up."

He heard her sigh laboriously, making no attempt to disguise her frustration. "Well, I've nothing here for her. She'll have to come home with me. Is it still raining?"

"No. Look, I'm really sorry, Vivienne. I just can't think what else to do."

"Christ, you blokes do get yourselves in some good scrapes!"

"Well, this wasn't anything I did, I'm just - "

"All right, all right, I know." She was silent for a moment, but he heard her breathing into the phone. "I don't even know the girl. Perhaps if you come with us."

"This is kind of crazy, I know."

"Yes, it's a pretty good imitation. What does she do for an encore?"

"I know she'd be really grateful."

Through the sighs and clicks, the small intakes and exhalations of breath, he could almost hear her mind working in the room above his head. The machinery unnerved and intimidated him. Yet the question, when she fired it at him, came as a complete surprise.

"Okay Gavin, I'll only ask you this once, so I shall expect you to be straight with me. Is this just so you can get on with your job, or have you got something with this girl?"

"What?"

"You heard me, Gavin. Don't ask me to repeat myself."

"You - you're asking me if I'm committed to her?"

"Bollocks, Gavin! I'm asking you if you're fucking her!"

"No, absolutely not, ever!" His hands were starting to shake, his chest fluttering. "I'm just trying to solve a problem, that's all." He wiped a hand across his brow. "No, honestly, it's all right, if you can't do it I quite understand. I've made no promises."

"Oh, don't go all sulky. Have you heard me refuse? It was a reasonable question."

"On the contrary, I think it was an unfair and rather impudent question, but I've given you my answer."

He waited, listening to her breath rasping, wishing her mouth was really that close to his ear, imagining what it would feel like, the dewy heat of it, the soft, slicked point of her tongue darting out to flick his earlobe.

"Gavin, I don't want to be upstaged, that's all. I need to know where I stand."

He had to stifle a snort of ironic laughter. "You want to know where *you* stand? What about - "

"What about what?"

"Doesn't matter."

"Okay, look, you helped me out at the flat. I'll return the favour. Meet me downstairs in five minutes."

"Thanks."

"Don't forget to bring her with you."

Slanting its thin lemony light beneath a barrage of mud-coloured cloud, the winter sun seemed to spotlight the three of them as they trudged uphill to Vivienne's house. A gusting breeze ruffled Gavin's hair, fanned Carolyn's scarf into her face and daubed the pavement with grey-brown stains of drying rainwater. It felt odd almost to the point of impropriety to be out walking at this time of the morning, the traffic diminishing and the streets bleakly empty of the sodden commuters who had so manically jostled one another an hour before. Few words passed between them as they walked. Carolyn, uncomfortable in her wet clothes, just wanted the ordeal to be over. Vivienne felt vaguely that she owed Gavin at least a perfunctory good turn, but the distraction was a nuisance, an irritation. As for Gavin himself, he was embarrassed that he had needed to solicit her aid, though underlying this awkwardness was a thin strata of excitement at finding himself the pivotal character in the game.

Though she had made no direct reference to her predicament, in the present company, Carolyn's stance, head down and tight-lipped, betrayed her inevitable sense of dismayed insecurity at having been manoeuvred into a state of dependence on someone she scarcely knew. Unsure of what to say, she said nothing. Whether Vivienne thought her rude, or merely disadvantaged, no-one could determine or articulate, but the aura of lumpish detachment enveloping the group seemed to expand the minutes into hours, the silence into a barrier of almost physical pain surrounding each one of them.

Gavin heaved a sigh of relief as they reached the house. Vivienne pushed open the door and ushered Gavin and Carolyn into the hall. The place seemed gloomy and rather cold. Gavin recalled the last time he was here, the strange confrontation in the bathroom.

Vivienne closed the door and switched on the hall light. "If you'd like to sit in the front room," she told Gavin. She rested one hand on Carolyn's shoulder, looking her up and down. "I don't know," she said, "you're a different build. Lizzie's more - willowy." She glanced up the stairs. "Perhaps some of her older things, when she was - well, anyway."

She told the girl to follow her upstairs. Gavin went to sit on the front room settee. Yesterday's paper lay on the coffee table, and he picked it up, flicking through the pages without seeing what was there. Overhead, he heard their voices, then the boom and scrape of drawers being opened and closed. The newsprint swam before his eyes, as he asked himself - what am I doing here? An exaggerated sense of duty to one woman, a morbid addiction to another; these were the forces to which he responded, and he waited silently in awe of his frailty.

A peal of laughter rang in the stairwell, her laughter, Vivienne's laughter. He had never known her laugh, not like that. When she was with him, there was no room for laughter. He folded the newspaper into a neat rectangle and slapped it down on the coffee table.

Really, there was no need for this. He had done all that could reasonably be expected of him. Now he need only call up the stairs, tell them he was returning to the office, and leave the pair of them to resolve matters in their own way. Neither of them would give his departure a second thought.

Another sound intruded, this one closer, crisper, the rasp of a key in the door-lock. What if this was the infamous Jack? He sat hunched on the edge of the seat, holding his breath.

It was a woman's voice. Softly, as if to no-one else, it asked, "Why is the light on?"

Gavin allowed himself the shallowest escape of breath. Animated voices spilled down the staircase.

"Mum? Is that you?"

Footsteps sounded at the head of the stairs, then Vivienne's voice. "Hello Lizzie. You're back soon. How did it go?"

"Yeah, it was good. I got the job."

"Oh Lizzie! That's marvellous!"

"Yeah, right. Mum, what are you - is something wrong?"

"Wrong? Oh no, no. Actually - look, you'd better come up."

"What's happened? Why are you home?"

"Just come up, love. There's someone you need to meet."

"What? Who?"

"It's all right. I'll explain."

Gavin heard the girl sigh heavily as she approached the stairs. Low voices drifted back to him as she reached the top landing, her feet thudding loudly on the last two steps, as though to underscore her apprehension. He heard Vivienne say, "This is Carolyn," and then the voices faded and fragmented as the three of them moved into a bedroom.

Gavin checked his watch, leaned forward with his head in his hands and gazed down at the carpet between his feet. The earlier rain had left white scuffs on his shoes, and he studied them irritably. The marks, he knew, would be a pain to remove. This whole morning had become a pain. A shaft of pale sunshine tilted in at the bay window behind him, licking his shoulders like a warm tongue, more a taunt than a comfort.

A single set of footsteps on the stairs made him sit up, watching the doorway. Vivienne appeared, carrying her coat. "I think we're okay," she said, "they seem to be getting along famously."

"Was that your daughter?"

"Yes. She went for an interview. They offered her the job straight away, so she's all fired up. Research trainee for a TV company."

"Sounds interesting," he said, hoping to appear enthusiastic.

A chorus of laughter chimed above them. "See what I mean," Vivienne said, pointing over her shoulder with her thumb.

"How long will they be?" he asked her.

"Not long. She's got some things." She draped her coat over an armchair. "Can I make you a drink?"

"No thanks. I need to be getting back."

She shrugged. "Up to you. I can walk back with her if you want. If you're in a hurry to get away."

That last remark seemed barbed. "I'm not in a hurry," he said. "I'm not anxious to get away from you, Vivienne. I've told you that before."

"Yes, of course. Only we won't talk about that now."

"No. So - so when will we talk about it? Will we ever talk about it - about us?"

"Gavin, there is no 'us'. Please don't push this. I can't handle it right now."

"All right. It's just that I don't know where I stand with you. At the party - do you remember? - you said, 'I want you to hold me.' Ever since then, you seem intent on keeping me at arm's length." He covered his face with his hands. "I suppose I'm confused, that's all."

"Oh, well I'm sorry you find me so difficult to get on with. Perhaps if you tried giving me some space."

"Some space?" He sat with his hands fanned out either side of his face. "The whole holiday, I never spoke to you. I never wished you a Happy Christmas or a Happy New Year. How much space do you need?"

"I need as much as I want. I have to keep control. That's the kind of person I am."

For what seemed a moment suspended in time, he sat there, just quietly looking at her, while she stood with one hand resting on the back of the chair, her legs crossed at the ankles, poised, perfectly balanced, graceful as a dancer. As the seconds ticked by, he found himself trying not to like her, not to want her in his life. If only the choice had been his to make. There was no denying the chemistry within his own heart. Slow, sure, inexorable processes had been set in motion, and now he was as a passenger aboard an accelerating machine, helplessly entangled in the relentless mechanism.

He eased himself up and walked slowly past her into the hall. "I'll go. Thanks for helping Carolyn. Thank your daughter for me."

She turned to stand beside him. She nodded up the stairs. "Thank her yourself, she's coming down."

Carolyn came down towards them, carrying a plastic bag. The girl behind her was taller, slimmer, her dark hair bouncing softly in a tangle of wild curls. In her hand she clasped a red hat.

"All done," Carolyn said, cheerfully.

Vivienne extended a hand to her daughter's shoulder. "Gavin, this is Lizzie." She touched Gavin's chest. "Lizzie, Gavin's a friend of mine from work, and Carolyn - well, you get the picture."

Lizzie stopped on the bottom step, one foot in the air. She and Gavin stared at each other. Gavin's mouth hung open.

"What's up?" Carolyn said.

Lizzie stepped to the floor. "We've met," she said.

"Oh, my God!" Gavin murmured.

"How can you have met?" Vivienne was scratching her forehead in puzzlement. "I don't understand."

"We - uh - we bumped into each other in the street. Me and - Lizzie."

Lizzie put the red hat back on and pulled it down to her ears. "All coming back to you now, is it?"

"Yes. I suppose I ought - "

"No, please, let me," Lizzie interrupted. "I need to explain."

"Well, I wish somebody would." Vivienne was frowning at each of them in turn, while Carolyn, hugging her bag of damp clothes to her chest, stood gazing awkwardly at the floor.

"I was in a hurry," Lizzie went on. "See, I had this interview and I thought I was late. I wasn't late, but I *thought* I was late. Then this guy, he had a newspaper up to his face, he crashes into me, gets me all rattled. Oh Christ!"

"This guy?" Vivienne massaged her temples as if to clear her head. "What guy?"

Lizzie flapped a hand under Gavin's chin. "*This* guy!"

"I need to get back," Carolyn said.

"You two go on ahead," Vivienne urged them, one hand on Carolyn's back. "I'll get the full story from Lizzie." She reached behind Gavin and opened the door. "If you see Ross, tell him I'll be there in time for his meeting."

Gavin turned to face the street's chill draught, but before he could move to the door, Lizzie caught his arm. "No, wait."

"What is it?" He saw her face in close-up, just as he had done in the rain when they first met. There were tiny speckles, silver silica, in her brown eyes, and the lightest brush of down over her upper lip.

"I just wanted to say - I shouldn't have called you that. I'm sorry - okay?" He felt her breath on his face. "You must think I'm very rude, only I'm not, not really."

"It's okay. It was my fault."

"Yeah, but. I behaved like shit. I'm sorry."

At his back, he felt Vivienne's eyes on him, heard her brief grunt of sympathetic laughter. He didn't know why he did it, but he reached out and touched Lizzie's cheek.

As he and Carolyn reached the pavement, Vivienne, standing with one arm round Lizzie's shoulders, called out to him. "Meant to tell you. The flat - I'm taking it. I'll be in Saturday." She cupped a hand to her mouth. "Bring a paintbrush!"

8

A STEADY pulse of relaxed satisfaction coursed through him as he felt the sun's warmth, amplified by the glass, anointing the skin of his wrist and bared forearm, the muscles tensing, flexing rhythmically, carrying the brush with measured strokes along the planes and interstices of the window-frame.

A secondary heat, lighter and more fragile, touched the back of his neck. He found the sensation surprising and not unpleasant. He had no need to turn round, for he knew she was standing close behind him, watching him work. It was quiet in the room, and he could hear her breathing. If he stepped back, he might bump against her, then there would be a gentle exchange of apologies, perhaps a tinkle of shy laughter, the touch of a hand.

"It's very kind of you to help me," she said. "I don't mind painting doors, but windows are just too fiddly."

"Windows are interesting," he said. "You can pause and look out, see the world."

That made her chuckle. "The world? A drab street in North London. I don't call that the world."

"All right, so I've led a sheltered life." He stopped painting to roll back his sleeve more securely. "What did you say this was - Soft Peach?"

"Vanilla Peach. Do you like it?"

"It's warm. Sort of friendly."

"Yes. I thought of waking up in the summer, with the sun falling on it, if I did the walls as well. I'd lie in bed and feel warm, kind of protected. Do you think?"

He didn't reply. He imagined what she had described, sunshine flaring yellow on russet-pink, the spears of light rebounding on to the bed where she lay, her dark eyes blinking away the sleep, the tawny branches of her thin arms thrown outside the duvet, her tangled hair seething over the pillow like a spiralling fire, a skimpy T-shirt rucked up by the bedclothes, underneath maybe a tiny pair of white cotton knickers scarcely containing the moisture of the night.

She was prodding his arm lightly with her forefinger. "You listening to me?"

"Mm? I'm sorry, I was...somewhere else."

"I noticed. I asked you if you wanted a drink. You were miles away."

He turned to face her.

"Ah-ah. Don't lean against the window."

He raised his hands submissively. "Of course. Stripes like peach pyjamas."

"Well, would you?"

"Would I what?"

She rolled her eyes, making them huge. "Shall I make us some coffee. I can't offer you anything stronger, the fridge is nearly empty."

"Coffee would be fine. One sugar. What about your mother?"

"I'll do one for her as well." She looked around her. "We'll have to sit on the floor, pretend we're Japanese."

Gavin dunked his brush in a jam-jar of white spirit resting on a newspaper spread on the floorboards. Lizzie's footsteps trailed downstairs to the kitchen. Faintly, he heard her voice, then Vivienne's, echoing thinly in the room below. A large cardboard box sat in the far corner, Lizzie's blue fleece jacket thrown over it. He picked up the jacket, peered at the box, then held the garment against his chest, inhaling her scent from the collar.

Funny how things worked out, he thought. He'd been in the flat over an hour and only seen Vivienne for a few minutes, hardly said a dozen words to her. Lizzie had sort of commandeered him as soon as he arrived, taken his coat to hang it in a safe place, almost as if she was taking charge of him. He recalled that brief flash of venom, when she had called him a pillock, and he shook his head and smiled.

She brought in a tray, two mugs on it and a crumpled packet. "I found some biscuits."

They sat cross-legged on the cold floor, facing each other, the steaming mugs between them.

Lizzie clasped her mug in both hands, holding it up to her face, and looked at him over the rim. "So - are you an old friend of Mum's?"

"No, I'm sort of a new friend."

"I see." She took a sip of coffee and went on gazing at him. "She must think a lot of you."

"Why do you say that?"

"You're the only person from work I've ever seen. She says you came with her to see the flat before Christmas."

"That's right. I was surprised to be asked."

"Then Dad turned up."

"Yes. Well."

"Bastard."

"Pardon?"

"Not you. Him."

He sighed. "He is her husband."

"Not for much longer." She shuddered. "Gives me the creeps."

"I - uh - am I allowed to ask why?"

She carried on staring at him like that, as if she was trying to see inside his head. She unwrapped the pack of biscuits, still gazing into his eyes, and slid one into her mouth.

"I did broach the subject with your mother," he said, "but I didn't get much response. She sort of made me feel it was none of my business."

"Well, it isn't, is it? You don't wanna know." She stuck out her tongue, coated with brown paste. "These are stale."

"Might just be the top ones. Try - "

"Yeah, okay."

She carefully prised a biscuit from near the bottom of the pack, snapped it in half and held out one piece between her thumb and forefinger. "Open," she said.

Nervously, Gavin opened his mouth, watching her eyes. She slid the biscuit on to his tongue, leaving a dusting of crumbs on his lower lip. He closed his mouth, and she smiled and traced her finger from left to right along the curve of his lip to remove the crumbs, then from right to left, and back again.

"Lick my finger," she said.

He chewed the biscuit and swallowed. Tiny crumbs adhered to the pad of her finger, poised before his face.

"Lick my finger," Lizzie repeated.

His tongue flicked out and took the grains from her soft flesh. He wanted to kiss her finger, maybe kiss all her fingers, grasp them in his hand and kiss them separately, but he didn't dare to. He told himself he wasn't ready for this.

"I'm getting these - vibes," he said, trying to still the quaver in his voice. "Like there's some dark secret in the family. With Jack, I mean."

"Hmm. Sounds a bit melodramatic. Skeletons in the cupboard and all that."

"I notice you're not denying it." He drank the dregs of his coffee. "Sorry, I really shouldn't be asking."

"I think we've established that. The point is, you don't *need* to know. It doesn't alter anything." She squinted over his shoulder. "Did you finish that window?"

"Nearly. Five minutes." He hoisted himself up, flapping at his jeans to remove the dust. "What do you want doing next?"

"I'm not sure."

She stood up and walked to the window. Her grey wool sweater had ridden up while she was sitting, and a thin crescent of bare flesh showed above the waistband of her jeans. Standing behind her, he pondered the temptation for a moment. Probably it wouldn't matter, he thought, it was hardly important. He stepped beside her and gingerly traced a finger along the line of cool skin.

Lizzie flinched, shaking her head. "You touching my body?" she said, staring out of the window.

Suddenly he felt embarrassed, perhaps because she hadn't smiled. "I'm sorry. I don't know why I did that."

"Why are you sorry?" she asked, turning to look at him. "Is that how you are with her - with Mum? Faint heart, Gavin, faint heart. You'll have to be strong, go for it. It's the language she understands."

"Right. Trouble is, she told me she needs her space. I don't want to crowd her."

"From him, she needs her space, not from you. All that 'I need my space' crap is just baloney, she's just trying to convince herself she can adjust to being on her own again, even though she doesn't want to. What Mum wants is support, not isolation, for God's sake."

He nodded. "I'm sure you're right. I'm afraid I haven't had much practice at this."

She arched her eyebrows then, and her unblinking gaze seemed to penetrate the very core of him. "Then I think you should finish here, and go downstairs and see her. Get some practice in, eh?"

"Okay. I am very fond of her, you know."

"Yes, I know. Don't give up on her."

Gavin picked up the brush and carried on painting. The job was trickier now, for his hand was trembling. The sun had gone in, and the room felt colder. Music drifted up the stairs. Vivienne must have turned on the radio, perhaps for company. Very shortly, he would go down to her.

Lizzie's voice rang hollow over the floorboards. He turned and saw her at the door. "I'm going to the loo," she said. She smiled quickly. "Think I'm starting."

"Starting?"

"Yes. Don't you know anything about women?"

"Oh. Sorry. I - yes, of course."

For a while they stood staring at each other. Lizzie chewed her little finger, her head on one side, so her curls hung down. "Come here," she said quietly.

He rested the brush carefully on the window ledge, and walked over to her. She was running her tongue across her lips, corner to corner.

"What's the matter?" he asked.

She shook her head. "I want to tell you something, that's all."

"I see."

Quite gently, almost gracefully, she placed both hands upon his shoulders and drew him towards her. "Gavin, you are a good man. You know, if I was your schoolteacher, I'd have to say something like..." She scanned the ceiling for inspiration. "I'd say: 'A promising pupil, but must try harder.' Does that sound too patronising?"

"Depends what you mean."

"Oh, you know what I mean." She gripped him tightly. "You're shaking."

"I can't help it. You're amazing."

"We're all amazing, Gavin. We just have to find a way of showing it - of releasing the energy. You're full of pent-up energy."

"Am I?"

"Yes, I think so. But I can help you unlock it." She moved slowly towards him, parting her lips a little, and as her face covered his, he felt the warm wetness of her lips working against his, easing open his mouth, and the quick, hot dance of her tongue inside him, light as a butterfly.

Then she let him go, just standing there with a strange, questioning smile on her face. Gavin marvelled again at the silvery speckles in her brown eyes, sparks of liquid light.

"Thank you," he said. "I think you're beautiful."

Her smile broadened. "Yeah, well I won't be so beautiful if I stand here much longer. There's junk coming out. Must be all this emotion."

"Oh, right. You be okay?"

"Course. You come back soon now."

"Yes."

"You and Mum - you deserve each other." She bent down and picked up her bag from the floor. "And thanks for coming to help."

"Maybe I'll see you again," he said. "If there's something else I can do."

"Depends what else you're good at," she said, and grinned. "Remember what I said about practice."

Gavin painted the last few inches of the window frame, then he went downstairs and found Vivienne hanging curtains in the front room. A small portable radio stood on the mantelpiece, tuned to a classical music station. Out of atonal orchestral turmoil, a small, brave trumpet sounded, like a cry for help.

"*Poem of Ecstasy*," he intoned, gazing up at her silhouette against the window.

Vivienne dropped a box of plastic hooks, the contents scattering across the bare floor. "Damn!" she cursed.

"It's all right. I'll get them."

"Turn that down if you want."

"Let's at least hear the end. One of the greatest C major chords in the entire literature of music."

She came down from the stepladder and helped him, the two of them scrabbling about on the gritty floor. "Where's Lizzie?" she asked.

"Gone to the toilet. I finished her window."

"Thanks. You didn't have to."

Clutching a handful of hooks, she sat back on her heels, peering at him. "What's that on your face?"

Hesitantly, he touched his cheek.

"Not there. Round your mouth."

"Don't know. Could be paint."

"It doesn't look like paint to me. It looks more like Lizzie's lipstick."

He felt his face swarm with sudden warmth.

"Now your whole face is red. Bit of a give-away, Gavin."

They stood up, and he helped her pour the hooks back in the box.

"So. Were you painting, or snogging my daughter?"

"No need to make it sound so sordid. She said she was grateful, that's all."

"For what?"

"I did the window frame. It's no big deal."

Vivienne laughed, a kind of ironic snort. "Huh. Good job she didn't ask you to paint a wall; it's a bit chilly up there for taking all your clothes off."

He allowed himself a small sigh of despair, which he didn't bother to disguise. "I think I should treat that remark with - "

"With the contempt it deserves, yes, I know. Sometimes, you see, I can be quite contemptible."

"Only I don't believe you're really contemptible at all." He took the box of hooks from her hand and put it on the mantelpiece. "I've already told you how I feel, and you chose to ignore it."

"I know. Tell me I'm a cow."

"Don't. I wouldn't love you if you were a cow."

"You used that word again. I don't think you should use that word."

"No, maybe I shouldn't use any words, not any more. Maybe there's just too much talking." He took her arm and tried to draw her closer, but she resisted, unyielding as a stubborn child. "Vivienne, please," he sighed.

"What are you doing?"

"I want to kiss you. Is that so unreasonable?"

"Yes. I'm all grubby, and so are you. You've got slime on your face."

"Okay, okay." He turned aside, wiping his mouth with his hand. "Let's just listen to the music, eh?"

"I think that would be better. We can sit down. I'm sorry I've no chairs yet."

They sat on the floor with their backs to the radiator. Vivienne leaned her head back against the warm metal and closed her eyes. *Poem of Ecstasy* raged towards its final apotheosis.

"Can I hold your hand?" he asked her.

His eyes, too, were closed, but he felt her shrug against him. "If you want."

They sat without speaking, letting the music fill their darkness. While he was so close to her, he thought he might turn and kiss her cheek, catch her unawares, but that could so easily lead to an argument. So he held her hand, enjoying the steady warmth of it, and when the great organ-crowned deliverance rang out, he tightened his grip and felt her sympathetic response, like a compression in his heart.

For what seemed a long time, neither of them moved or spoke. Gavin squeezed her hand, and released it. Vivienne shivered.

"You're cold," he said.

"A little. I don't think the heating is quite right. I must get them to look at it."

Then he lifted her hand, lightly kissed her fingers.

"You'll get germs," she said. "My hands are filthy."

"Only the best germs," he murmured.

She snatched her hand away. "Tell me what Lizzie said to you."

"Nothing, really. I was painting, she was in and out. We didn't talk that much."

"Right. Too busy snogging, perhaps. It's as well the bed hasn't arrived yet."

"Vivienne, you know that's nonsense."

"Do I? She didn't - did she say anything about Jack?"

"No. Well, actually, she called him a bastard."

"So she did talk about him?"

"I told you, no."

"Come on. She didn't just blurt out, 'By the way, my dad's a bastard.'"

"I don't remember how she came to mention him. I would have listened, but she obviously didn't want to say any more." He touched her shoulder. "That's the truth."

He could see the muscles working in her jaw, highlighting her cheekbones. "She never mentioned the photographs? Tell me she never - "

"Photographs? What photographs?"

"The clothes." There were tears in her eyes. "Did she say about the clothes?"

"Vivienne, please, I don't know anything about any clothes."

"He can't sing, you know, not a note." Her voice was strained, almost strangled, tensed to breaking point. A tear slid slowly down her cheek. "Still, of course, he knows that, that's why he - well, I mean, it wasn't his own voice, was it? Wasn't meant to be." She let out a muffled moan, and banged the floor hard with the side of her fist. "Bastard! Fucking bastard!"

There was, he knew now, too much pain and anger here for him not to do it. So he threw his arms around her and held her close to him as she began to weep. He felt her tears running wet on the side of his neck, her body shaking, convulsing against his chest. She whimpered like a small animal, and he held her there, waiting, feeling her weight hang limply against him, amazed at how much he loved her.

We're all amazing, Gavin. We just have to find a way of showing it.

When next she spoke, her voice seemed to boom in the hollow of his shoulder. "On the kitchen shelf. A box of tissues. I need to clean my face."

Standing, he rested her securely against the radiator, as if she were a large doll. "I'll be right back," he said.

He helped her wipe her face, and she did not resist his attention. He turned off the radio.

She dabbed her eyes repeatedly with a bunched tissue. "It was sort of sad about poor Scriabin - don't you think?"

"Too complex for his time, perhaps," he ventured.

"I think so. All that mad piano music no-one could play." The tears brimmed in her eyes again. "Lizzie - did she mention Jasper? Did she?"

"Who's Jasper, Vivienne?"

"Jasper? No, Jasper's dead. Poor Jasper." Shaking her head, she covered her eyes with her hand, as if to blot out a memory. "Why do you bother with me? Why don't you just walk away?"

"I've already told you that. Whether you believe me or not, it doesn't make any difference."

"I mean...there's Tchaikovsky, mired in his sexual confusion; and Shostakovich, battling his political demons; and Rachmaninov, wallowing on a sea of overblown romanticism." She paused, chewing her top lip, grey-faced, haunted. "And then poor Scriabin - well, he was insane, wasn't he? The Russian establishment, they could take anything, but not that. All that magnificent madness. All gone to waste."

"Perhaps it should be *Poem of Lunacy,*" he said, stroking her hair.

"So she never said - about Jasper?"

"No."

"Poor Jasper. She loved him so much."

"Was he - was Jasper her boyfriend?"

"What? No, I mean Jasper."

"I know." He held her tightly, her face in the crook of his shoulder. "One day you'll tell me, won't you?"

"One day," she said, "I'll tell you everything."

"Can I wipe your face again, Vivienne?"

"No, I haven't finished yet. Why do you think they did that to poor Scriabin?"

"Because they didn't understand him. We still don't."

"It's all right," she said. "One day I'll tell you all about it."

"About Jack and - ?"

"Yes, of course. If you're still here."

"I'll be here," he said.

"Poor Scriabin. I do miss him. He was amazing. Amazing."

The tears ran down her face like rain.

9

HE STARED at her in sullen disbelief. A solid numbness seemed lodged in his chest, immobilizing him. "I find that extraordinary," he said, meaning that he found it both inexplicable and hurtful. "Are you sure you got the date right?"

Carolyn nodded, waving her hands, exasperated. "Yes. I've just told you. I saw her in the supermarket last week. She said 'Hello' and told me she was shopping for a party at the weekend."

"And she specifically said it was a house-warming?"

"Yes, I'm not deaf." She began opening and shutting her desk drawers, slamming files down on her blotter. "I'm sorry I mentioned it now."

"I think I am too," he muttered.

"Right, can I get you a coffee?"

"Please. Why didn't you say anything last week?"

"Because I naturally assumed you'd be going, that you knew all about it. I would never have thought for a moment she hadn't asked you." She held the tray in front of her face, peering at him apologetically over the top of it. "I'm sorry. If I'd known, I wouldn't have asked you if you'd had a good time."

"Obviously."

"I'll get the coffee. I'm sorry, Gavin."

"It's not your fault."

"No, but I feel bad about it now. I wish I'd kept my mouth shut."

"It was only natural you'd ask."

"I should have thought. I should have waited for you to mention it."

"Well, I wouldn't have done, would I?"

"No, but..." Her eyes narrowed as she struggled to focus her thoughts. "I wonder why she didn't invite you? See, I told you I had my doubts about her."

"Well, anyway. I'd like a cup of coffee, please."

"Course." She turned to the door, stopped and looked back at him. "Gavin, I'm really sorry."

"I told you, it's not your fault."

"I know that. I mean, I'm sorry - well, I'm sorry she's hurt you. That's what I mean."

"Who says she's hurt me?"

"Come on, Gavin. I know you better than that. She's supposed to be your friend."

"Yeah. I'm beginning to wonder," he said, absently.

Against that part of his better judgment that told him what was done was done, Gavin turned Carolyn's disclosure over and over in his mind, trying to make some sense of it, until it threatened to become a neurosis akin to self-torture. There was no need, he reasoned, for Vivienne to have told Carolyn of the party if she had no intention of inviting him. The fact that she had spoken of it, however casually, seemed a calculated ploy to remind him of his insignificance, for she could be in no doubt that Carolyn would feel free to discuss the event. Had Vivienne elected to remain silent in the matter, or even to solicit Carolyn's confidence, he might at least have been allowed to enjoy the bliss of ignorance. In his interpretation of the incident, he was left to brood over the imperious spectre of a woman who quietly declared, 'I can do what I like, he is not important to me, it is none of his business, I need not trouble myself with the complication of concealment.'

Or was he, just possibly, being unfair to her? Though he was suspicious of the proposition, it demanded to be examined, if only because it might mitigate the damage to his self-esteem. So his enquiry was a kind of selfishness, a half-hearted attempt at self-protection.

Here, then, was a woman bringing up two teenaged children with, presumably, scant support from a man she despised. She held down a full-time job, and now suffered the emotional turmoil of an imminent divorce. Simultaneously, she was moving out of the family home to re-establish herself - re-invent herself? - in an unfurnished flat in the middle of winter. Perhaps - he screwed up his fingers into loose fists and slitted his eyes as he considered these conditions - *perhaps*...there was a case for a more measured, more sympathetic response to an apparent slight. If that case were to be proven, or even coloured with the palest shading of validity, then he must charge himself with indecent haste in condemning her. Whoever she had invited to the flat at the weekend, they were probably close friends of long-standing or people from her office. He was, at best, on the periphery of that circle.

"Here. I've brought you an extra biscuit." Carolyn patted his arm, a small act of consolation.

He offered his reflections for her consideration. She perched on the spare chair, the one used by occasional visitors or interviewees, and gazed at him sternly. When she crossed her legs, he tried not to be distracted by the brief flash of her thighs.

"I mean, I wouldn't want to over-react," he explained.

"You wanna know what I think, Gavin?"

"Well, yes."

"I think she's a stuck-up bitch. All that stuff you said, that's just because you're desperate to let her off the hook. But really, you're kidding yourself."

"Am I?"

"Yes. Only you can't kid me. I can see through it."

"I thought you might. So you don't see these as mitigating circumstances?"

"No, I'm afraid I don't. More like feeble excuses."

He smiled. "Who're you calling feeble?"

"Not you personally." She jiggled around on the chair, crossed her legs the other way. "Gavin, you've got to get a grip on this situation. Do you really fancy her? I mean, be honest."

"Carolyn, I'm really very fond of her. I'd like to make something of the friendship."

"Hmm. Your coffee's getting cold," she said.

"You don't approve."

"Are you telling me or asking me?"

"I know you don't like her. But she did help you out when you got soaked in the rain."

"Yes, because she felt she owed you one after you'd checked out the flat with her. She wasn't doing it for me."

"So it was all down to a matter of obligation?"

"Absolutely. Sorry, Gavin, if that's not what you wanted to hear."

"No, it's okay. At least you've been honest with me."

"Well, you don't have to agree with me. I don't even expect you to agree with me."

"Maybe it would lessen your respect for me if I agreed with you."

"Oh now you're getting too philosophical." She stood up, brushing the creases from her skirt. "One thing I know for sure."

"And what's that?"

"You're going to have to decide what to do next. When you see her, or speak to her, do you mention the party? Do you play it deadpan and just ask her if it went well? I wonder how she'd react? Or do you ignore the whole thing and try to move on, pretend it never happened?"

"God," he said, grinding his teeth, "I could have done without this." He looked up at her, anxiously. "What would you do?"

"Gavin, you really shouldn't be asking me that. Like I said, you need to take the initiative. Don't look to me for guidance. Don't involve me in your relationships."

As the morning wore on, this edict was to bruise his conscience, worrying him almost as deeply as the situation which had engendered it. For sure, he was being unfair to Carolyn, expecting her to adopt the role of counsellor in his private life, and he was equally certain that, the longer he leaned on her for what amounted to romantic advice, the more his credibility would be damaged.

Whatever he decided to say to Vivienne about the house-warming - and whether he might bring himself to approach her on the subject at all - there could be no doubt as to his feelings for her. Did it matter, then, why she had excluded him from the party? Perhaps, if she gave him a reason, he would not like the sound of it, and it would still make no difference to the way he felt. The truth was that she could ignore him, reject him, even insult him, and it would be as a lapping wave washing harmlessly over the rock of his affections. By now she could almost hurt him with impunity.

Carolyn was on the phone as he came in from lunch, but she fixed him with a steely gaze and waggled her fingers at him. Covering the mouthpiece with her hand, she told him, "Message on your desk," before continuing her conversation.

A square of paper under a paperweight bore the terse instruction, in large capitals: 'Ring Lizzie. Mobile 07752 412676'.

Frowning, he dialled the number. She answered after three rings, her voice guarded, hushed. "Hello. This is Lizzie Drexler."

"Lizzie. Is it all right to talk?"

"Who's this?"

"It's Gavin Lake. Where are you?"

"Oh. I'm in the library. Stuff to research for my job."

"I see. So it's not a good time?"

"No, no, wait. I'll come out. I'll go in the lobby. Don't ring off."

He waited. There were distant, scattered voices, a sound like a door banging. In the ensuing silence, he heard his heart beating, drumming in his ears.

"Hi! Thanks for ringing."

"It's okay. Surprise, surprise. What can I do for you - plaster a wall?"

"No, I can get plastered on my own, thanks," and he heard the suppressed laughter in her voice, loving it. "It's just - I missed you, that's all."

"Really? That's very flattering."

"I mean, on Saturday. I looked for you."

"Only I wasn't there."

"I know. I thought you would be."

"Well, if I'd been invited."

"What?"

"I didn't know anything about it, Lizzie. I only found out when Carolyn told me afterwards."

The silence on the end of the line lasted so long, he thought they'd been disconnected. "You still there?" he checked.

"What? Yes. Gavin, are you seriously telling me she never asked you, never mentioned it?"

"Not a word."

"But - "

"Carolyn asked me if I'd enjoyed it. She didn't realise. Otherwise I'd never have known."

Another silence. "Gavin, I don't believe this. It's like some kind of bad dream."

"Didn't you think to ask her where I was?"

"No. When I turned up it was late and she was buzzing around, you know, with her friends, and I hardly got to speak to her. I saw you weren't there, then Daniel walked in - he's my boyfriend - and we ended up going out for a kebab. Half the people there I didn't even know."

"I see. Oh well, it's over and done with now."

"Is it? Is it?" She sounded petulant, almost tearful. "What is it with her?"

"Don't get upset about it. It's not that important."

"Not that - Gavin, you went to inspect the flat with her, then you came round to help her after she'd moved in, then she doesn't even invite you to her bloody house-warming. Don't tell me it's not important!"

"She's had a lot to think about, Lizzie. A lot's going on in her life just now."

"Gavin, you are supposed to be going on in her life. The way she's going, she won't have a life."

"I think that's a slight exaggeration. I think - "

"You know what I think, Gavin? I think you should stop thinking. You're letting her piss you about. Don't make excuses for her. She's treating you like shit!"

He waited, hearing her panting with anger. "Maybe you're right," he said. "Maybe I'm doing this all wrong."

"Well, somebody is." A loud, gasping exhalation roared in his ear. "Just wait till I see her!"

"No, Lizzie, don't say anything! You'll only make things worse."

"Worse? How can they get any worse? If you ask me, the pair of you want your heads knocking together."

"It's just - before you go chastising her, I think we ought to talk about this and see if - "

"We are talking, Gavin. We're talking right now." She interjected a weary, long-suffering sigh, and he imagined her standing there, fists clenched, stamping her foot in frustration. "Right, okay, you want to talk, we'll talk, we'll do it properly. What time do you finish?"

"Five o'clock. Why?"

"Right. Do you know a place called Marble Rainbow? It's round the corner from Hain's, Plaxton Road."

"Do you mean the wine bar?"

"That's it. I go there with Dan sometimes."

"I know it. I haven't been in there."

"Now's your chance. I'll meet you inside at five-thirty. Get us a table if you're there first."

"Well, I don't know."

"You're doing something else?"

"No, it's not that."

"Gavin, please. Do something amazing. Make a decision."

"You're the amazing one, Lizzie, remember?"

"Be there, Gavin. We can sit in the corner and be amazing together."

"I like the sound of that," he said, with a smile.

So early in the evening, Marble Rainbow was nearly empty, and he had his pick of the tables. He strolled to the back and sat at a table with a raffia screen behind it. A large potted plant, foliage like palm fronds, curled protectively towards him. Peering myopically at the menu in the dimly-lit gloom, he didn't notice Lizzie come in.

"You ashamed to be seen with me?" She dropped her suede shoulder bag on the table and ran her fingers through her hair.

"Hi! You said to sit in the corner."

"Yeah. This is in the corner all right. Perhaps they'll bring torches."

"We can move," he said, half rising from his seat.

She waved him down with a flattened hand. "It was a joke, Gavin. I don't care where we sit, really."

He nodded, smiling sheepishly. "It's good to see you again."

"You too." She sat opposite him, moving her bag to the adjacent chair. "Here's another major decision you've made."

"I'm getting the hang of it," he said, reaching for the menu again. "Are you having something to eat?"

"What I usually have. Chicken and apricot panini, no mayonnaise. You gonna treat me?"

"Sure. And a bottle of - what?"

"Yeah, a bottle of what. They do a Chilean Riesling that's pretty good. I mean, well, I'm no connoisseur, but it's really kind of - warm and rounded. It's called...Valdivia."

They waited, not saying much, making small talk, while a young man with ginger hair and acne brought the wine, the panini and Gavin's pasta. Gavin smiled at him sympathetically. A mixed group, looking like office workers, came in and sat by the door. The two girls chattered in high voices, occasionally hooting with laughter at something the men had said.

Gavin and Lizzie touched glasses. "Great idea," Gavin said.

"If it works," said Lizzie, ambiguously.

She was wearing a split-neck kaftan-style shirt in blue cotton, over black jeans. On her broad lips gleamed the same copper-red lipstick she'd worn before. He found himself staring at her between forkfuls of pasta, his eyes trailing down through her cascading hair, black in the subdued light, over her vaguely aquiline nose, to the pale V at her throat and the swellings below. Lizzie's breasts, as far as he could make out, were neatly rounded, much smaller than her mother's, almost as if they were still developing.

"So," she said, over a mouthful of food, "what's new in your world?"

"Not as much as I'd like, I suppose is the answer." He wondered if she wore a bra. "I've got to put that right, haven't I?"

"Aha. I'm going to ask you a direct question. You've got to be honest."

"Okay."

A shriek of laughter from the distant table distracted her, and for a moment she stared at the group disapprovingly.

"Sounds like they're pissed already," Gavin said.

"Yes. Anyway. My mother."

"What about her?"

"I want to know - I shouldn't be asking you this, it's between you and her really - but is all this *kosher*? You know? I mean, well, I know I have a go at her, but she is my mum, and I love her, and I don't want to stand by while she gets hurt."

He rested his fork in the plate. "Lizzie, believe me, there is no way I would ever hurt your mother. I am really very fond of her. I would like to make something of our friendship - if she'll only let me."

"So it's not just sex?"

"Lizzie, please! How can you even think that? She won't even let me kiss her, for Christ's sake!"

"Bloody Hell! What is the matter with her? Good-looking bloke like you. Don't tell me she's going frigid."

"I don't know," he said, stirring his pasta listlessly. "Sometimes I think it would be best for both of us if I just gave it up as a bad job, walked away from the problem."

"No, you mustn't do that. You mustn't even consider it." She slid her hand across the table and took hold of his wrist. "Trust me. One day soon, in that big flat all on her own, she'll wake up in the dark and it'll come to her, kind of a vision, and then she'll realise how much she needs someone to enrich her life, someone to make up for all the lost years."

He placed his other hand over hers, making a small pile of warm fingers on the table-top. "But am I that person?"

"I don't know. There's one way to find out." She squeezed his wrist. "Don't run away and hide, Gavin. That way, everybody loses."

Without knowing for sure that he was going to do it, Gavin picked up Lizzie's hand from his wrist, lifted it to his lips and gently kissed it. She offered no resistance as he drew the slender hand towards his face and, afterwards, made no attempt to pull it back to her side of the table. He wondered if he might kiss it again, one kiss for each finger, but then he saw the gravity in her eyes, and he relaxed his hold until she slowly withdrew, her lips slightly parted, as if an unasked question lingered there.

They sat in silence for a minute or two. When their plates were empty, they drank more wine, smiling quietly, almost secretively, at each other. Lizzie drained her glass, twirled the stem in her fingers and emptied the bottle.

"You ought to ask her out," she said.

"You mean, like a date?"

"Call it what you like. Invite her out one evening. Be firm."

"Lizzie, she's a married woman."

"Don't be silly. You know that's just an excuse." She rolled her eyes dramatically. "Ooh, I feel a bit squiffy."

"Can I get you a coffee?"

"Maybe. Not yet."

He watched the glow from two green and amber lights falling down the planes of her face, a mystic decoration on her left cheek. Something was happening here, he thought, and it was difficult to control, because he knew he didn't want it to be controllable. All the same, this was not how any of this was supposed to be. This was ridiculous, and he ought to make it go away, but he couldn't see that happening now, couldn't bring himself even to think about doing it. He didn't want to try to change how he felt, because he liked the feeling too much. That was how he was, and he couldn't change himself.

"Tell me about this job of yours," he said.

"I start next week." She picked up the wine bottle, shook it and put it down again. "I think I need a drink."

"No you don't. Tell me what you'll be doing."

"Company called Running Fox. They make TV films, documentaries mainly. Quite a lot of wildlife stuff, but mostly in this country. Oh, and some historical things too. I'll be their research assistant."

"Sounds interesting."

"Yeah. I'll be in the office mostly to start with, but then I can go out to places like the British Library or museums, and possibly go on location later."

"Good prospects?"

"Dunno. I think." She dragged a coil of hair from her temple, straightening it in her fingers, and peered at it almost cross-eyed. "I fancy a chilled Tia Maria."

"Hmm. I don't know if theirs would be chilled."

"No? I know where there is one."

"Where's that?"

"At home, in the fridge. There's a bottle in the fridge."

"You want to go?"

"Yeah. Coming?"

Gavin paid the bill, tipped the raddled boy two pounds and held the door open for Lizzie to pass through into the cold draught. "Which way are you going?" he asked.

"Which way am *I* going? Aren't you coming with me?"

"Oh. I thought you were going home."

"Where do you think I'm going?"

"But - "

"What's the matter, Gavin? You bored with me all of a sudden?"

He felt a violent constriction in his throat, and swallowed hard. "What about - you know?"

Lizzie had produced the red hat from her coat pocket and was tugging it down over her wayward curls. "Don't worry about it. Darts night. He won't be back from the pub till they throw him out." She slotted one arm through his. "Let's walk. Keep warm."

After a few yards she stumbled and fell against him. He gripped her arm and held her upright. "Fresh air getting to you?"

"Mm, I reckon so."

He steadied her, both hands on her arms, holding her tightly. The hat was slipping down to her eyebrows, a few stray curls poking out under the front like tendrils of black smoke. She looked so edibly beautiful, he thought.

"You want something?" she asked, mischievously.

He closed his eyes, paused, opened them again. "Yes, I want something quite badly."

"Really? At least wait until we get home."

"Lizzie, I want to know what happened to Jasper."

What?" She knitted her brow, bringing the hat down still further over her eyes. "What do you know about Jasper?"

"Nothing. That's why I'm asking."

She shivered, and he felt the tremor through his hands. "Take me home," she said, "and I'll tell you. I'll tell you all of it, everything."

10

"Christmas 1998. That's when it all started to go wrong." Lizzie leaned back on the settee, clutching a glass of ice-cold Tia Maria to her chest. "Well, anyway, that's when I remember. That's what set it all off."

Gavin sat in the armchair opposite her. He picked up his Scotch, sipped at it and replaced the glass on the small side table beside the wing of the chair.

"Did I put enough ginger in that?" she asked him.

"It's fine. Go on."

"Maybe you don't want to hear this."

"Maybe I need to hear it," he said. "To help me understand."

She stared at him for a moment. Then she closed her eyes and nodded, as if assembling her thoughts.

"But if it's too painful," he said, "I don't expect you to - "

"No. It's all right. It's time I did this. It's time I told the story to somebody." She shook her head, hunched into a spasm. "It's like I'm purging myself - you know?"

"You make it sound like an enema," he said, laughing nervously.

She was staring at him again. "Yes. Yes, I suppose it is, in a way. Now's when all the shit comes out."

"How old were you?"

"Twelve. I was twelve."

She had shuffled off her boots, sprawling back on the settee with her legs thrust out. Her mauve wool socks were rumpled round her ankles, and her big toe protruded through a hole in one of them.

"At school, some of the teachers organised a nativity play. I wanted to be an angel."

"You are an angel," he said.

"Thank you." She smiled quickly. "Don't interrupt."

"Sorry. Carry on."

"They said they already had enough angels, but I could be one of the animals that came to the stable. There was a vacancy for a lamb, so that was me. Mum made me a lamb costume, a short white frock with cotton wool balls stuck all over it, and pink leggings. I had these really skinny legs, so I looked more like a flamingo. I even had a wad of pipe-cleaners for a tail. The teachers blacked my cheeks and forehead, and there I was, a little lamb."

Gavin nodded appreciatively, waiting, giving her time, all the time she wanted. After all, he was in no hurry to leave her.

"All the animals clustered round baby Jesus. Then we had to sing 'Away in a Manger'. My teacher took a picture of us, and when I went back to the school years later, to see her because her husband had died, that picture was framed and still hanging in the hall."

"Did your mum and dad go?"

"To the nativity? Yes, they sat in the front row. Mum was smiling, taking it all in, but Dad - he just sat there motionless, staring at me with those gimlet eyes. Whenever I looked at him, he was sort of glaring at me. I remember that, those little eyes boring into me. That was before he had his glasses."

"Do you have a copy of the photo?" he asked.

"No. Don't know why." She finished her drink and put the glass on the floor. "Look at my bloody toe sticking out."

"Lizzie, I think your toenails need cutting."

"Yeah, right. When I was twelve, I could bite them. Don't think I could do it now."

He drank the rest of his Scotch and waited for her to continue. It was good, just watching her, just being there. For now he didn't want to talk or make conversation with Lizzie, he was locked comfortably into listening to what she had to say.

"Anyway," she went on, "it was a few days after Christmas, and I was going to have my bath. I always loved having my bath. Mum used to put her bath salts in and make the water go all silky and a nice colour, with lots of bubbles. Used to make my skin go all slippy and smooth."

Gavin lowered his eyes, imagining Lizzie's warm, wet skin turning all slippy and smooth. Then he blinked repeatedly, banishing the vision. Instead, he gazed at the white stub of her big toe.

"So I was in my bedroom, undressing, and there's a knock at the door, and without hesitation Dad comes in. He's got this ugly grey thing in his hand, this Polaroid camera, and he sort of smiles at me, and he says he meant to take a photo of the play - and can he do it now? I didn't understand, then he asks me to put on the little lamb costume - it's hanging in my wardrobe - with the pink leggings, so he can take my picture. Well, I really just wanted to get in the bath, but there didn't seem any much reason not to, so I slipped the frock thing on over my knickers and I tugged the pink legs on - course I didn't have a black face - and he took about three photos and ran them out. He made me sing the song again, 'Away in a Manger', and he stood there holding the photos in his hand and staring at me, not smiling or looking pleased at all, just - staring at me, like he had done in school. It seemed all right in school, but then, in the bedroom, I didn't like the way he stared at me, it felt funny."

She paused, watching his face. He looked away for a second or two, composing his thoughts.

"Was that the first time you felt uneasy in his company?" he asked.

"I think. Probably. Would you get me another drink, please?" She held out her glass. "You can have one, too."

Gavin went to the kitchen, took the bottle of Tia Maria from the fridge and poured Lizzie a full glass. He came back to the lounge and got another Scotch from the sideboard, but he didn't put any ginger in it. For a moment he stood with his back to her, thinking.

"Come and sit down," she said, "I can't talk to your back."

He handed her the drink and rested his on the side table. He glanced surreptitiously at his watch. The house was very quiet.

"Then - then I got in the bath and I was in there quite a long time, and I got out and started drying myself. Mum always told me not to lock the bathroom door - in case I had an accident and they couldn't get in, she said - and the next I knew, he was back again, my dad, and he said, 'I've brought you a nice clean towel, all warm from the airing cupboard.' Well, actually, I could see it was two towels, draped over his arm, one on top for me, and under it he had that bloody Polaroid hidden under the second towel."

Gavin frowned. "Why did he bother to hide the camera?"

"In case Mum saw when he carried it across the landing."

"I see." He shook his head. "I don't think I like where this is going."

"Pretty much what I thought at the time." She sipped her drink and continued her recollection with glazed eyes. "Anyway, I took the towel from him and hung the wet one over the side of the bath. I went on drying myself, not liking him being there, and then he said to sit on the bath edge, and he pulled the new towel away from me and stood there gawping at me. I said to him, 'Dad, will you go please, I don't want you in here,' but he was hanging about, fiddling with his damned camera, and obviously I knew what he wanted to do or he wouldn't have brought it in, so it got like I just wanted to get it over with, you know. Then he said - he said something like, 'You're getting all grown-up, Lizzie. You're not my little girl any more,' which was a bit scarey, if you think about it. Yeah. And he took a photo and ran it out and looked at it for a second, then he said - he asked me if I could lick my knee."

"Lick your knee?"

"Yeah, lick my knee. Well, I was only twelve, but when I thought about it I could get what he was meaning, you know, if you've got nothing on and you try to lick your knee..."

"Right."

"So there's another photo, and another. 'There's a good girl,' he says, 'there's my good girl.'"

Lizzie let out a long, deep sigh and sat quite still for a while with her eyes closed. It looked almost as if she had fallen asleep. Gavin gazed at her, not moving, not speaking, and soon he could see the wet glimmer of tears creeping under her lashes. When the wetness sparkled on her cheeks, she opened her eyes once more and rubbed at the moisture with her knuckles.

"Lizzie, are you all right?" he asked quietly.

She nodded, pursing her lips as if to hold something back. "I will be in a minute," she said.

"Your dad - did he try to - you know?"

"No." She shook her head emphatically. "No, never. That's the odd thing. He never once tried to touch me. He never asked me to touch him. It was almost like he was scared to."

"What happened to the photographs?"

"For years I never saw them. I nearly forgot about them. Well, sometimes."

"Don't tell me. He said, 'You mustn't tell your mum. It'll be our secret.' He made you promise. Yes?"

"Something like that. I don't exactly remember what he said. But the photos kind of vanished for years."

"But not for ever. Did she find them?"

"Mum? Yes. In one of his drawers, mixed up with some papers. She was looking for something, quite innocently, I don't know."

"What happened?"

"Well, we're getting ahead. There was stuff before that." She finished her drink and let the empty glass fall lazily on to the carpet. "Before I was thirteen, we had all the trouble starting with Dad's drinking. I mean, he always liked a drink, nothing wrong with that, but then Mum got this part-time job to help with the money, and Dad seemed to resent it, saw it as some kind of independence crusade, and he was coming home pissed, falling about, sometimes he even had to be brought home. Shambles. One day Mum and me, we had to put him to bed, he was in such a state, but he got up again while we were downstairs and he went into my room and he got that lamb frock, you know, out of the wardrobe and he was trying to put it on over his vest and pants. We heard him crashing about upstairs, and when we went up, he'd got it on over his head - he couldn't get the arms in, obviously - and he was rocking from side to side, sitting on my bed, singing that carol, 'Away in a Manger', only in this weird little-girl voice, all high and squeaky, his mouth was all wide and funny, stuff coming out of his lips, and we were trying to stop him, shut him up, and he started - he started weeing his pants, wetting himself, and all the time he wouldn't stop singing this bloody song."

"Pissed out of his mind," Gavin said.

"Yes. Literally. I can't stand that bloody carol now, can't listen to it. So we had to tear the dress off him, drag him to the bathroom. He wee'd all on the landing carpet, everywhere. I was just a kid, Gavin, I was twelve and there I was, helping clean up my dad's wee, picking up his stinky pants, and all he could do was keep on screeching this stupid bloody song."

"Your mum - when we were in the flat, she said something about him singing a song in a funny voice."

"Well, there you are then." She sat back, biting the knuckle of her forefinger, chewing at the flesh. "That's how bad it was. That was before it came out about the photographs." Lizzie propped one elbow on the settee arm and let her head fall into her hand so her fingers masked her eyes. "Gavin."

"What is it?"

"Would you come and sit next to me, please?" she asked, in a small voice.

For a while they sat quietly side by side. Slowly, cautiously, Gavin slid his arm around her shoulders and let her lean against him. The side of her cheek pressed into his ribs. He held her there, feeling her weight fusing with his own body. He loved the feel of her so close against him, the small vibrations that coursed through her, the tingling defencelessness of her.

"You don't have to say any more," he said. "You've told me so much."

"No. I haven't, not yet. I haven't told you about Jasper."

Through her shirt, he could feel the imprint of the side of her bra under his fingertips. In his nostrils was the ferny scent of her hair. As he gently slid his hand up to support her under her arm, he touched a dampness of perspiration, a humidity that quickly cooled but lingered there, a breath of memory.

"Who was he?" he asked her. "Who was Jasper?"

"Jasper. Jasper," she whispered, and she settled more firmly against him. "Poor Jasper."

He waited. He didn't want to ask her again, to urge her. He would just wait for it to come out, no matter how long it took. In the meantime, he would have the feel of her lying on his chest, under his arm, the sweet chill of her sweat on his fingertips. This was like nothing he could ever have imagined.

"Is it me, or is it hot in here?" she asked.

"It's okay," he said, hugging her, "don't worry."

"You know, I really, truly loved that dog."

"Jasper?"

"Jasper."

"Tell me. Did something bad happen to Jasper?"

"Something very bad. Something you don't want to hear about."

Despite these words of warning, Lizzie's tone made it apparent that she wished to withhold the story no longer. Again, Gavin waited. He stretched up his hand and stroked her hair. It felt wiry and a little oily. Like the dampness under Lizzie's arm, it felt alive. Carefully, without disturbing her, he brought up his fingertips and dipped his head, so he could inhale the scent of her. The words formed silently, unseen, on his lips: *My God.*

"I always used to say he was the colour of a ginger biscuit that's been dunked in syrup," Lizzie said. Her voice seemed to boom against his chest. "He was a cocker spaniel, hardly more than a puppy, and he was a reddish-goldy colour. He had these big floppy ears like furry mittens."

"And you called him Jasper?"

"No, he was already called Jasper. We got him from the RSPCA centre."

"You rescued him."

"And then we killed him." Lightly, with one curled fist, she pummelled his chest. "We saved his life so we could destroy it."

Gavin began to wonder if this was, indeed, a story he would rather not hear. Only his anxiety to be there for Lizzie, to be her comforter, sustained him as she prepared to embark upon her last revelation. His right arm tightly cradling her, he drew his free hand across his chest so that Lizzie's cheek rested upon it, trapping it there.

"Comfortable?" he asked her.

"Yes. This is nice. Am I too heavy for you?"

"Course not." He gave her a reassuring hug. "This is amazing."

"That word again." She made a little squeaking sound and rubbed her face into his shirt. "Now then."

"At first I thought Jasper was your boyfriend," he said.

He felt her head rock against him. "No. But, in a way, I loved him."

"You going to tell me what happened?"

"If you want."

"Do you want to sit up?"

"No, I'm all right. I can close my eyes and remember."

Gavin stroked her hair and the side of her head, as though this might draw the story out of her, ease the flow of memories.

"When I was thirteen," she said, "I wanted a dog for my birthday. Dad wasn't keen - he doesn't like animals - but Mum said it would be all right so long as I looked after it properly."

"And that was when you got him - Jasper?"

"Yes. He was gorgeous, Gavin. He was like a big puppy, with these soft, floppy paws and melty eyes. By the time I went to bed the day he arrived, I was in love with him. He went everywhere with me - well, not to school, obviously. In the summer I used to take him to the park so he could have a run, then I'd sit down on a bench, or maybe on the grass, to do my homework, and Jasper would just wait there with me so calmly, like he knew it was important and he had to sit still and be quiet for a while until I'd finished. He was so patient, so trusting. He'd just lie there with his head resting on his front paws, his eyes flicking left and right, watching the world, or what he thought was the world."

"So he really was your dog, your companion?"

"Yes. Mum was fond of him too, but Dad had no time for him, and I think Jasper always sensed that, because sometimes if Dad came too close, he'd growl at him."

"Probably protecting you."

"In his own way, yes. But he was always gentle, never snapped or tried to bite anyone. He was a darling."

When the words failed to come, Gavin looked down, and saw the tears on her face. He felt her trembling under his encircling arm. "You know, you don't have to do this if it hurts too much," he told her.

"No, I want to. I said I would. There's a tissue in my bag."

He reached down by his feet, felt in Lizzie's suede bag and found a pack of tissues. He pulled a couple out and put them in her hand.

"Thanks," she murmured, wiping her eyes. "It's just - I can see him so clearly. It sort of makes him real again."

"I can make you a warm drink, if you like. You feel a bit cold."

"No, I'm okay. Just don't let go of me."

"I won't. I've got you."

She let out a deep, shuddering sigh. "Around this time, Dad's drinking was getting worse. He'd come home and shout at Mum and - "

"Lizzie, did he hit her?"

"No, I never saw him do that. Sometimes I thought he might, but I never saw him do it. I saw him kick Jasper once or twice. He almost seemed to grow to hate him, poor little thing. I mean, Jasper never did him any harm, never asked anything of him except to be left alone. The drinking and all that - I think that's why James - he's my brother - went along with the idea of going to boarding school. James is at Saint Luke's. His friend Simon goes there. Probably James thought it was a way out of all the ugliness. He hasn't got much resilience, James, he couldn't hack it."

"Do you see much of him?"

"James? In the holidays, mainly, except then he sometimes goes away with Simon and his parents. I suppose we don't see that much of him, really."

"You must miss him. It sounds like he's sort of opted out."

"Well, that's James. I don't blame him."

"Vivi - your mother said he played cricket and chess at school. I didn't realise he was at boarding school. She didn't say."

"Well, she plays things close to her chest, doesn't she? I mean, that's agreed, isn't it? The drastically edited version of absolutely everything."

"Hmm. It has a familiar ring to it. Anyway, we were talking about you."

"No, we were talking about Jasper."

"Like picking at a sore."

"Sometimes there's precious little difference between recollection and masochism," she said. "Like now, for instance. Where was I?"

"Jack was kicking Jasper. He kicked a dog, for God's sake."

"That's right. I mean, it wasn't right. A few days before my fourteenth birthday, Mum found the photographs in one of his drawers, hidden in an envelope under some socks. Don't ask me what she was looking for, it doesn't matter. She came into my room with the photos in her hand, riffling through them like they were a pack of cards. I noticed her face; it was grey, washed-out. She asked me, quite politely, who had taken them. Whether it was the right thing to do, I don't know, but I told her the truth. I told her Dad had taken them. That was the first time I had even seen the photos."

"What about the dressing up and singing? She'd seen that, your mum. She must have known he was a bit peculiar."

"Well, whatever. She wouldn't have guessed about the photos. I don't think she even knew he had a Polaroid."

"Did she - accuse you of anything?"

"Me? No. 'Dad wanted to do it - take the pictures - so I let him.' That's all I said to her. Well, of course, she went straight downstairs and confronted him, and they had this enormous row, they even knocked the clock off the wall and broke it. I sat upstairs and heard it all, didn't dare to go down. Then it went quiet, and I heard a door bang. I waited a while longer - nothing. I got a bit worried, in case one of them was dead or something, and I crept down to the lounge, to this room, and peeped in, and Mum was sitting on her own in the armchair, gazing sort of dreamily at the floor. The broken clock was on the settee with all its works hanging out."

"Where'd Dad gone? Up the pub?"

"Must have done. A couple of hours late he came back, staggering about as usual and cursing us both under his breath. I got hold of Jasper and carried him up to bed with me. Funny, the fact that she, that Mum, never tackled me directly about the photos, never suggested anything was, you know, going on - well, that made it seem worse somehow, like a silent condemnation. All night, I lay there wide awake with Jasper curled up next to me, and I just couldn't sleep for - for wondering if I *had* done something wrong. You know - was it all my fault?"

"I can imagine," he said. "Must have been awful. Terrifying."

"I got up to be sick during the night. I tried not to let anyone hear." She shifted her position, waving one arm to dispel a cramp. "I think I need to sit up now."

He helped her move, holding her as if she were a fragile doll.

"Hold on to me, please. Keep your arm round me."

"It's okay, Lizzie. Don't worry."

She licked her lips before continuing. "The day before my birthday, Mum decided she would bake me a cake and ice it. A birthday cake. She had candles and everything. After about an hour she opened the oven and checked the cake, and said it needed another five minutes. She went to the cupboard to get the wire rack to put the cake on, only she couldn't find it. She could have sworn she had one. So she phoned Maggie next door to borrow hers. 'I'll go round and fetch it,' she said, 'I'll be right back.' Well, anyway, she'd hardly gone out the door when he started on me. He had this bottle of *Laphroaig* he found at the back of the sideboard, more's the pity, and he was slurping away at it, getting more and more red-eyed, and when he heard the back door go he came lurching into the kitchen and started accusing me of grassing him up to Mum about the pictures, which I hadn't done. I got scared then, because he was looking all wild-eyed and he was, you know, all stinky, and he kept doing these little punches on my arm as he was talking, and in the end he was hurting me - and - and..."

Gavin waited for a while as Lizzie's chest heaved and her tears flowed again, bringing thin black streaks of mascara in spidery lines down her cheeks. He took the discarded pack of tissues and she leaned back, unprotesting, and let him wipe her eyes.

"'Spect I look like a clown," she said hoarsely. "Give me another one, I want to blow my nose."

"Will he be drunk when he comes back tonight?" he asked her.

"Course. Except probably no-one'll notice hardly." She stuffed the balled tissue under her sleeve. "I'll make sure I'm in bed by then. I don't want to see him. I'm moving out, by the way. I'm taking my stuff round to Mum's now my room's done."

"I'm amazed you've put up with being here with him - after what you've told me, I mean."

"Inertia, Gavin. Plus the man with the van who moved Mum's things has disappeared. Daniel's sorting something out for me for Saturday."

"So then he'll be rattling around here on his own?"

"He's not fit company for anybody else." She blew her nose again, staring straight ahead out of smoke-rimmed, bloodshot eyes. "Mum - she always blamed herself, you know. She said, if she hadn't thought about that bloody cake...I mean, it's not as if we ever got to eat the cake, anyway."

"While she was out, getting the rack - did he try to hurt you?"

"Not directly. But he was hanging about in the kitchen, getting in the way, and little Jasper, I don't know, perhaps he sort of sensed I was in trouble, and he was rubbing round my feet all the time. Mum didn't come, so I said I had to take the cake out before it burned. I think Jasper had been eating grass in the garden. Anyway, I got the oven door open, and I heard Jasper being sick, that kind of whooping noise, and of course it went on Dad's shoe and his sock, and he went mad, starting kicking Jasper really hard in his tummy, so I left the cake and tried to rescue my dog, only...only he lashed out with his foot and knocked me over, I think it was a mistake, but I couldn't get up quick enough, oh Gavin, I just - and I saw him at the oven, and he pulled that shelf out with his bare hands like some kind of madman and chucked it on the floor, then he lunged at Jasper and poor Jasper, he was scrabbling in Dad's arms, he was trapped, and he - he just stuffed Jasper in the oven and slammed the door on him. I tried to get there, but he's a big man and he was sort of snarling at me and he pushed me down and sat on my back. I got my head twisted round but there was no way I could get up, he was crushing me, and I had to look at the glass window in the oven and I could see Jasper thrashing about in there, his mouth, it was clacking open and shut like a ventriloquist's dummy and his eyes were just huge, the whites rolling up, and when I looked at him he was staring back at me with this mad terror just pouring out of him, oh Gavin, it was terrible, and next I knew his tail must have gone in the burner at the back and that set it on fire, oh my God, and the flames, they came crawling up his back like orange foam, I heard him screaming, I've never heard an animal make a noise like that, like when a machine goes berserk and blows up and all the screeching metal, only it wasn't a machine, it was my dog, it was Jasper, and I saw his head disappear then in a ball of flame and the whole oven was jumping about on the floor as he struggled to get out, and next there was just this awful - fizzing noise, and smoke and a smell of burning fat and, oh Christ, it was just too...I saw his paw by the glass pane and it was still waving, like he was, you know, saying goodbye to me, and I didn't - I just...oh Gavin, I loved him so much, I loved him so much."

All the time she was speaking, Gavin had felt the blood draining from his face, to leave but a grey mask pearled with cold breath of perspiration, and he clasped Lizzie fiercely to his side, until he feared he would squeeze the last drop of air from her lungs. Eyes staring, he chewed wildly at the loose flesh in the palm of his free hand, shuddering as if he might vomit.

Then he felt her tears wetting his shoulder, even as he tasted the trickling salt on his own lips. "Your father is not a man," he said icily, "he's a monster."

"I know. And now you know. Now you can understand."

"But I'm not sure I do," he said.

"How do you mean?"

"All that time your mother put up with him. So much time, so much of her life. She let it go on and on." He brushed a couple of Lizzie's stray hairs from his trousers. "Why do women do that?"

"I suppose because they're afraid of upsetting the status quo," she said, without conviction. "You have to remember, your knowledge of him amounts to a few minutes. Right? Mum's been with him for twenty years. I've known him all my life."

"Meaning?"

"Meaning, you don't just brush all that away, give up on it, because of a few beers and arguments."

"Now it sounds as if you're defending him."

"Never. I'd never do that, not now. He's getting worse, following her about. He's used up all his chances."

"He followed her to the flat before Christmas. She had to tell him I was Mr Lord, the house agent."

"I know. Mum said. He's cunning, but he's not very bright."

"I still wonder - why now?"

"Why what now?"

"The great escape. After all these blighted years."

"Because, Gavin" - she reached out and ran her fingers lightly across his brow - "you are now. You are here and now. You are in her life."

"That's crazy. She hardly acknowledges me."

"Perhaps she doesn't dare to. Perhaps she can't quite bring herself to believe it. You have to convince her it's real - you're real." She jumped up suddenly and sat on the arm of the settee. "I think this is where we came in, don't you?"

While she perched up there, he felt himself somehow isolated, disadvantaged. He missed the contact, the warmth of her. A little nervously, he ran his hand along the length of her slender thigh towards her hip.

"What was that?" He started as a soft thump and a rattle sounded through the wall. "Someone coming in?"

"It's okay. The heating's going off, that's all."

90

He glanced at his watch. "It's getting late," he said.

"I know." She stretched out her arms and sighed. "Gavin, I think I'm going to go up. I'm tired."

"Yes, sure. Time I was heading home. Train to catch."

She stood up, gazing at him, her mouth slightly open. "Come up with me. Just for a moment. Put me to bed."

"Lizzie." He felt his throat tighten. "Maybe that's not such a good idea. You know I can't stay."

She nodded, smiling artfully. "Gavin, I said put me to bed, not take me to bed."

"Lizzie, please don't think I - "

"It's all right. You don't have to say it. I understand." She reached for his hand. "Come on now."

Gavin, uncertain of his role, sat primly at the end of the bed while Lizzie splashed water in the bathroom. His mind raced forward and back, jagged, disconnected flashes of film spewing crazily from his brain's projector. Here was Jack Drexler reeling into the room, face suffused with purplish blood, a froth of vomit on his chin, 'Ah! Mister Lord, I presume!' and then the black hole of Lizzie's nightmare, Jasper tumbling in his steel-and-glass pyre, eyes crackling with monstrous madness amid a spitting corona of fire, and of course Vivienne, his vision of untouchable serenity, Vivienne with the freckles like coffee grounds sprinkled under her eyes and a blouse pulled tight by inaccessible promise, her bearing so damnably immaculate...and Lizzie, Lizzie with the exploding smoke-bomb of wild hair and the face full of wise laughter.

She stood beside him, bent over, drawing back the sheets, patting her pillows. The T-shirt reached halfway down her tanned thighs, and when she slid sideways into bed, she lifted her trailing leg just for a second, pinioning herself on the heel, and his heart skipped at a glimpse of jet-black softness in the shadow beneath the blue cotton, and then she was tugging at the covers, Gavin feebly helping her, reaching behind her to plump the pillows again.

"Thanks," she murmured, leaning back against the headboard. "Now give me your hand."

"Here."

"You're trembling."

She prised apart his shaking fingers and took them, one by one, into her mouth, wetting them softly.

"You like doing that, don't you?" he said.

"Sort of baby things," she said, and giggled.

"And now I must go, Lizzie."

"Yes, now you must go."

He stood up, one hand moist with her saliva. "Thank you."

"What for?"

"Shall I put the light out?"

"No, leave it. I don't want it to be dark in here when he comes back."

"Will I see you again?" he asked her.

"Don't be daft. Course you will."

"I mean - well, can I, you know, *see* you some time, perhaps? And if you feel like I do..."

"Oh, I see. I don't know, Gavin. We have to get our priorities right."

"You're amazing, Lizzie."

"That makes two of us," she said. She turned and pounded the pillow once more. "Close the door after you."

Gavin went out and closed her door quietly and leaned hard against it and shut his eyes. The splintered film began again, at double speed, running on its own, out of control.

11

CAROLYN sat sideways on her chair, studying him over folded arms. One white bra strap dangled from the shoulder of her sleeveless blouse, and her grey skirt, not unusually, was rather on the short side. Above her left knee, inside her broad thigh, a leaf-shaped tear showed in her stocking.

"A barbecue, you say? You've bought her a barbecue?"

"Yes. For her new place."

She blinked at him silently for several seconds. "That's very generous. Considering."

"Considering what?"

"Considering she never even invited you to her flat-warming. Considering she never so much as mentioned it to you."

"Yes, well. You've got a hole, by the way."

"A hole? Where?"

"Your left leg. Sort of halfway up."

She bent to inspect herself. "So I have. Damn."

"Don't worry about it. No-one'll notice."

She moved her thighs apart, touching the bare spot with one finger. "You shouldn't be looking up my legs."

"I wasn't looking up your legs."

"You must have been, else you wouldn't have seen." She brought her legs sharply together. "What colour knickers I got on?"

"For goodness' sake! How should I know?"

"You've obviously been having a good old gawp. Reckon you're getting frustrated."

"Now you're being ridiculous. Why don't you get me a coffee, eh?"

"Hmm. So where is it then, this barbecue?"

"At home. Top of the range. Perfect for when the better weather comes."

"Yeah, see you clambering on to the tube with that."

"No, I'll drive in with it one weekend."

"Right. Is it a gas one?"

"Yes."

"My dad's got one. We use it loads." She stood up. "There's no biscuits, 'less you want me to go out and get some."

"Don't bother."

"Right. Don't want people staring at my leg, do I?" She picked up the tray and opened the door. Over her shoulder, she said, "They're white with pink flowers on. Okay? So it doesn't prey on your mind."

Gavin smiled, shaking his head. Carolyn was all right. Carolyn was Carolyn. She was slickly efficient, good at her job, and she took her role as his P.A. quite seriously, to the extent of always seeing to his morning coffee and afternoon tea and checking that he'd had a proper lunch. Once, he recalled, she had even produced a tiny repair kit from her handbag and sewn a button back on his shirt cuff. At times she could seem acerbic, but mostly that was out of a commonsense concern for his welfare. She would make someone a good wife, he thought. She would manage her children with ease, and they would love her for her steadfastness.

He would have to speak to Vivienne, of course. He couldn't just turn up unannounced with a barbecue in a box. While Carolyn was out, he should ring her. Right now.

"Hello there," he said, putting a lilt in his voice. "It's that man again."

"Oh. Well hello, that man. How are you?"

"Okay. I've got a present for you."

"A present? What sort of a present?"

"Wait and see. I can't - it's a bit big, so I can't bring it in on the train."

"Gosh! Whatever is it?"

"A surprise. Vivienne, can I drive to your place - to the flat, I mean - and deliver it? One Saturday, perhaps?"

There was a silence, during which he tried, inevitably, to divine her thoughts. It was strange how many interpretations could be placed upon the apparent nothingness of silence. Perhaps she had no wish to entertain him and was stalling to invent an excuse. Or was she stunned, lost for words, at the exciting prospect of reunion? Or searching her imagination for the likely identity of the gift? Could it be that she had had enough of him and now struggled within herself to find the words that would finally dissolve a tenuous and tiresome relationship?

Carolyn was back with his coffee. She placed the cup and saucer carefully in front of him, smiled briefly, and from behind her back, as by some deft conjuring trick, produced a cellophane-wrapped walnut whip, which she set down beside the saucer. She patted the back of his hand and returned to her desk.

"You still there, Vivienne?" he asked.

"Yes. Only it sounds like a lot of bother."

"For you or for me?"

"For you, of course. You shouldn't be buying me presents."

"It's sort of a moving-in present," he told her, and wondered if this might elicit a response based upon a residue of guilt.

"I see. That's very kind of you."

He had resolved to say nothing about the party or his meeting with Lizzie. He could see no mileage in any of it. These distractions were over and done with - except...no, that wasn't exactly true. Lizzie was not over and done with. Lizzie was here and now, trapped inside his head, a kind of inflammation.

Cradling the phone between his head and shoulder, he unwrapped the walnut whip and bit the walnut off the top. "I could make it Sunday, if you'd rather," he offered nervously.

"Sunday. Er...I've got Maria coming over for lunch."

"Who's Maria?"

"My sister."

"I didn't know you had a sister."

"Gavin, there's lots about me you don't know."

"Of course. How's Jack, by the way?"

"Gavin, please. I suppose - why don't you come Sunday morning? Then, if you feel like lunch..."

"You're inviting me to lunch?"

"Yes, in a round-about way. Let's hope it's more successful than the last time. I'm intrigued by this present, the one that's so huge it won't fit on a tube train."

"Yes, well."

"Are you going to hire a van?"

"I don't think that'll be necessary," he said. "Anyway, I look forward to meeting your sister."

"Really? Aren't you looking forward to meeting me?"

"Depends on your mood," he said bravely.

Then he heard her breath pumping, and he wondered for a moment if she was angry or tearful, but in the next instant his ear was filled with squealing laughter. "Oh Gavin! That's about the boldest thing I've heard you say!"

Gavin smiled warmly to himself, heartened by her laughter. This time her mirth seemed untainted by bitterness or malice, and it was as if she laughed in surprise, a reaction which gave her pleasure in its unexpectedness.

For the rest of the week he deliberately avoided her, making no attempt at contact, anxious to preserve the almost palpable memory of her amusement, that cheerful music. He wanted no doubt or denial to intervene. Each day, when he awoke, he could hear her laughter, could see her smiling. He longed to kiss that smile.

To his relief and delight, it was still there when the door swung open to reveal her face. The morning sun picked out the freckles beside her nose and glinted in her eyes. Nothing had changed. The pink bow of her lips flexed and curved in welcome, and Gavin leaned towards her, closing his eyes, and kissed her softly there, and his wordless greeting met with no resistance. She opened the door wide to let him in, and he stepped on to the mat, listening to the frenzied drumming of his heart.

"It's good to see you," she said. "You smell nice."

"Do I? *Obsession*. Calvin Klein."

She closed the door and waved him towards the kitchen. "Come in the warm and talk to me. Tell me about this mysterious present."

"It's in the boot of the car. Shall I bring it now?"

"No, we'll have coffee first. Sit down. I've baked scones."

"When does your sister arrive?"

"Soon. Please stay." She turned and began clattering plates, speaking over her shoulder. "Is it something for the flat?"

"Sort of."

"For the kitchen?"

"No. To do with food, though."

"It's a coffee table," she said, with an air of triumph.

"It goes outdoors."

"It's an aluminium coffee table. That's brilliant. It won't go rusty, and you can leave - "

"Vivienne, it's not a coffee table."

"I haven't got a coffee table. I could do with a coffee table."

"Well, you still haven't got a coffee table."

"Here." She handed him a plate and mug, and carried a loaded tray from the worktop. "It's good to see you. Did I say that?"

"Yes. But I like to hear you say it. I can stand the repetition."

They drank coffee and munched warm buttered scones dripping with honey. Over her blue jeans Vivienne wore a close-fitting red sweater bearing the unmistakable imprint of her nipples. Noting these tantalizing protrusions, Gavin wondered whether her bra was of an unusually sheer fabric, or if she was naked under her top. Without complete success, he tried not to be fixated upon the question.

His fingers found a sliver of paper, the edge of a label, under the rim of his plate. He picked at the paper and removed it, inspecting it on his fingernail.

Vivienne peered at his extended finger. "I should have taken that off," she said. "It's a set I got at my hou-"

"Your house-warming?"

"Yes." Her eyes fell to the table top. "Oh dear. This is awkward."

"Awkward? How?"

"If you must know, I've already been given the third degree."

"Who by?"

"Who do you think? Lizzie. She called me a mean bitch."

"Did she now?"

"Do you think I'm a mean bitch? Do you?"

"Vivienne, if I thought you were a mean bitch, I wouldn't be here." He propped his head in his hand, elbow on the table, shielding his face. "If I thought you were a mean bitch, I wouldn't love you."

"That word again."

"It's not a word, Vivienne, it's an emotion. It could be a commitment, even."

"Now that sounds ominous. It sounds like things could get complicated."

"So - you're frightened of getting involved with me. Is that it?"

"Gavin, I thought you came to bring me a present. I didn't know we were - "

"Oh, very well," he said, testily. "I can just go across the road and fetch your box and it'll all be over. I can go home and you can get on with your lunch and - "

He stopped when she grabbed his hand. "Don't do this, Gavin," she urged him. There were tears standing in her eyes. "Don't give in to me.

96

Don't let me kill everything like this. Can't you see, it isn't what I want?" The tears spilled over and tracked slowly down her cheeks. "For God's sake, help me to stop doing this!"

Gently, he unpeeled her hand from his and stood up. The urge to throw himself across the table and gather her into his arms was overpowering, yet somehow he backed away, pushing the chair in, and avoided her eyes.

"You're not going?" she asked, hoarsely.

"I'm going to get your present. Leave the door for me."

A few minutes later, his face and hands pinked from the street, he brought the large box in, cradled awkwardly in both arms, and strode past her into the kitchen.

"Whatever is it?" she asked, sounding excited.

"I'm sorry about the brown paper. I didn't have enough gift wrap left over."

"Don't worry about it." She began tearing off the paper until the coloured box appeared, then she stopped to read the lettering. "Gavin, this is marvellous!"

"It's their premier model," he told her. "I'll go to the garage later, get you a gas bottle."

Vivienne cut open the flaps and found the brochure and manual. She sat at the table, flicking through the pages. "Why?" she said, and her eyes misted over again.

"Why what?"

"Why do you insist on being nice to me? You know I don't deserve it."

"I don't know any such thing." He pulled out the chair and sat down facing her. "All I ask is, when spring comes and you want to have a barbecue, invite me over."

She nodded thoughtfully. "Like I didn't before, you mean."

"It doesn't matter about before."

"Actually, it does. I owe you an explanation."

"Because of Lizzie?"

"No. Leave her out of this. All she did was remind me what I should be doing - should have done."

"Vivienne, there's no rights or wrongs in this. There's nothing you have to get all upset about."

"I wanted you to come," she said, stifling fresh tears. "I really wanted you to be there."

"I see."

"No you don't. Of course you don't. How can you? God, I must be the most maddening woman you've ever met."

"Well, you're a prime contender for the title," he said, pleasantly.

His good-natured agreement made her smile, and she slid her hand across the table and stroked his fingers with little dabbing movements, soft as brush-strokes. He wanted so much to reach out for her, but he didn't trust himself, didn't dare to risk spoiling the new-found oasis of understanding into which they had somehow wandered.

"Do you remember when we were listening to Scriabin?" she said.

"Yes. You were upset."

"Mm. I couldn't get you out of my head after that."

"What?"

"You heard. I couldn't stop thinking about you."

He allowed himself a cynical smile. "It's taken long enough," he said.

"No. Not for me to feel it, only for me to admit it."

Some crumbs had fallen on the table, and he bent his head and traced a forefinger through the remains, drawing doodles as his thoughts raced. "So - uh - where does that leave us?" he asked.

"Where it leaves you, I don't know," she replied. "Only you can answer that. As for me, well, there are still things that need attending to, aren't there? For a start, I still owe you an explanation about the other day."

"I'm not pressing you for one."

"Maybe not, but I owe it, just the same. Let's say I have to clear the air - clear my conscience. Here, let me get you some more coffee."

While she stood with her back to him, refilling his cup from the flask, Gavin watched her and wondered where all this was leading. The signals seemed clear enough, but he could not afford to misread them. If he presumed an affection Vivienne did not sincerely feel, he could be taking a retrograde step back into the void. Conversely, were he to ignore or dismiss her implications, a vital opportunity might be squandered for ever. Lizzie, he recalled, had counselled him against the futility of faint-heartedness. Oddly, he felt that he owed it to her, as much as to himself, to claim Vivienne Drexler as his own.

She handed him his mug and took her seat again, clasping her hands on the table in front of her. He saw a warmth in her eyes that hadn't been there in a long time, as though she sensed some kind of resolution.

"I really did want you to be with me," she said.

"You said. I didn't know what to think."

"I invited about twenty people. Ross Glaister, my boss, he came, and his brother Paul. Paul's an electrician and we used his van to move my stuff in. Some of the girls in my office came too. Then there were a few neighbours from Launceston Road. Oh, Lorne Mowler looked in with some ideas for the garden."

"What about Jack?"

"Please. Don't try to be provocative, it doesn't suit you."

"And Lizzie and Daniel," he prompted.

"Yes, they dropped in, but they didn't stay." She peered at him quizzically. "How did you know that?"

"Lizzie told me."

"Oh. When did you speak to her?"

"Recently. I don't remember."

98

"Well, anyway. The point is, I missed you, and that's the truth. And you know something?" Again her eyes swam with tears. "I spent the evening cursing myself for my - for my greed."

"Your greed?"

"Yes. Because, Gavin, I couldn't bear the thought of having to share you. Maria was there, and she always makes a bee-line for an eligible man. I know one of the girls I work with - well, she keeps going on about you. And, anyway, while I was going round making small talk with these not very interesting people, I wouldn't be able to - to get close to you. I couldn't imagine anything more frustrating." She shook her head and clumsily wiped her eyes. "Oh, right, yes, I know it all sounds ridiculous."

His heart was beating fast, and a strange acidic taste had oozed into his mouth. "So - are you saying you didn't invite me simply because of how strongly you felt about me?"

"What else? I wanted you all to myself. I was selfish and greedy." She rubbed her knuckles under her eyes, smudging tears. "Now I've paid the price. I've pissed it all away."

"Who told you that? Lizzie?"

"No, she didn't say that. She said a lot of things, but she didn't say that. I worked that out for myself."

"Really? Then you worked it out wrong."

He got up and walked behind her chair so he could rest his hands on her shoulders and gently massage them. As his fingers worked into the flesh and muscle, she tipped her head back against his chest and closed her eyes. Gavin leaned over and kissed her cheek, and his gaze fell naturally to the swell of her breasts, the promontory rising and falling with the gradually more rapid motion of her breathing. He pressed himself into the back of the chair, moving rhythmically to the pulse of his clenching hands. It would seem, he thought, a normal, natural act, the most perfectly reasonable movement in the world, to allow his hands to slide down from Vivienne's shoulders until they cupped her breasts; but for all the warm submissiveness in her posture, he could not quite bring himself to take her acquiescence for granted.

She reached up and covered his right hand with hers. "That's nice," she murmured. "I could let you do that all day."

"But sitting on a wooden chair," he said. "You could be more comfortable."

"Maybe. I'm all right."

"You know what I'd like to do?" he said, and he heard his voice tighten.

"Don't know. Put my barbecue together, perhaps."

"Of course. Soon." He cleared his throat. "I - we could go somewhere else."

"Somewhere else? To the coast? To see the fairies at the bottom of the garden?"

"No. I meant - we could go upstairs."

She squeezed his hand affectionately. "I don't think so, Gavin. My sister will be here soon. We don't have time."

He nodded, smiling to mask his disappointment. "Some other time - will we have time?"

"I expect so," she said.

He kissed her again, then he turned and began unpacking the barbecue from the box. Vivienne went to the hall and brought him a plastic case containing a set of tools. A label taped to the lid read 'Jack Drexler'. Gavin knelt on the floor and worked quietly, pausing occasionally to smile at Vivienne over his shoulder. She was still sitting at the table, looking pale and serene. Once she stretched both hands behind her head to smooth her hair, making her breasts lift.

When he had finished, she leaned towards him, resting her forearms on her thighs. "It's superb," she said. "I shall be the envy of all my neighbours. However much did it cost you?"

"Thousands," he replied, and they laughed together. "And now I'm going up to the garage to get you a gas bottle. You won't need it yet, but it's incomplete without. A car with no petrol."

"Gavin, why are you so good to me?"

"You know why," he said.

"You've forgiven me, then?"

"Let's say I'm getting around to it."

When he returned she was setting the dining room table for three.

"I found the side entrance," he said. "Your gas is by that old shed."

"Thanks. I'll put it inside later." She looked engrossed in her task. "I thought we'd eat in here. Help me do this."

"Just don't ask me to fold napkins. I'm useless at origami."

"Wine glasses are in the kitchen cupboard. There's red wine and white. Uncork the red and bring it in here." She hesitated, hovering over the table, and stared at him. "Why are you looking at me like that?"

"Can't I look at you?"

"If you want. You make me feel uneasy, that's all."

"Can I kiss you?"

"You did earlier."

"What, is there a quota?"

"Don't be silly."

He went to open the wine. He found three glasses and brought them to the table and put the bottle on the sideboard.

"Help me pull the table over a bit, Gavin, there's not enough room."

It was hard for him to concentrate on anything now. He wanted to touch her breasts. Not roughly or hungrily, but just to feel their softness in his hands, mould their weight in his palms. He wondered about the colour and texture of her nipples. His imagination was running away with him, accelerating his heartbeat. There was a sheen of sweat on his brow.

The doorbell rang.

Vivienne was adjusting the cutlery. "That'll be Maria," she said, her eyes still roaming the table. "You can let her in for me. Introduce yourself."

He strode to the door and drew it open with a flourish. On the step, facing the street with his back to the door, stood a short man with a glossy lick of black hair combed over a balding pate. The man turned slowly to face the doorway. Something sour and indigestible lurched into Gavin's stomach. He recognised the mottled beard and the black-framed glasses.

A sneering grin seethed across the man's face, distorting his features, revealing an uneven row of brown-stained teeth, pitiful as fallen soldiers.

"Well, Lordy-Lord!" the man growled. "If it ain't Mister Lord!"

12

JACK DREXLER stared malevolently at Gavin Lake. Gavin Lake stared in shocked disbelief at Jack Drexler. The lurching sensation in Gavin's stomach plunged in a wrenching spiral to his bowels, where it flared into a searing ball of pain, the kind of nauseous ache he had sometimes felt when looking down from a great height over a wall or parapet.

"You gonna let me in?" Jack said. It was more a challenge than a question.

"Why should I?" Gavin's heart was wedged in his mouth. In the draught from the street, he could feel the blood draining from his face.

"I wanna see Viv," Jack said. "I wanna see my wife."

Gavin moistened his lips, considering the dilemma. "As I understand it," he said, "she soon won't be your wife. I doubt she wants to see you."

"Freezin' out 'ere, mate." He put one hand on the door-post, as though to claim some right of access. "Go on, let us in."

Gavin felt a movement behind him, then a sharp intake of breath. "What the Hell are you doing here?"

"'Allo Viv. Didn't expect to see me, did you?"

Gavin stood aside, his eyes darting between Vivienne and her husband. He could feel himself starting to shake.

Vivienne sensed his vulnerability. "Gavin, would you check there's nothing burning in the oven, please?"

"Sure. Are you all right here?"

"I'm fine, thank you."

"We can't talk out 'ere," Jack said.

With a toss of her head, Vivienne indicated that he should step inside. She closed the door and stood barring his way. "You know the score," she told him. "We're to let the solicitors do the talking. You're not supposed to contact me."

"Not supposed to - ? You're my bloody wife!"

"The solicitors are - "

"I an't got a solicitor."

"Then that's your look-out. Mine will write direct to you. Meanwhile, we've nothing to discuss."

He craned his neck past her towards the kitchen. "Who's that bloke?"

"None of your business. Time to leave, Jack."

"Look, we need to talk. There's things to sort out. Kids an' that."

"For Christ's sake, Jack! We've had twenty years to talk. Now we're all talked out."

"Food smells nice. You always was a good cook."

"Yes, and you always were a wanker. Now get going before I lose my temper."

"Ah, come on, Viv." He took hold of her arm, but she smacked his hand away. "Oh, don't be like that," he whined.

Gavin walked slowly towards them. "I've basted the meat," he said. "Do you want some help here?"

"It's all right," she said briskly. "Jack was just leaving."

"This is not your house, Mr Drexler," Gavin said, struggling to control his voice. "I think you should - "

"It's not your 'ouse, neither," Jack retorted. "Who are you, anyway?"

Gavin opened his mouth to reply, but Vivienne put out a hand to cut him off. "Just - don't get involved."

"I think I am involved," Gavin said quietly.

"Yeah, reckon you are," said Jack, and there was an edge of menace in his tone. "You shaggin' my wife?"

Vivienne had both hands on Jack's shoulders, trying to steer him back to the door.

"As a matter of fact, I'm not," Gavin replied. In some small part of him, he imagined himself adding: 'Unfortunately I have yet to be presented with a reasonable opportunity'; but he divined that the elaboration would be ill-advised.

The doorbell rang again. Vivienne pushed past her husband and yanked the door open.

"Morning Viv," Maria said, chirpily. She thrust out a bottle wrapped in white tissue paper. "Here. Stick it in the fridge while it's still cold." She stepped inside, tugging at her scarf. "I just missed - oh Christ! What's he doing here?"

"Good morning, Maria, my love," Jack said, with mock solemnity.

"I could be any number of things to many people, Jack, but I am certainly not your love." She turned, unbuttoning her coat. "And you must be Gavin." Darting forward, she pecked him on the cheek. "Nice to meet you at last."

"I'll take the bottle," Gavin said to Vivienne, "while you - er - sort this out."

The door stood open, admitting a freezing draught. Vivienne had managed to manoeuvre Jack to the doormat. His face was a pale, scowling mask of sullen anger. Despite the chill, he was sweating, panting for breath.

Gavin poured Maria a coffee and sat facing her at the kitchen table. "This is crazy," he said.

"You don't know the half of it, darling," she assured him. "Believe me, I'd have swung for that man long ago."

"Should I intervene, do you think?" he asked. "I mean, perhaps I ought - "

"Leave it, Gavin. Don't muddy the water. He'll only try to score points off you. Don't give him the satisfaction."

Maria took off her glasses, blew on the lenses and put them on again. They were a simple lightweight design with titanium frames and small oval lenses, allowing her strong face to dominate in spite of them.

Studying her discreetly, Gavin thought her a handsome woman. She wore a sleeveless cotton V-neck in pale turquoise over a candy-striped seersucker shirt with two gold bangles at the right cuff. There was a kind of informal elegance about her. Already, Gavin found himself liking her.

Vivienne and Jack were arguing at the front door. Gavin frowned at the sound of raised voices. "Why has she let this go on so long?" he asked, speaking as much to himself as to Maria.

"Women do," Maria said. "Whatever our talents, we're always good at martyrdom."

"Maybe. But I wouldn't have put Vivienne down as a martyr."

"As a matter of fact, neither would I. Marriage, commitment, they do strange things to people."

"But why didn't she want to salvage something? If not for herself, for her kids?"

Maria clasped her hands round her coffee mug and gazed at him. "Do you know why? Do you know why women really do this - put up with all this crap?"

"That's what I'm trying to find out," he said, unhappily.

"Because they can't believe that, for them, there's something better. Their misery becomes a kind of comfort, shielding them from the emotional trauma of taking that defiant leap into the void."

Gavin smiled and nodded. "You've really thought this through, haven't you?"

"Believe me, Gavin, I've been there. Vivienne's strong, yes, but I'm ten times stronger. Jack Drexler - he'd have lasted about half an hour with me. Then it'd have been my foot in his bollocks, end of story." She shook her head and took another drink. "Jack knows that. That's why he hates me."

"Me too, no doubt. He sees me as the culprit in all this, the man who's broken it all up."

"Rubbish! You haven't broken anything. You're the one who's putting it all together. It's just, he's the part that's left over. You know, the bit you chuck back in the box." She glared down the hall, drumming her fingertips on the table. "Sod this! I'm going to kick him out."

Almost capsizing the chair in her haste, Maria lunged for the door and hurried down the hall to join her sister. Gavin waited for a few seconds, then he moved to the doorway and hovered there, shifting awkwardly from one foot to the other.

Maria brushed Vivienne aside with the back of her hand. Jack tried to duck past her towards the kitchen, but Maria seized his upper arm and shoved him back into the wall.

"Don't get physical," Vivienne told her, "you'll only inflame the situation."

"Shut up!" Maria said, over her shoulder. "I'm taking charge of this."

"Lay off me!" Jack snarled. "Smacked my 'ead on the bloody wall!"

"I'll smack your head in a minute. First of all, a character reference. You are a drunk and a pervert. Stop squirming, or I'll get Gavin to hold your other arm. You are lower and slimier than a worm, and more useless. At least worms dig the garden. You stink of booze already - or is that your brain cells decaying? Don't answer that. Now the constructive advice. This comes from the heart, and I earnestly recommend that you act upon it without delay. Fuck off!"

Jack let out a strangled roar of rage and thrust both hands at her face as if to throttle her, but Maria slammed the flat of her hand into his shoulder, whiplashing his head against the wall once more.

Gavin had moved up to join the group. Something about Jack's colour and the expression in his eyes worried him. He wanted the altercation to be over. Jack's face had changed under Maria's onslaught, no longer showing anger or resentment, but a wild-eyed alarm as he felt his strength, his very presence, diminishing. To Gavin, he seemed unsteady on his feet, as if dazed, and the possibility of drunkenness as a logical diagnosis somehow failed to explain his appearance.

Vivienne stood behind her sister, pulling gently but insistently at her shoulder. "Come on, Maria, that's enough. He's got the message."

Slowly, with laboured breathing, Jack dragged himself to the door. The lick of black hair combed across his balding head was sealed to the thin white skin with a patina of perspiration. He rubbed obsessively at his left arm.

"I'll be back," he growled, baring his teeth at Vivienne. "Unfinished business."

"Best to stay away," Gavin said, hoping his voice would not crack. "What's wrong with your arm?"

"Dunno. Touch of cramp." Jack hesitated, one hand on the door knob. He pointed a trembling finger at Gavin's face. "You're makin' a big mistake, sonny. She'll eat you for breakfast, chew you up, swallow the bits, spit you out for lunch."

Maria was crowding him again. "I told you to - "

"Yeah, all right, I'm goin'." His black eyes, magnified by his glasses, burned into Gavin's brain. "I got your car number," he said. "Watch your back!"

They watched him go down the steps to the pavement, stumbling slightly as he reached the bottom. Vivienne and Maria returned to the kitchen, but Gavin waited, peering up the road, wanting to see Jack Drexler drive away. The car was parked about a hundred yards along the opposite kerb, facing the wrong way. Jack got in, slammed the door and sat mopping his face with his handkerchief.

"Shut the door!" Vivienne called. "We're sitting in a draught."

He moved on to the top step, pulling the door against his back. Jack had an old Fiesta. He had the engine running and he was cranking on left lock to clear the car parked in front. Gavin stood there, just watching. He heard Vivienne call out again, but he ignored her and carried on watching Jack's car, for it was important to him to see the man go, disappear from sight, so he stayed rooted to the spot, staring into the road with no expression on his face. His eyes were locked on the car as

Jack looped left in a high-revving arc, then spun the wheel right to straighten up, and just went on roaring away to the right at frightening speed, and Gavin's mouth dropped open in horrified disbelief as the Fiesta speared into the side of a white van parked outside a builder's merchant. The huge hollow bang made him flinch and clench his fists, and he went on staring at the smashed car, half buried in the van's side, as the front bumper seemed to detach itself in slow motion and clatter on to the tarmac.

Then there was nothing, just silence. He waited, but the driver's door stayed shut. Jack wasn't moving. From where he stood, Gavin couldn't see the man's head, the car was at the wrong angle and there were watery reflections in the glass.

"Gavin, please! Come in, for God's sake!"

He wheeled round, pushing open the door. "Get out here! Now!"

"What?"

"Come here!"

"What's the matter?"

"Just come!"

The three of them huddled close together as they crossed the road. When they reached the car, Gavin could hear the engine still running, and he tugged open the distorted door to switch off the ignition. Around his feet, green water was dribbling from the crushed radiator and trickling towards the gutter. Jack's head was bent over, his face buried in the steering wheel. The visible flesh was unbloodied, but it had a greasy grey pallor, like oiled putty. Gavin felt for a pulse at the side of the driver's neck.

"Nothing," he said. "I think he's dead."

Vivienne stared at Jack impassively. "I'm sure he's dead," she said.

"I hope he's dead," Maria said.

Vivienne eyed her sister coldly. "Thank you, Maria."

Maria puffed out her cheeks ambiguously. "I may be tactless," she said, "but I'm no hypocrite."

"Do something useful," Vivienne told her. "Run back to the house and call for an ambulance."

Maria turned aside. "I'll call for a breakdown truck."

"Maria!"

"What's the point...if he's dead?"

"We're not doctors," Gavin said. "We don't know if he's dead. He could just be unconscious."

"You said he had no pulse." Maria looked irritated. She leaned forward, frowning. "He looks extremely dead to me."

A man came running from a nearby house. "I've called for an ambulance," he said, panting. "And the police. They're coming as well."

"What a performance," Maria muttered.

"The van's destroyed," said Gavin.

"Yes, so's our lunch, at this rate," Maria added, with a smirk. "Jack always did know how to break up a good party."

The paramedics' names were George and Luke. Behind his glasses, George had rheumy eyes, and a peppery grey moustache bristled under his mottled nose. Luke, a generation younger, was tall, black and vaguely beautiful. On his skin the scents of antiseptic and after-shave were subtly combined.

Luke, quicker off the mark than George, dropped his medical kit on the ground and squatted by the open car door. "The man's name, please?"

"Jack," Vivienne told him. "Jack Drexler."

"Okay. Just gonna move your head, Jack. There we go. Speak if you can hear me, Jack. My name's Luke."

Luke pressed two fingers to Jack's neck, waited and grunted. He lifted Jack's eyelids with his thumb. A thin line of blood oozed from the stricken man's nose.

The neighbour who had called for help was standing back, screwing up his eyes. "Do you all mind if I cut loose?" he asked. "I'm not very good at this sort of thing."

"That's all right," Gavin said. "Thanks for helping."

The man spread his hands dejectedly, and walked away.

Luke was standing up, talking quietly to George. "Can I ask who you people are?" he said. He looked worried.

Vivienne said, "I'm his wife, and this lady is my sister. This is Gavin, a friend of ours."

Luke sighed and moved his case away from the door. "What's your first name, Mrs Dexler?"

"Drexler. It's Vivienne."

"Is he dead?" Maria asked.

Luke glanced at her, then fixed his eyes on Vivienne's ashen face. "Vivienne, I'm afraid there's nothing we can do for Jack. He's not breathing and there's no pulse. Probably a heart attack. I'm very sorry."

Gavin had wrapped one arm around Vivienne's shoulders. He could feel her shivering. "Is he injured?" he asked Luke.

"Doesn't appear to be. Hit his nose on the steering wheel, otherwise..."

A police car pulled up opposite, blue light flashing. Two officers got out. The driver was putting his hat on. The policemen spoke briefly to the paramedics, listened and nodded sympathetically.

"I can't believe this is happening," Vivienne said.

"If I stand out here much longer, I shall be dead from frostbite," Maria complained.

Vivienne ignored her.

"Go and get your coat," Gavin said.

The police car driver approached them, removing his hat again. Maria turned and started walking back to the flat. The second officer reached inside the car and turned off the blue light.

"Good afternoon," the police driver said, "I'm PC Sean Burrows. Could I have your names, please?"

Gavin gave him their names and explained who they were. PC Burrows wrote everything down. While he was writing, Maria came back, huddled in her coat with the collar up. A small crowd was gathering, gossiping about the accident. Gavin wondered where the van owner was.

"Now," said the constable, "did anyone see the accident?"

"I did," Gavin replied. "I saw it all." Suddenly, he felt important.

"Tell me what you saw, please, Mr Lake."

PC Burrows scribbled frantically as Gavin described what he had seen.

George and Luke were carefully extricating Jack's body from the car. Both ambulance doors stood open.

The constable tapped his teeth with his pencil. "Mr Lake, do you recall if Mr Drexler applied his brakes? Did you notice his brake lights?"

Gavin thought about this for a moment. "No, I don't think he did. I can't be sure, of course."

"I understand. You see, I notice there are no skid marks."

"Try looking in his pants," Maria mumbled.

Gavin stepped away from her, still hugging Vivienne. "The ambulance man mentioned something about a heart attack."

"Yes, that's the theory. He seems to have made no attempt to avoid the collision. The consensus is, already dead on impact."

Luke moved up behind the policeman. "Almost ready," he said.

"What happens now?" Vivienne asked him.

"We'll take him to St David's. There'll have to be a post-mortem. I'm sorry."

Vivienne gazed at the ground, shaking her head. "Can I go with him?"

"Of course. George will sit with you. Would you like anyone else to come?"

"No. I'd just - I'd like a little while on my own with him."

She eased herself out of Gavin's embrace. There were tears in her eyes and she was very pale.

Maria was fumbling in her pocket. "Anyone want a bit of chocolate?" she yelped. "I found some on the sideboard."

No-one replied.

"Suit yourselves," Maria said, tearing at the foil.

"Are you sure you'll be all right, Vivienne?" Gavin asked. "Do you want me to come with you?"

"No," she said firmly. "I don't want anyone else. Just Jack."

"All right. Ring me if you want a lift home. I'll be here. I'll wait for you."

George came forward and put an arm out to her. "Time to go, my love."

A few yards from the ambulance, she stopped and called back. "One of you call Lizzie. Tell her what's happened. Try and get James too."

George put a hand at the small of her back to guide her up the step. Luke started the engine. The two policemen came over to wait with Gavin while he watched the ambulance move off. The onlookers began to disperse in little knots, muttering amongst themselves, heads down in quiet reflection. When Gavin looked round, Maria had disappeared.

He found her in the kitchen, ladling roast potatoes on to two plates. The large empty box and the barbecue were outside, dimly visible through the patio doors.

"Did you buy that?" Maria asked, jerking her thumb at the garden.

"Yes. I hadn't long finished putting it together when..."

"Hmm. You must think a lot of her."

"I do."

"That's good. Now come and sit down. We'll eat here. No standing on ceremony."

He brought the red wine from the other room. "I think I may have lost my appetite."

"Can't waste good food," Maria said, pouring herself a large glass of wine. "There's people starving."

"There's people dying," said Gavin. He cut a few cubes of meat from his pork steak and stared at them morosely. "Do you think she'll be all right?"

Maria juggled a hot potato in her mouth. "Wha-? Do you mean this afternoon, or in the future?"

"Both, I suppose."

She poured him some wine. "She'll cope. It'll get better and better. There's nothing to be miserable about."

"Yes. It's just - I'm not sure she saw it that way."

"Give it time." She drank half of her wine and sat gazing at him over the rim of the glass. "You think I killed him, don't you? You think it was my fault."

"What? Of course not."

She put down her glass and propped her elbows on the table, resting her chin on her tented fingertips. "Well, Mr Lake, perhaps you'd care to hear my version of events."

"Up to you. I'm sure you're about to tell me anyway."

"Only to avoid any misunderstanding." She paused, gathering her thoughts. "Jack's been on the brink for weeks. Booze and blood pressure. No, I didn't kill him, but I'm glad he's gone. Sorry if that appals you. I tell you something - if I really did believe I was responsible for his death, which I don't, I would accept the charge without feeling one iota, one infinitesimal scrap of regret or remorse. You see, that man stole away the best years of my sister's life. That's a kind of murder, don't you think? He went out of his way to pollute everything that family held dear. He made that vile obsession into an art form." Tears were brimming in her eyes, and she pulled off her spectacles and blinked them back. "So don't ask me to mourn him. To me, Jack Drexler was the embodiment of a popular myth: that there is virtue in all of us. Well, I'm afraid there isn't, Gavin. That is a lie." She shook her head, flicking out the tears. "May God forgive him, because I won't."

They sat quietly, not eating, sipping their wine, replenishing the glasses, until the bottle was empty. Maria's tears had dried, leaving grey stains on her cheeks. Her eyes were puffed and pink.

"I think I've finished," Gavin said.

"Yes. Me too. Look, it's getting dark."

"I wonder if she'll ring."

"Well, if you don't mind, I'm going up for a bath - get out of these clothes. I feel sort of - tawdry."

Gavin began clearing the table. He saw his reflection in the glass doors, a ghostly transparency, as the darkness settled outside.

Maria hesitated in the doorway. "I meant to ask..."

"Yes?"

"Are you sleeping with her?"

"No. She keeps me at arm's length."

"Whatever for? She must be mad."

He rinsed the cutlery and plates and stacked the dishwasher. Then he went into the front room and pulled the curtains across. The settee was strewn with newspapers. He tossed them to the floor and sat down. There was the sound of water running in the bathroom and the plod of Maria's bare feet on the landing. He turned on the television and flicked from channel to channel, but the noise and the images quickly became an intrusion rather than a comfort, and he switched the set off and tried to relax in the solace of his own company.

What would she be doing at the hospital? How long might it take, this loveless farewell? In its bleak finality, death was also open-ended and arbitrary. It stripped away etiquette and commitment. So he could see Vivienne, free as she was to wait with the man on the trolley or leave him without a word or a backward glance, vacuously suspended in time and space, helplessly immersed in the unreality of being there. She would surely talk to Jack, probably more earnestly, more meaningfully, than she had done for years; and she would hear his response, accepting it without question, even when it seemed to embody anger or criticism directed at her. This was no time for argument. Possibly she would forgive him - although Gavin's imagination balked at the enormity of such a gesture. Then again, could it be that *she* would seek forgiveness from *him*? When there was nothing left to say, sometimes that simple humility, suddenly bereft of consequence, was at last affordable, in the manner of self-purification. He was sure that she would take his hand and bend and kiss him on his cold cheek, and there would be tears in her eyes and, in her heart, a suspicion of failure as powerful as the stark relief of unburdening. And then, finally, she would softly walk away, not knowing if it was the right thing to do, not even sure who she was any more.

Maria's appearance in the doorway rescued him from the warm fringes of sleep. She had put on a pink silk dressing gown, a little too large for her, and a pair of tattered slippers.

"Vivienne's," she said, tugging at the loose folds. "I'm sure she won't mind." She sat next to him and sighed. Her skin smelled of soap. "What a day, eh?"

"Are you planning to stay tonight?" he asked.

"I don't know. I'll see. Now I've had a bath..."

"Of course. I wonder what's happening?"

"She can't be much longer, surely. Will you pick her up?"

"If she asks me."

In a sudden flurry of rustling silk and bouncing cushions, Maria made herself a backrest against the arm of the settee and threw her legs sideways across Gavin's lap. His eyes traced the sculpted line of her slender ankles and the blue veins in her feet.

"You don't mind, do you? I do so like to relax."

"So I see."

"So -uh - tell me." She jiggled up and down, making herself comfortable. "What is it that attracts you to Vivienne?"

"It's hard to put into words," he said. "She's quite vulnerable, I think. She needs protecting."

"Who from? He's dead."

"Maybe from herself."

"Possibly. Go on."

"She's sensitive and intelligent. She has a certain charisma about her. She's not charming, but there's a kind of allure."

"And do you find her physically appealing, Gavin?"

He thought the question, or the manner of its presentation, slightly strange, but he answered, "Yes, I do."

"That's good. Do you find me appealing?"

"Pardon?"

"Surely a simple enough question. Am I attractive?"

"Well, I don't quite know how to - "

"Just answer, yes or no. If you say no, I shan't be offended." She smiled at him kindly and adjusted the position of her legs on his thighs. "You can be quite honest."

"I suppose I do, in a way," he said, avoiding her gaze.

"A shade non-committal," she said. "You'll need to be more direct with Vivienne. But I think you already know that. Are my legs too heavy for you?"

"No, it's - it's all right."

"Then I think we should close our eyes for a while. Get some rest. You must be tired." She snuggled back into the cushions. "I'm very comfy here."

Gavin let his eyes droop shut, only opening them again when he heard a change in the rhythm of Maria's breathing. She appeared to be asleep, her mouth slightly open. He placed one hand lightly on her left thigh, feeling the thin silk move under his palm. Then he dozed for a while.

He awoke when the sound of her voice intruded into a fragmented dream. His hand was still on her thigh.

"Gavin?"

"I'm sorry. I didn't hear you."

"It's all right. I wondered what the time was."

He checked his watch. "It's ten past five."

She swung her legs to the floor and stretched her arms high above her head. "I think I'll lie down in the spare room. Will you stay on?"

"For now, yes. I said I'd wait for her. Oh, you should ring Lizzie."

Maria stood up. She reached for his hand. "That can wait," she said firmly. "Come on, I'll show you what you've been missing."

He got up to follow her, leaving his hand in hers. Already he felt the first stirring of an erection.

The telephone was on a small table by the door, and it rang as they reached it. Gavin freed his hand and picked up the receiver. Maria waited, a tight-lipped smile on her face.

Vivienne's voice was a thin metallic scratching in his ear.

"Of course," he said, "I'll come and fetch you."

Vivienne carried on speaking.

There was a note block by the phone, a ballpoint balanced on top of it. While he listened, Maria picked up the pad and wrote four words on it. Then she held her message before Gavin's face.

'Saved By The Bell', it said.

13

WITH a slow, measured tread, its metronomic precision born of years of practice and stoically perfected through sun and rain, wind and snow, Mrs Margaret Groves ushered the procession of vehicles silently away from the kerb. She wore a black suit with a straight skirt that fell just below the knee. A broad-brimmed black hat was pinned to her hair, casting a faint grey shadow over her white blouse and neatly-knotted grey silk tie. Her laced shoes were black leather, rubber-soled and sensible. The sun peeped out from behind banks of smutty cloud, thrown about the sky like abandoned bags of dirty laundry, and in the brittle air there was a welcome brightness but only the merest vestige of warmth.

Two shiny black Volvos headed the cortege. The first was the hearse containing the coffin and a scattering of small wreaths. Behind it, a limousine carried five mourners: Vivienne Drexler, her sister Maria, her son James, Jack Drexler's brother Stanley and Mrs Alice Stamp, the landlady from the Wilton Arms.

Following the funeral cars were two private ones, almost stalling in low gear, their passengers mostly friends of Jack's from the pub darts club. In these last cars, hardly anyone wore sombre clothing, and their faces were confused rather than grief-stricken.

After perhaps a hundred yards, Mrs Margaret Groves stepped aside and waited in the road. The driver of the hearse moved up beside her and brought the cortege to a halt. Mrs Groves opened the left-hand door and slid deftly into the seat behind the driver's companion, taking care to arrange the hem of her skirt so that no more than an inch or two of her dark-stockinged thighs could be seen, even though there was no-one next to her to see anything, apart from Jack Drexler. When she had adjusted her clothing, the procession moved off, the Volvos gliding noiselessly past small knots of respectful neighbours waiting on the pavement. Some of the onlookers bowed their heads, and a tall man bent low and removed his hat.

In the chapel the people's breath plumed out before them in the stagnant chill. The coffin was brought in to the strains of *Londonderry Air*, the deceased's favourite melody. Maria whispered, a little too loudly, that in this particular instance the title should be spelt as *London Derriere*, a none-too-oblique reference to the fact that those present were now about to see the back of Jack Drexler once and for all. There were a few smiles but, significantly, no tears. The vicar said a few words, a hopeless expression hanging from his face like a death mask, and the coffin was removed while the organist played a faltering hymn which hardly anyone could be bothered to sing.

The sun blinked out behind a pall of cloud as they gathered at the graveside. To left and right of the vicar, there were thirteen people, all with their hands in their pockets. The coffin was lowered and a prayer intoned. With a willingness scarcely distinguishable from haste, the mourners dispersed, grimacing uncharitably at the mud on their shoes. Before she followed them, Maria picked up a spade, rammed it into a mound of earth and tossed the contents on to the coffin lid with a thud. She dropped the spade and smiled, smacking her hands together.

He could see the scene unfold in his mind's eye as clearly as if he had been there. When Lizzie recounted the story, it was exactly as if he *had* been there. The extraordinary part of it was, obviously, that Lizzie herself had declined to go. Yet her narration sounded totally authentic and word-perfect.

"How do you do that?" he asked her.

"Do what?"

"Recite it like that, so flawlessly."

"Gavin, if you'd sat and listened to my mum going over it again and again, telling the bloke next door and Lorne Mowler and me and Daniel, and then writing it all down in her diary - God knows why - like some news report. Well, anyway. I reckon she can't convince herself it's really happened, so she has to keep going through it all in the minutest detail. I tell you, it's getting spooky."

"Is she all right, d'you think?"

"Oh, I don't know," she said wearily. "I think so."

They waited while the young man with the acne, who had served them before, brought their pasta and a bottle of mineral water.

"His face isn't getting any better," Lizzie observed.

"I'm surprised Maria went," Gavin said.

"Anxious to see him off the premises." She pointed her fork at the waiter. "Do you suppose he's got spots all over?"

"I'd rather not speculate, if you don't mind."

"I mean, imagine if you had to snog his face." She stuffed a forkful of pasta into her mouth. "Would you want to snog me - if I had spots like that? Well, would you?"

"Eat your pasta, Lizzie."

"Yeah, right." She chewed hungrily, keeping her eyes on his face. "Mmm. This is good."

Gavin poured two glasses of water.

There were dribbles of sauce on Lizzie's chin. "I mean, there must be creams and stuff you can get," she insisted. "I wonder if - "

"Lizzie, please. He's only the waiter. It doesn't matter."

"Yeah, I know." She handed him her napkin. "Will you wipe my face, please? There's sticky stuff on my chin."

He reached out and dabbed a corner of the napkin at the orange streaks below her lip. "You're like a child," he said.

She giggled. "Did you say, would I like a child?"

"No," he said, with emphasis, "that's not what I said." He flattened the stained napkin and placed it next to his. "I don't think you're ready for a child. I think you still need looking after yourself."

"Do I? You looked after me the other day. You were kind."

"I listened, that's all."

"You were a real gentleman."

"Was I?"

"Yes. Some blokes, all they want to do is grope you." She shuddered. "I like a bit of respect. I get that from you."

"Hmm. A respectful gentleman. It doesn't sound very - cool."

"No, no, that's where you're wrong. No, really. Gentlemen are cool, absolutely. A mature man who cares about other people. That's you, Gavin. You're a class act.   Feel good about it."

"Lizzie, you certainly know how to massage my ego."

An impish grin flickered on her face. "Yes, and I don't only do egos."

"Really?" He felt his face warming with unexpected pleasure. "Like I said, you're amazing."

A red lamp on the wall behind her head glowed through the coils of her hair, creating a simmering crown of burning coals. She had painted her fingernails green. The tip of her tongue slipped out like a slow pink flame and licked the sauce from her lips.

"Can I say something?" he asked quietly.

"You just did."

"No, seriously."

"I don't know if I want to hear it if it's something serious."

"Lizzie."

"What?"

"I think you're beautiful."

"Wow! That's - well, thank you."

"Can I kiss you?"

"You don't have to ask. Just do it. Don't overdo the gentleman. Don't let him take over."

Closing his eyes, he leaned across the table and found her lips. For what felt to him like a sweet eternity, they hung on their elbows and kissed, working their mouths in slow, wet circles, tasting each other's tongues, bumping heads in soft collisions of affection.

At last he sat back in his chair, licking his lips, tasting her wetness on his mouth. He fiddled with his plate, reached for the water bottle and then pushed it aside. His heart was thumping, blood drumming in his ears.

"What's the matter?" she asked him.

Somehow, her voice seemed to have come from a long way away. "Nothing," he said. "I think I'm confused, that's all."

"Oh? What about?"

"About us. About where we're going."

"I see. And is there an 'us'? I don't think there's supposed to be an 'us'."

"No. I just feel there is, that's all."

"I'm supposed to be encouraging you to get closer to my mother."

"I know. But something else is happening."

"To us?"

"To us."

Lizzie took a last forkful of pasta and pushed her plate aside. "So what do you think we should do about it?"

Gavin swallowed and made no reply. Somehow he felt excited but unhappy. This wasn't meant to happen, this churning in the pit of his stomach. He touched a trembling finger to his lips, feeling the moist place where she had been. Covering his mouth with his hand, he licked his lips, sucking at her lipstick, tasting her inside him.

The waiter returned, asking if they would like anything else.

"Bring us another bottle of water," he said.

Lizzie tapped the table with her fingertips. "I know. I wanted to ask you a favour."

"A favour?"

"Yes. Would you take me to the cemetery?"

"To the cemetery?"

"Yes. It sounds strange, I realise."

"Why on earth?"

"Well, I'm not going there to pay homage."

"Then why?"

"You'll see," she said. "I want to leave something on his grave."

"Such as what?"

"Gavin, please don't keep asking questions. It's just something I need to do. It'll make me feel better - about the whole thing."

The waiter brought the water. Gavin poured two more glasses. They drank in silence for a while. The sudden chill in his stomach calmed him.

"I could take you on Sunday," he offered.

"I'd really appreciate it. We could go early. They open at nine."

"Shall I come to the house?"

She thought for a moment. "No. Pick me up at the top of the road. I don't want Mum to know I'm going there."

"Whatever. Eight-thirty?"

"Yes. Is - do you have a blanket or rug or something in the back of your car?"

He looked puzzled. "I think so. Why?"

"Like I said, you'll see."

Anticipating Sunday with mixed emotions, he asked himself constantly if his agreement had really been a good idea. These meetings with Lizzie, enjoyable as they might be, served little useful purpose in the scheme of things. If it was his serious intention to forge a more intimate relationship with Vivienne, the point had surely been reached at which her daughter was a dangerous distraction, a dalliance setting all his responses at a tangent to the true path. He told himself, without conviction, that he was not in love with Lizzie Drexler, but he could not escape the bruising reality that he was telling himself lies to salve his guilt. He cowered before his own transparency.

On Saturday he even considered ringing to tell her he couldn't do it after all. Something had come up unexpectedly - an illness, a death, a forgotten prior commitment. This, though, would be tantamount to cutting off his nose to spite his face. It would let him off the hook, but his friendship with Lizzie might be tainted, or even irreparably damaged. The prospect was more than he could bear. In any case, he needed her to smooth the way with Vivienne, needed that determined empathy. He was trapped inside a delusion. Tangential love.

It was the first time he had seen her in a skirt. She was hardly dressed for the weather, he reflected. It was short, in blue denim, exposing her slender, sun-tanned legs. She wore scuffed trainers with no socks, and a mauve fleece with the collar pulled up.

"Aren't you cold?" he asked, as she slid into the passenger seat.

"A bit. Don't worry about it." She leaned over and pecked him on the cheek. "Hi. Thanks for this."

"You'll have to direct me."

"No problem."

He accelerated away, already aware that her fleece had slid open as her skirt had ridden up, revealing a bright flash of pale gold thigh, which he struggled to ignore.

"How's your mum?"

"In bed with the paper. She's started wearing these funny little reading glasses perched on the end of her nose. Looks very - secretarial."

"Trouble with her eyes?" He spared another glance at Lizzie's legs.

"Don't think so. She's never mentioned it. I reckon they're just a fashion accessory."

"But in bed? She's on her own. No-one can see."

"At the moment. Perhaps she's hoping someone'll join her. A gentleman with good manners and impeccable taste." She nudged him in the arm, making the steering wobble. "Trust me, I'm working on it."

"I know. I appreciate it. What's that?"

She was unfolding a piece of paper and peering at something pencilled on it. "It's the plot number. There's no headstone yet."

"No, of course."

"K662. Remember that."

Opposite the main entrance to the cemetery a flower seller was setting up his stall, unloading bags and boxes from a van parked nearby. A plastic chair stood on the pavement with a vacuum flask balanced on it.

"Do you want to stop?" Gavin asked.

"What, here? What for?"

He pointed with his thumb. "Flowers."

"What do I want with flowers?"

"You said about putting something on the grave."

"I wouldn't waste my money," Lizzie said, haughtily.

A groundsman in a donkey jacket was unlocking the gates as they pulled up. He stood back to let them pass through. Gavin drove slowly up the narrow roadway. This was odd, he thought. Lizzie had brought nothing with her, unless it was concealed in her pocket, and she didn't want any flowers. He wondered what they were doing here.

"I saw a K over there," she said, inclining her head. "Park under that tree."

He pulled over and turned the engine off. "K662," he reminded her.

"Yeah, right." She looked around uneasily. "Just a minute."

"Problem?"

"I don't think so."

"You ready?"

"Not quite. Something I have to do."

"Okay. No hurry."

She sat quite still, staring ahead at the massed ranks of gravestones lightly bleached by the early morning sun. The car engine ticked and clicked as it cooled. A woman in a hooded coat and rubber boots walked past, towing a large box on a trolley.

"Look, you're going to think this is really weird." She turned to him, gesticulating with outstretched hands. "But I'm doing it for a reason. You gotta trust me, Gavin."

The car lurched as Lizzie dug her shoulders into the seat back, arching her bottom in the air. Thrusting both hands under her skirt, she pulled down her knickers, tugged them over her trainers and stuffed the small blue bundle into the glovebox.

Gavin stared, open-mouthed. "Lizzie, what in heaven's name -?"

"It'll all make sense, you'll see. It's important."

"How can it be important to take your knickers off in a cemetery, for Christ's sake?"

She was opening the door. "Come on. You got a blanket?"

"What? Yes, there's a tartan rug thing in the back."

"Perfect. Bring it. Follow me."

Gavin stumbled along behind her, the blanket draped over his arm. "This is insane," he muttered, catching his foot in the dangling folds.

She was running on now, putting space between them. "Six-two-two or six-six-two?" she called over her shoulder.

"Six-six-two. What's with this damned blanket?"

"You'll find out. Keep up."

With the blanket hanging hazardously from his arm, he was content to let her hurry on, while he watched her bare legs skipping ahead, catching the light. Mud was sticking to his shoes, the ground slippery with dew.

She stopped suddenly when she found the place. He moved up beside her. She was staring at the raised earth, her arms hanging limply at her sides. A few bedraggled bunches of dead flowers littered the ground. A wooden stake with the number on it protruded from the clods of soil.

"Right," she said, not looking at him, "is there anyone about?"

"Man over there with a bike," he said, pointing.

Lizzie's eyes followed his finger. "He's miles away."

"What are you going to do?"

"Just - hold the blanket up in front of me."

"What?"

"Like a screen. Go on. This won't take a minute."

He did as she had asked. By peeking over the outstretched fabric, he could just see the top of her head. She was squatting on the ground, her bottom slightly raised. He heard her grunting, then a hissing sound, which became a liquid gurgle. The man in the distance had his back to them, tending a grave.

She stood up, licking her lips, smoothing down her skirt. "All done. Race you back to the car."

He folded the blanket into a large square. The grave was steaming, a humid ammoniac smell issuing from the glistening earth. Lizzie had vanished.

Gavin walked slowly back, unlocked the car and let her in. He threw the blanket in the boot and stood for a moment, kicking the mud from his shoes.

She was staring ahead through the windscreen, not moving. He slid in next to her and sat quietly, thinking. He heard the breeze in the trees and the whistle of a train far away. Already the car interior was growing cold.

She kept her eyes straight ahead when she spoke, almost as if she were in a trance. "I suppose you've gone off me now."

"No, of course not."

"Thank you for bringing me." She touched his knee. "You'll never understand how much better I feel. You can't imagine."

He shrugged. "I could try."

Gavin glanced at her face. There were tears in her eyes, jewel-bright. He put out his left hand and slid it under her skirt until he felt a wetness at the top of her thigh.

"Don't. Not here. Not in a cemetery."

He gave in to an impulsive laughter. "That's rich. When you've just pissed on someone's grave."

"No, I haven't. I've pissed on no-one's grave. The grave of a nobody."

"Whatever. You know, I can't believe you did that."

"Are you ashamed of me?"

"No, I told you." There was a lick of moisture on his hand. "You - there must be a lot of hate behind that lovely exterior."

"Yeah, and hate's destructive, I know. Only I don't feel destroyed, not now."

"That's good. What do you feel?"

"I feel - clean inside, that's what I feel. Like something dirty's come out of me."

The tears were spilling over, trickling down her cheeks. Her face looked streaked with silver in the cloud-filtered sunlight. She caught some of the tears in her mouth.

"Will there come a time, perhaps, when you can let him rest in peace?" he asked her.

"I'm letting him rest in piss," she replied. "That'll do for now."

"You must have been planning this for a long time. Yes?"

"I don't know, Gavin. I don't remember."

"Do you think you'll ever really forgive him? I mean, I know you won't forget."

"Forgiveness isn't something I'm considering right now." She pulled a tissue from her pocket and wiped her face. "I am thinking about him, though. Oh yes, I'm thinking about him a lot." Her voice began to falter and crack.

"Tell me. It helps if you talk to people."

"Well. I shall say a prayer for him tonight. A prayer for - for the permanence of pain."

"Meaning?"

"Meaning...what'll happen when he gets to Hell. Meaning - this is like in my dreams, only dreams can come true, so - they tie him to a wooden post with rusty nails embedded in it, and they put sulphuric acid in his eyes with a dropper. Then they light a fire at his feet. He's naked, and the flames lick slowly up his legs to his balls, and he shrinks back out of the heat, only the nails spear his back until the blood runs, and he can't get any release from all this pain, because he can't black out, it's there all the time, the pain, and no matter what he does, what he thinks, he's still conscious, still feeling the nails in his flesh and the fire clawing at his legs, climbing like flaming snakes up over his chest, and in his eyes there's this black surge of agony, like his whole brain is full of needles, driving him to madness and beyond madness - because he can't let go, the pain won't stop, it's for ever." She paused, shivering. "Can you imagine that - a pain that's unbearable, but it goes on for ever and ever. And you can't escape by dying, because, of course, you're dead already. Can you imagine that?"

"I hardly dare to," he said. "What I can't imagine is, I can't imagine hating anybody enough that I would wish that on them. It's almost beyond humanity."

"Hmm. So what does that make me? Some kind of monster?"

"It makes you amazing - remember?"

"How could I ever forget?"

Gavin leaned across and kissed her on her damp cheek. "What am I going to do if I'm in love with you?" he said.

"You're not allowed to be in love with me. It would scramble all the codes." She sat back and fastened her seatbelt. "We would be mired in confusion."

"But what if I can't help myself? What if-?"

"Shush!" She put a hand over his mouth. "Don't say another word. Just drive me home."

He asked her if he should drop her off where he had met her, but she said that Vivienne was meeting Maria for morning coffee at the South

Bank, so it would be perfect if he could take her to the house. He drove with the radio playing to calm his tortured mind. Lizzie leaned back into the headrest, eyes closed. There was a red scratch on her knee, and her trainers were caked with mud.

"I feel funny," she murmured.

"Funny?"

"Sort of - empty."

"It's all right. You'll soon be home. It's all done now."

Lizzie was right. There was no-one in. She made coffee and they sipped it quietly. They didn't mention the morning.

"I haven't been here since I painted your window," he said.

"The room's finished now. I did the walls the same colour, just like I said."

"Can I see?"

"If you want."

He followed her up the stairs, his eyes fixed on the back of her legs.

Lizzie sat on the edge of the bed, watching him. "So what do you think?" she asked.

He looked down at her. Tousled hair, pale lips, smudged eyes, scratched knee, muddied ankles.

"I think - I want to make love to you," he said.

"Oh, I see. You don't like the paintwork, then?"

"Don't be ridiculous, Lizzie."

"Don't tease you, you mean."

"Lizzie, if I have to go out of this house - "

"All right, I know, I heard you. But - I'm not going to let you make love to me. It would take too long. All that protestation, all that soul-searching and questing after the truth. All that pain."

"So? What am I supposed to do?"

"Do? Gavin, please." She held out her hand and he took it. "Just fuck me, for Christ's sake. This has gone on long enough."

14

Spring

WITH the onset of spring, the thaws came one after the other in quick succession.

In his sister's cottage garden in Dorset, the weekend had been frost-free. The coloured blades of crocus heads thrust through the corners of the dew-sodden lawn, and at the foot of the rockery a scattering of snowdrops glinted in the early sunlight. Clinging to the dry stone wall that ran down to the apple orchard, a pink blush of cyclamen seemed to enhance the sun's frail warmth. The garden was crisp and quiet and lightly fragrant with the tangs of wood and grass and night creatures recently departed. In the garden there hung in the brittle air the scent of hope.

Yet, for all its aura of promise, of better times soon to come, the thaw he observed in Amanda's garden paled into insignificance alongside the unmistakable mellowing of his relationship with Vivienne. By April he dared to believe that he could count on her regular companionship. Unless he was sorely deluded, she was warming to him, becoming more open and spontaneous in his presence, more delicately tactile.

Knowing and appreciating her taste in music, he bought two tickets for a concert at the Barbican, the Leipzig Gewandhaus playing the Mahler Seventh Symphony.

"I'd love to come," she said.

"Of course, the Seventh isn't everyone's first choice," he conceded.

"Agreed. But perhaps - perhaps you think it suitable for someone like me. You know, troublesome, enigmatic and inaccessible."

"I couldn't have put it better," he said, wondering if there was a measure of self-condemnation here.

After the concert, she invited him back. "Time to unwind," she said.

They sat in the kitchen, facing each other across the table. Vivienne made coffee and heated up pizza from the fridge. He stayed half an hour, then stood up and kissed her goodnight. With the back of his knuckles, he stroked her cheek and allowed his hand to drop so that it brushed her left breast. She smiled knowingly, returning his kiss, and whispered "Thank you" in his ear.

A week later he took her for a Chinese meal in the West End. It was late when they returned to the house. The place was in darkness.

"Lizzie's staying over with friends," she explained. "Girls from college."

She made hot chocolate. The kitchen was warm and bright and smelled of fresh bread.

Gavin finished his drink and looked at his watch. "I ought to be going," he said. "I'll miss my train."

"Yes," she said, flatly. "Except..."

"Except? Except what?"

"Except, maybe you don't have to go at all."

"You mean, stay here?"

"Don't look so nervous, Gavin," she said, with a short laugh. "Doesn't the idea appeal to you?"

"It's always appealed to me," he replied, feeling his throat constrict.

"Well then. I could do with the company."

How amazing it felt, he thought, to be lying in Vivienne's bed, naked but for his boxer shorts. He listened to the noises she made in the bathroom, to the ticking of the bedside clock and the occasional rumble of a passing car in the street below. He listened to his own breathing, laboured in anticipation.

She slid in beside him in her blue silk nightdress. For several minutes they lay side by side on their backs. "I loved the meal," she said. "You're good to me."

He rolled on to his side and kissed her cheek.

"We've got all night," she said.

They kissed for a long time, exploring each other's lips and chins, cheeks and necks. He couldn't get enough of her.

He felt her hand burrowing down in the dark. "You're not hard," she murmured.

"I'm nervous," he said. There was a sheen of sweat on his brow.

They slept. Once he awoke, peered around in the darkness, remembered where he was and went back to sleep. At two in the morning something disturbed him. Vivienne was awake, gazing at him, her eyes unblinking. She had thrown one leg over his hip. Her discarded nightdress was a pale cloud on the pillow.

"Hi," he whispered.

"Come on," she said. "Come on top of me."

He rolled over her, burying his face in her glorious breasts. They moved together in the shadows.

In the morning he had to use Jack Drexler's old electric razor, which Vivienne had salvaged, before dressing in the clothes he had worn the previous day. He left while Vivienne was still in bed, almost as if embarrassed to confront her at breakfast.

Carolyn looked him up and down, seeming to take a deliberate interest in his appearance.

"You all right?" she enquired.

"Yes. Why shouldn't I be?"

"No reason. You look a bit washed-out, that's all."

"I - uh - had a late night."

"Seems like it. That's the same shirt and tie you had on yesterday."

"Is it?"

She rolled her eyes with a smirk. "Been playing away, have we?"

"What's it to you?"

"Ooh, pardon me. Mister Sensitive."

She brought his coffee and two chocolate digestives. Gavin sat back, thinking about last night, wondering if it had all been a bizarre dream. He wondered if there would be another time, another dream. His senses somehow retained the scent of her breasts, the feel of the skin behind her shoulder-blades as he held her against him.

He didn't notice her come in. She was staring at him, but less sternly than before.

"What is it, Carolyn?"

"Mrs Whats-her-face."

"Yes?"

"I reckon you must be good for her, after all. She gave me this big smile the other day. Asked how I was. Could have knocked me down with a feather."

"She's complicated," he said. "You have to give her a chance."

"Yeah? That what you been giving her - a chance to get her hand in your trousers?"

"I don't think I shall dignify that question with a serious reply," he said, slapping irritably at the files on his desk.

"Up to you." She turned to go, then paused, glancing back at him. "By the way, I'll need some petty cash. That's the last of the biscuits and we're nearly out of sugar."

A phone call from his mother set him musing upon Amanda's role in the development of his friendship with Vivienne. He suspected that his sister had broached the subject with their mother after his recent trips to Dorset, for Mrs Lake seemed persistent and well-informed. Her references to Vivienne as "this woman friend" he found mildly irritating, for he could not help but draw the inference that, in Mum's estimation, Vivienne was too old for him.

"Why don't you bring her over? I ought to meet her." She waited while Gavin considered the matter in silence. "I'll get a nice piece of beef. She's not a vegetarian, is she?"

"No, she's not a vegetarian."

"Well then."

"Is this a firm invitation?"

"Of course. I mean, you seem keen on her."

If Janet Lake was no less than kind and polite to Vivienne, she managed to evince a certain cool detachment. Gavin was well aware that his mother's indulgence of their guest was essentially an act of deference to her son, an attitude quite unconnected with any concept of conventional friendship. It was as if, rather than wishing to join her son and *this woman friend* in their happiness, she sought to place some abstract construction upon the liaison. Inevitably, Gavin found this posture unnerving, for it invested the entire meeting with a brooding sense of suspicion and unease.

"A delicious fish pie, Mrs Lake. Your own recipe?"

"Yes. No Delia Smith for me. I hope you've room for dessert. It's fresh trifle - home-made, not shop-bought."

"Then I shall manage a little, I'm sure."

Janet Lake removed Vivienne's plate. "I always say, it's nice to be treated."

"Oh, but I couldn't agree more."

Gavin smarted, as though a seething rash inflamed a deep inner layer of his skin, at the women's falsely decorous banter. His nostrils flared in the acrid waft of the fish pie, which had filled the downstairs rooms with the reek of a trawler.

His mother presented the trifle in a glass bowl, with a jade-handled silver serving spoon. "Do help yourself, Vivienne."

"Thank you, Mrs Lake."

"Please. Call me Janet."

"Very well."

Gavin sighed and studied his watch under the table.

Janet Lake sat with her elbows propped on the table, her chin supported on clasped hands. "So - er - tell me, Vivienne: do you have family?"

Vivienne took two modest spoonfuls of trifle. "Actually, my husband died recently. I don't know if Gavin told you."

Janet shot her son a swift, reproachful glance. "No, I'm afraid not. I'm sorry to hear it."

"Really, it's quite all right." She paused to sample the trifle. "Mmm. I love the texture. And - well, I have a teenage son and daughter, and a sister who lives nearby."

Janet afforded the situation a respectful flicker of the eyelids, nodding her head sympathetically. "I see. They must be a great comfort to you. And Gavin too, of course."

"Indeed," Vivienne said, with a thoughtful smile, which made Gavin feel uneasy. "Gavin has been there to comfort me when I've needed it."

"I'm sure," Janet assented. "That's always been his strength."

Methodically working the tip of his tongue around a sliver of fish lodged between his teeth, Gavin was content to let them drone on, suspecting that he hardly needed to be there at all. In a moment he would smile perfunctorily, excuse himself and go to the toilet. There, he could pick the fish from his teeth, urinate, wash his face and hands and comb his hair. Then he could check his watch again and go downstairs, wearing the same vacant smile. The women would continue their shallow discussion without acknowledging his return, as though in his brief absence he had, by some subtle metamorphosis, attained a merciful invisibility.

"Thank God that's over," he declared, driving out through deserted back streets afterwards. It was nearly midnight.

"Gavin, that's unkind."

"Hmm? Yes, I suppose it is. Now you're seeing the worst of me."

He hoped, and was reasonably confident, that if he drove her back into London instead of putting her on the last train, she would ask him to stay the night. Along mile after mile of obsidian streets, the prospect warmed him. He put out a hand, its movement glimpsed under flickering amber shadows, and let it rest on her lamplit thigh, feeling the cool firmness under his palm.

"Mind if I put on the radio?" she asked, and he liked the way she reached over his hand without disturbing it.

Orchestral music swelled into the car, smothering the sound of the engine.

"Bruckner Te Deum," he intoned, keeping his eyes on the road.

Cresting the summit of a railway bridge, they saw the trouble looming, less than a mile away. A red glaze of brake lights stabbed the darkness and, ahead of the braking traffic, the blue beacons of emergency vehicles flashed from either side of the road. Gavin slowed, and a howling police car raced past in the next carriageway. The Bruckner chorus thundered on. Gavin reluctantly retrieved his hand as the car inched to a halt.

They waited in silence for a while. He had no way of knowing, then, that the steady thaw was about to regress. Vivienne smiled across at him and squeezed his arm. He turned the radio down to a hum.

"I wonder what's happened," she said, peering through the side of the windscreen.

Five minutes passed. The car ahead moved forward a few yards, then stopped. In the distance, Gavin could see people getting out of their vehicles, standing in the road. An ambulance rushed by, siren wailing. A police motorcyclist came up on the inside, threading his way through the queue, boots kicking at the ground.

"D'you think there's a way out of this?" Gavin asked her.

"Probably." She pointed across him. "There's a right turn there, if you can get over. Have you an A to Z?"

He started moving out of the line, indicating right. "In the door pocket. Where does this go?"

"Tell you in a minute." She had the book on her lap, head down, squinting. "I can't read in the dark."

Gavin was driving slowly uphill along a residential street. "Should be a Maglite in the back of the glovebox."

"Well - take the next left, then we're running parallel." She had the flap open, fumbling behind papers and CDs. "Got it."

He caught sight of it in the corner of his eye, trapped in her hand as the torch came out. Feather-light. A scrunch of blue cotton. A tiny, limp pennant.

"Damn," he groaned, under his faltering breath.

Vivienne switched the light on, but she didn't shine it on the A to Z; she shone it on the piece of blue cotton in her hand. "What is *this*?"

Gavin knew perfectly well what it was, which was the very reason he was unable to reply.

Vivienne lifted the soft bundle to her face, sniffed it and lowered it into her lap. "I recognise these," she said. "I bought them. They're Lizzie's."

"Ah," Gavin said.

She glared at him indignantly. "Is that all you can say?"

"I thought you were directing me."

"Pull up anywhere."

"What?"

"I said, pull up. Stop the car."

He drew into the kerb. His mouth was suddenly very dry.

"Turn the engine off," she said.

He did as she had asked.

"Radio off, please."

In the quiet, he heard her sharp intake of breath. "Gavin, what's been going on?"

"This is difficult," he said.

"Difficult? Is that for you or for me?" She dangled the knickers in front of his face. "Gavin, I want to know how a not particularly clean pair of my daughter's knickers comes to be hidden in the glovebox of your car."

"Vivienne, honestly, it's not what you think."

"Not what I think," she repeated slowly. "So what exactly do you think I think? What can you possibly expect me to think?"

"Look, there is a perfectly innocent explanation. Only..."

"Only what? Okay, let me put the question more specifically. Are you going to deny that you and Lizzie have had sex in your car?"

"Yes," he replied, zealously.

"Yes, he says. Is that a denial or an admission?"

A man plodded past, walking his dog. Gavin watched him until he disappeared into the gloom. "It's late," he said. "Can't we go home? I don't want to do this in the middle of nowhere."

"Home? We've just come from your home, Gavin. Do you want to go back there, is that it? Tell your mother, who presumably believes we can forge some kind of lasting relationship, that her beloved son has been having it off in his car with my daughter? Do you think that would impress her?"

"I could tell you the truth," he sighed, "only I don't think Lizzie would want me to. I know she - "

"Oh, this is good. Instead of being honest with me, you prefer to lie to protect her. Oh, great. Now I know where I stand in the pecking order."

Gavin raised both hands in a gesture of defeat. He started the engine. Vivienne muttered something inaudible under her breath, and pushed the knickers into her handbag. "Go on," she said, "get going."

"Where to? Where do you want me to - ?"

"Gavin, it's the middle of the fucking night. Just get me home."

They set off in icy silence. After a mile or so, Gavin switched the radio on again. A few more bars of the Bruckner Te Deum reverberated in the car, then Vivienne reached down and turned it off. "I need to think," she said.

Gavin needed to think, as well. Most of all, he needed to think about the disingenuous manner in which he had leapt to take advantage of a fortuitous misuse of words. Unwittingly, Vivienne had elicited from him a specious denial of an offence which he had nonetheless committed in another context. The deception left a bad taste in his mouth, a sense of guilt that festered in his mind. If he disliked her accusation, he disliked himself still more for his opportunistic dishonesty.

The house felt cold, unwelcoming, as if that were the best he deserved. The heating had clicked off, though she had thought to leave a light on in the hall.

"Go in the kitchen," she said, "it'll be warmer."

He walked ahead of her and sat at the table, fiddling nervously with his hands. She came in behind him and draped her coat over the back of a chair.

"Can I stay the night?" he asked.

"If you want. I'll make us a drink."

"It's late, that's all."

"Oh, diddums."

"Yeah, well."

She made two mugs of coffee and sat opposite him. She looked tired, he thought, with a touch of greyness about the eyes, the whites flecked with red threads in the corners.

He didn't want all this to go wrong, not now. He didn't want to have to start again, clawing his way back into her affections.

Vivienne reached into her handbag, extracted the knickers and placed them on the table. She gazed at them briefly, shook her head and smiled, a tight-lipped breath of muffled laughter.

"Don't," Gavin said.

She poked the cotton with her forefinger, pushed the scrap of blue towards him. "Will you return them to her or will I? I mean - you might want slip them on for her. I expect you enjoy seeing my daughter naked, don't you? I expect you - "

"Vivienne, please don't. It's not helping."

"Huh. A bit late for that, don't you think?"

"If you'll give me a chance, I'll tell you," he said. He took a long drink from the steaming mug, scalding his throat. "I'll tell you what happened. Of course, I can't make you believe me."

"If you tell people the truth, generally they believe you."

"Lizzie didn't want you to know, you see."

"What, that you'd had sex in the car?"

"No. I mean, we didn't. I told you. See, already you don't believe me."

"I'm finding it difficult, Gavin." She wrapped both hands around her mug and lifted it to her lips. "Go on."

"This was weeks ago - months ago. You'd just buried Jack."

"Right."

"Lizzie - got in touch with me. She asked me if I would take her to the cemetery."

"Take her to the cemetery? Lizzie? Whatever for?"

"I wondered that myself."

"If she wanted to go to the cemetery, why didn't she just ask me? I'd have taken her."

"Because of what she wanted to do."

Vivienne frowned. "What do you mean?"

"I thought it was a bit odd. I picked her up, and she didn't have anything with her to - well, to put on the grave or anything. When we got there, I offered to stop by the flower-seller, but she wasn't interested, didn't want to know. So we drove in - it was early and there was no-one much about - and parked quite near Jack's grave."

Vivienne was shaking her head. "Please don't tell me you did it in the cemetery."

"Course not." He paused, drawing a deep breath. "She - Lizzie asked me beforehand if I had a blanket in the car. Which I did. So, anyway, we were sitting there, I was waiting for her to get out and go to find the place."

"Yes. Well?"

"She - I couldn't believe it. She just yanked off her knickers and chucked them in the glovebox. I tell you, I couldn't believe it."

Vivienne was sitting motionless with her eyes closed. "No, neither can I, Gavin. What exactly is this nonsense?"

"Just listen. I swear to God I - "

"All right. Go on then."

"I followed her round to the grave. She made me bring the blanket."

Vivienne sighed heavily.

"We had to check there was no-one near us. She didn't want to be seen, you see. Then she squatted down on Jack's grave, lifted up her skirt - she had this short denim skirt on - and got me to shield her with the blanket while she - she pissed on where Jack was. I'd never seen anything like it. I mean, she hated him that much. It was, you know, all steaming in the cold. Then - well, that was it, really. We came back to the car, we got talking, I drove her home."

"I didn't see you. Either of you."

"It was that Sunday. You went to the South Bank with Maria."

"I remember."

"Stupid," he said. "The knickers. Neither of us gave them a thought afterwards. Idiots!"

"Right."

"What I can't understand..."

"Is what?"

"How come she didn't miss them when she undressed? You'd have thought - "

"Probably because she doesn't always wear them. I keep on at her about it. I think it's a horrible habit, but you can't tell her. That's Lizzie."

"Oh, I see." He nodded thoughtfully, wondering whether he was making any headway. He looked up at her, guardedly. "You do believe me, don't you? Please say you believe me."

"And if I don't?"

"Then you can ask your daughter. She didn't want you to know what she'd done. But now I've let the cat out of the bag, you may as well talk to her about it. She'll tell you the same thing."

Vivienne cradled her head in her hands, elbows on the table. Gavin couldn't see her face properly, and she was silent for so long, he thought perhaps she was crying or even dozing. He wanted to reach out and touch her, move her hands away from her face, but he dared to believe that in this pregnant silence lay a spell that ought not to be broken, perhaps a prelude to resolution.

"Are you all right?" he asked, at length.

"Not really," she replied, from behind her hands.

"I'll go if you want me to," he said. "If you want me to leave you in peace."

"In pieces, more like," she said, sliding out from the warm cave of her hands. "Just - stay."

"Vivienne, I don't - "

"It's all right, Gavin. I believe you. I made a mistake."

"Talk to Lizzie."

"Maybe I will. Eventually."

He felt tears beginning to burn in his eyes. He wanted her - but did he deserve her? Did she deserve him - a man who disguised a lie in a mantle of deceit and called it the truth? After Jack, was this what he was offering her?

"Let's go up," she said. "Let's go to bed."

"You're sure this is what you want?"

She shook her head, laughing silently. "I don't know. All I do know is, there's no way you could have invented a crazy story like that. It's so unbelievable, I have to believe it."

He lay on his back in her bed, waiting for her. If she was too tired, too confused, to make love, that would be all right, he would understand, and they would simply sleep together, enfolded in each other's warmth. Sometimes it happened that way, and it didn't matter.

She came in from the bathroom and climbed on to his side of the bed. She was naked. In the soft glow of the bedside lamp, she was beautiful. She crouched on all fours, balancing over his legs, facing away from him.

"You'll get cold," he said.

"No I won't." She moved back, thrusting her bottom towards his face. "So long as you love me, I won't ever be cold."

"Vivienne, what are you doing?"

130

"Bite my bottom," she said.

"What?"

"I got it wrong. Punish me. Bite my bottom."

He chuckled nervously. "Are you sure?"

"Would I ask, otherwise?"

The two full, pale globes of her buttocks loomed close to his face, and he could smell the sweet, dark taint of her, could see the faint darkening of her orifice as she strained forward, stretching her back.

He clasped her hips in both hands. With pincer-like movements of his front teeth, he nibbled at the soft flesh of her left buttock.

"Harder," she said, her voice a hoarse whisper.

He moved to the other side, biting sharply into the centre of the mobile globe. Vivienne's body jerked backwards, and she cried out.

"Vivienne!"

"No, don't stop." She was panting, rocking backwards and forwards, mouth open. "Tell me what it's like."

"Like - like eating a peach," he said. He tasted blood on his lips.

"Yes, that's good. Do you like peaches, Gavin?"

"I love peaches. I love how the flesh feels when you pierce it with your teeth. Like biting someone's bottom."

"Yes."

Under the duvet, his erection was enormous.

"Do it again," she urged, breathlessly. "Bite me again."

"Yes," he said.

The blood trickled down her thigh on to the sheet.

"God, I love you," he said.

"Hurt me, Gavin."

"No, that's enough. We should sleep now."

"Is there blood? I can feel something wet."

"A little, on your leg."

"Lick it off."

"What?"

"Lick the blood off."

Gavin licked the thin line of blood from her thigh. Vivienne sighed, almost a gasp, and rolled over on to her side. She lay quite still. He could just see her back rising and falling against the lamplight.

"Come under the covers," he said. "We can keep each other warm."

He rolled on to his side, and she slid towards him, switched off the light and snuggled close. Soon they were drifting in and out of sleep. Her breath tickled his face. The metallic tang of her blood lay inside his lips, a tincture on his tongue.

He waited until he saw her eyes blink open. "Vivienne, will you marry me?"

"Hmm? Pardon?"

"I love you. I want you to marry me."

"Marry me?"

"Yes. I love you, remember."

She rested the flat of her hand on his bare chest. "Not now, Gavin. Don't ask me now. Don't ask me when you're biting my bum."

"I'm not. I've finished. I'm not biting your bum."

"Did it taste like a peach?"

"Like a peach with iron juice."

She tugged playfully at the hairs on his chest. "Ask me tomorrow. Ask me when we're not in bed. Ask me when it's daylight and we're walking in the clear air. Then, ask me."

"Do you think you might say yes?"

"That's not fair. That's cheating." She grabbed his chest hair and pulled until he squawked. "Anyway, why do you want to marry me?"

"Because. Because I don't know how to live my life without you in it. I can't imagine it."

"All right," she said.

They slept.

15

THE BOY bore no resemblance to his sister, Gavin thought. Contrasting with her slim frame, dark hair and flashing eyes, James was short and stocky, built almost like a small Rugby player, with a florid complexion, close-cropped fair hair and pale blue eyes. Gavin was drawn in particular to James' eyelashes, long, strangely elegant fans, lighter in colour than the rest of his hair, lending his eyes a disarming femininity.

Gavin smiled, trying not to focus on those eyelashes. "Glad you could make it, James. Can I get you a drink?"

"Thanks. What beer is there?"

"There's Stella, John Smith's or Bud."

"Yeah, right. Bud would be good."

He went to the kitchen, took a can of Budweiser from the fridge and brought it back to the patio for James. "Plenty in the fridge," he said. "Help yourself if I'm not around."

"Cool," James said. He tore the tab and tipped his head back for about ten seconds. "Sausages make me thirsty."

"Steak'll be ready shortly. Baguettes and stuff on the table there."

"Oh wow. Loadsa food."

"You're not a veggie, then?"

"Me? No way. I see a cow, that's it, I've got to eat it. I don't go for that vegetarian crap. Cows, sheep, pigs - industrial units. God's creatures go rampaging round the planet, eating one another to stay alive. That's pre-ordained, part of the original master plan. There's no exclusion clause for you and me; we're just animals with clothes on."

Gavin grinned and nodded. "Doesn't sound like you're a left-wing reactionary, then."

"Should I be? Do I look like one?"

"No, but then I don't know you. I have to learn as I go along."

"Me too." James took another tilt at his beer. "You, for instance."

"What about me?"

"Exactly. What about you? I don't know anything about you, except what Mum and Lizzie have told me."

"Isn't that enough?"

"Not for me, no. That lady" - he swung round and pointed at Vivienne with his can - "is my beloved mother, who's just escaped with her sanity from the purgatory of being shackled to a drunken slimeball. I have to be convinced that you're prepared to help her rebuild her life."

"James, I promise you, if she'll let me, I'll do that. No hidden agenda."

"She's not just an accessory?"

"No. In plain words, I love her. I've told her that."

James studied the flagstones, nodding pensively. "So how long have you been, you know, seeing her?"

"Oh, about four months. We're taking it slowly."

"Right." To Gavin's surprise, James extended his hand in belated greeting, and they shook hands, as if to seal an understanding. "Just one thing," he added.

"What's that?"

"Don't ever hurt her. Stay with her and be true to her. Leave her if you must. But don't ever hurt her like he did. If you do, none of us will ever speak to you again."

Gavin watched him as he moved off, melting back into the smiling group milling around the fume-wreathed barbecue. Maria was there, laughing at something a tall man had said, removing her glasses to wipe the tears from her eyes. Vivienne had her back to Gavin, but Lizzie, standing next to her, was facing him now, wide-eyed, waggling her fingers at him. James wandered up to the barbecue, speared a large steak and turned it over so that it sizzled fiercely.

He went into the kitchen and took a can of lager from the fridge. As he popped it open, he felt a movement behind him, and when he turned, Lizzie was there, smiling, half a sausage protruding from her mouth like a glossy cigar.

"What do you look like?" he said, shaking his head.

"Don't know. What do I look like?"

"If you had a hat on, you'd look like a cow-girl."

"You calling me a cow?"

"Course not."

"You gonna kiss me?"

"Not with that in your mouth."

"I'm practising," she said, sucking the sausage in and out over her lips.

"What for? Or shouldn't I ask?"

She spat the chewed sausage into her hand and dropped it in the waste bin. "Now you can kiss me."

He rested one hand on her shoulder, drawing her into him, and kissed her softly on the lips, letting his mouth crawl in a slow circle over hers.

"That was nice," she said, leaning back.

"You taste of sausage," he told her.

"Coo, you're an incurable romantic."

"I know. I don't get out much."

She laughed generously, and how he loved those sparkling eyes, iridescent as gemstones, and the wild black fire of her hair, billowing against the sunlight from the open door. Then, too, there was the memory of another time, the vision of her pubic hair, two neat crescents of tiny curls, almost as if she'd permed it, and the springiness of it under his fingers, coils of soft wire puckering the moist skin.

"I heard about the knickers," she said. "Gavin, I'm really sorry. That was careless of me."

"I should have thought. It was my fault as much as yours."

"Funny, I suppose, looking back."

"Yes. I hope you told the same story."

"It wasn't a story. It was the truth."

He smiled, but there was a gravity about it, a sadness. "Except, it wasn't entirely, was it? I deceived her. I made her believe something that was twisting the truth. Do you know how that makes me feel?"

"Okay. So what can we do now? Do you regret it all, regret it happened?"

"I regret lying to her. I don't regret making love to you. That's the truth. I need to tell the truth."

"Sometimes the truth can hurt someone else more than a lie can hurt you - don't you think?"

He thought about this, wanting to believe it, needing to believe it. "Sometimes, perhaps. The other times, probably it's just an excuse, a coward's way out."

"You're not a coward, Gavin." She kissed him fiercely, mashing his lips. "You're a saviour."

Clutching his lager, he followed her out to the garden. They met James coming towards them. "Mum wants you - both of you," he said.

The tall man he had seen earlier was re-arranging food on the barbecue. Standing next to him, Vivienne looked tense, but when she saw Lizzie emerge with Gavin she smiled and beckoned them over. She squeezed Gavin's arm and kissed him on the cheek. James, Lizzie and Maria went to stand between the barbecue and the kitchen door.

"Something happening?" Gavin asked Vivienne.

"I think - you haven't said anything to Lizzie, have you?"

"About what?"

"About us."

"No. You asked me not to."

"Good. Only I think perhaps now's as good a time as any. While we're all here."

Gavin wondered about this. There was something careless about it. *By the way, kids, this is your new dad. Take him or leave him. I've made my decision.*

"What's the matter?" she asked him. "You look doubtful."

"It's just - maybe we should have introduced the idea to James and Lizzie beforehand. This concerns them too."

"Oh, come on, Gavin. Lizzie's been on at me for months to let you into my life. She's hardly going to turn round and say she doesn't want you in hers."

"I know, I know. I just think we should all have sat down and discussed it. Getting married, I mean."

"Well, James was at school. Lizzie - she comes and goes. You live thirty miles away."

"I'd have made the effort to be here, to sit down with you."

"What do you want, a board meeting? I make the decisions in this house, Gavin. I decide what happens in my life. God knows, I've earned that right."

He touched her arm to pacify her. "We're being watched," he said. "Don't let them think we're arguing about this."

"We're not. It's been agreed. You asked me to marry you - remember?"

"And that's what I want to do. Yet, you know..."

"What is it, Gavin?"

"I can't recall you ever saying you loved me. I've said it to you lots of times."

She nodded, eyes downcast. "It's important to you, isn't it?"

"Yes," he said. "But I only want you to say it if you mean it, if it's the truth."

Maria, brandishing a chicken leg in the air, shouted for them to get on with it. "Come on, Viv! We're all stood here waiting."

Gavin gripped Vivienne's arm again, holding on until the pressure made her wince. "Of course it's important to me. It's the only thing that's important. People shouldn't get married for any other reason. When you feel so strongly about another person, you can't imagine living life without them. That's what being in love is. That's what I need from you."

"You make it sound so simple."

"So long as I make it sound true."

"You do," she said, and her voice was hardly more than a whisper. She kissed him on the side of the lips. "Gavin, you are a very special man, and I love you, and I want to marry you. If you'll have me."

"Since Christmas, that's all I've ever wanted."

He stood with one hand on her shoulder, a gesture of cautious possession, as she spoke to her guests. "I want this man in my life," she told them, "for me and for my family. I want him to help me forget the darkness of the past, and bring some sunshine into the future."

James applauded, and one by one the others joined in with a slow, uncertain handclap.

"Gavin will be moving in with me here very shortly," she continued, "and although we aren't planning a formal engagement, I'm very happy to tell you that he's asked me to marry him, and I've said yes." She squeezed Gavin's hand and swung his arm to and fro. "So expect an announcement quite soon."

"You must have some idea of a date," Maria called out.

"No, not yet," Gavin replied. "But this year. Probably within the next few months."

Vivienne was smiling broadly, looking happy and pleased with herself. She hadn't let go of Gavin's hand. "Enjoy the barbecue," she said, "and please have a drink on us. We aren't going to have a lavish wedding, but all of you here will be invited. In the meantime, I hope you'll think of us and wish us well."

A scattering of applause, more heartfelt this time, pattered across the garden, and the party broke up into small knots of gossiping friends and relations, muttering with their heads down, pausing now and then to munch on chunks of bread or peer critically at scorched and blackened sausages.

Vivienne introduced Gavin to the tall man he had noticed earlier. "Gavin, this is Lorne Mowler. I've told you about him. Lorne has some wonderful ideas for the garden."

Lorne, towering six foot-four in his heavy laced boots, bent down to shake Gavin's hand with a surprisingly gentle embrace.

"The man with the lawn mower," Gavin said.

Lorne laughed softly, obligingly. "Tell you the truth," he said, "I hate mowing lawns. The most tedious job in the garden. Outdoor hoovering. I'm a gardener, I create colour and space. Lawns are an intrusion, they try constantly to re-invent themselves."

Gavin smiled and shook his head non-committally. He had caught Lizzie's eye, and she was staring at him with her head on one side, as if seeing him anew, re-assessing him. He waited while Lorne and Vivienne strolled over to talk to Maria, then he saw Lizzie walking slowly towards him, still wearing the same quizzical expression.

"You all right?" he asked her.

"Shouldn't I be?"

"Yes. You should be more than all right. I've done what you wanted."

"What's that supposed to mean?"

"You told me to get closer to your mother, not to give up on her."

"Hmm. Sleeping with her's one thing, Gavin; marrying her is quite another."

"Sounds like something Oscar Wilde might have said."

There was a smear of ketchup under her lip, and he wiped it away with his thumb.

Lizzie put out her hands, palms up, and fanned her fingers under his chin. "Sticky paws, too," she said. "Lick me clean."

"What?"

"Lick my fingers. Do it one at a time."

"Is this a good place? There's people watching."

"Where?" She turned her head both ways.

"You know where. Everywhere."

"We can go inside."

Gavin shook his head in mock disbelief. "This girl is crazy. Private finger-licking, she wants."

She punched him affectionately on the chest. "That's not crazy. Not if I love you."

He eyed her sternly. "Don't, Lizzie. You know we can't get into this."

"Why, all of a sudden?" She puffed out her cheeks like a petulant child.

"You know perfectly well why. I think you're lovely, Lizzie, but I - "

"There always has to be a 'but', doesn't there? There always has to be something to spoil it."

He didn't resist as she took his hand and towed him through the kitchen to the deserted front room. The curtains were half-drawn and the room was cool. Lizzie sat on the settee. "On your knees," she said.

Gavin knelt in front of her.

"Now then." She held out her left hand, fingers rigidly extended. "Now lick them."

Gavin leaned forward and, clasping Lizzie's hand between his thumb and first three fingers, gradually drew each of her thin fingers slowly, methodically into his mouth, sliding it over his bottom teeth until it lay on top of his tongue, so he could roll the tip of his tongue around her finger, wetting it, warming it - then easing back his head to release the finger, before he carefully drew the next one over his lips and sucked that finger too, flicking the tip of it with his tongue, wet-tickling it, and letting it go again, shiny with his saliva. He could taste the salt on Lizzie's skin, and the bitter taint of the colour on her nails. When he had done this five times, he reached for her other hand, and did exactly the same with those fingers, pursing his lips to suck each one in and out of his mouth, penetration and release, wetness and air, the tiny scratch of her nail on his lip, dark and light, warm and cool, love-licking her until his mouth was full of the thick, sticky taste of this girl.

"Come and sit next to me," she said, patting the cushion, leaving dark marks there.

He sat and gazed at her. His hands were trembling. She was still in his mouth, the tang of her, the smell of her fingers above his lip.

"What'll happen to us?" she asked.

"We'll be friends," he said, the best of friends. You'll see."

"I don't know," she sighed, "I'm not sure that's enough any more."

"You must have known how this was going to go, Lizzie."

"Yes, but I didn't know how I was going to feel - about you and me."

"It'll work out, Lizzie." He squeezed her thigh. "We can be close, we can be - "

"Friends. Yes, I know, you said."

"Yes, and instead of seeing you occasionally, I'll be part of the family, I'll be here every day."

"Right, and you'll be my stepfather, Gavin. Do you know what that'll make me? I'll be Lizzie Drexler, or even Lizzie Lake, but whatever, I'll be the girl who had sex with her dad."

She collapsed against his shoulder, and he stroked her hair, running his fingers through the dense coils. As she started to shudder, he knew the tears were coming. For a while he sat still, letting her sob with her face buried in his chest.

"Lizzie, listen to me," he said, finally.

"What is it?" she moaned, her voice muffled in the folds of his shirt.

"Sit up, Lizzie."

Slowly, she eased herself upright, grey tracks of tears creasing her cheeks.

"Lizzie, all that's just a - a construction. I wasn't your dad then, anyway. I'm not your dad now. It doesn't make any difference to us, how we are, how we feel. It doesn't matter."

"Well, that's easy for you to say. It matters to me. How I feel about you - I don't feel like your daughter, see. I don't feel that way."

"So - what is it you want me to do now? How can we sort this out?"

"Come upstairs with me," she said, sniffing back her tears.

"I don't mean right now, this instant. I mean, from here on."

"You don't fancy me, do you? Not any more. Now you've got her, you couldn't give - "

"Lizzie, that's enough! You're only tormenting yourself."

"I can't help it. I don't know how to stop myself." She threw herself back on the settee, blinking away tears. "I just didn't think it would be like this."

"But you'll see more of me than you ever did before, Lizzie. We won't have to meet up in private. You'll just turn round and I'll be there."

"That's ridiculous. Everything will have changed. I'll be your daughter. It'll never be like before."

Vivienne's voice sounded in the hall. "Hello? Are you there, Gavin?"

"Front room," he called.

Lizzie hastily wiped her eyes with her knuckles.

"Ah, there you are." Vivienne stood in the doorway, a tea towel in her hand. "Wondered where you'd gone."

"Just talking," Gavin said.

Lizzie sniffed loudly.

"Are you all right?" her mother enquired.

"Course."

"Your eyes are red. You've been crying."

"Not exactly," Lizzie said.

"She's a bit emotional," said Gavin. "Quite a lot to take in, when you think about it."

"I see," Vivienne said, doubtfully. "Well don't think about it too long. Come and join the party, be sociable. James is putting more food on."

"We'll be right out," Gavin told her.

She turned to go, then hesitated. "I need a favour, Gavin. This is for later."

"Sure."

"Lorne's brought a DVD Maria wanted to see. Some trashy American thing. Apparently her player at home's gone on the blink. I said she could watch it here after we've done with the barbecue."

"Of course."

"It's just - well, I don't think she should be getting the bus home in the dark. So I said you'd run her back afterwards. I hope you don't mind."

"No, honestly, it's okay."

139

She nodded. "Good. I'll tell her. Now don't let that food go to waste."

"We won't," Lizzie said.

"Clean your face up before you come out, girl. You look like a panda."

He waited while Lizzie washed her face, obeying her mother's instruction like a well-mannered child. That, he reflected, was what she was: an appealing, vulnerable child, and he would do well not to forget it. Her reserves of sensuality and sexuality were well developed, but they masked an underlying insecurity, a repression rooted in the trauma of her past. Lizzie stalked the corridors of his imagination, a wilful adolescent impersonating a woman.

In the garden, James and Lizzie stood close together, speaking in low voices, and Gavin was sure that they were confiding their misgivings as they considered the future. Even as the early evening light's grey shawl slipped down around them, they went on talking, James kicking listlessly at stones on the path or digging his toe in the grass, Lizzie nodding or shaking her head, the wild mane of her hair the colour of black ink in the gathering gloom.

Maria sidled up to him, placing a hand on his arm. "Well, dear boy, are you pleased with your work?"

"What work?"

"You've finally won her over," she said, laughing. "Now you can start putting this whole sorry mess into some kind of order."

"First I have to gain their trust," he said, glancing at the children.

"Foregone conclusion, I think. Just give them their space. Learn to love them, a little at first, then layer by layer..."

He peered at Lizzie, hopping from one foot to the other, a spectral dancer in the thickening twilight. *Learn to love them.* The act of learning to love, as a process perfunctory and dutiful, had for him become hopelessly entangled in the reckless machinery of his emotions. He might try to love Lizzie as her father, but in his heart he knew that this resolve was doomed to failure, for all that had happened between them over the past months had set him inexorably on a different path.

Maria still had hold of his arm, applying gentle pressure to steer him towards the house. "I believe you're taking me home later," she said.

"Vivienne asked me, yes."

"You don't mind?"

"My pleasure."

"Hmm. Then I shall make it my business to attend to your pleasure, Gavin."

"What?"

She laughed, a crackle of delight in the hushed darkness. "Dear Gavin. Don't look so scared. I won't bite you - unless you really want me to."

"I'm not scared. You never cease to surprise me, that's all."

"Yes, I think I could surprise you." She leaned closer and pecked him on the cheek. "Come and watch the film with me. Sit with me."

She led him to the front room and told him to sit on the settee. Reaching over him, she drew the curtains together, then turned on the television and slotted a disk into the DVD player.

"What about the others?" he asked. "Are they joining us?"

"Up to them," Maria huffed, bouncing down beside him.

The film began. Soon the room was filled with strident music, men shouting and blasts of gunfire.

"Do you want the light on?" Gavin asked.

"What? No, leave it. It's nice in the dark."

He felt her hand resting warmly on his thigh. His eyes were on the screen, but the flickering scenes meant nothing to him, they were just a jumbled kaleidoscope of coloured shapes, enveloped in noise, an irritating distraction from his innermost thoughts.

Maria's hand crept further up his thigh. "Saw you chatting to Lizzie," she said quietly, her eyes still fixed on the screen. "Is she all right?"

"I don't know. I think so."

"She seems very fond of you."

"She's a wonderful girl."

"Yes. And you're a lovely man."

Her hand had inched so far along his thigh, the edge of her thumb now brushed his crotch. A strange fluttering welled up in the pit of his stomach.

"What are you doing, Maria?"

"Nothing. Nothing you need to worry about."

"There's people around, remember, just round the corner."

"They're in the dark and so are we. Relax."

"I thought you wanted to watch the film."

"I'm watching it."

"You're not concentrating."

He jolted in shock as her fingers tugged at his fly. He slapped her hand away, hearing the pounding of his heart in his ears.

Maria leaned back, chuckling in the dark. "Ooh dear. Don't you want to play with Maria, eh?"

"You're mad," he hissed. "Someone could come in at any moment."

She was shaking her head, tears of silent laughter glistening in her eyes. "You're right, of course. So calm, so sensible." She trailed her fingers down his back. "Bless you for loving my sister."

With the onset of night, the others began to drift in from the garden, finally abandoning the petrified barbecue. Vivienne sat next to Gavin, putting him between her and her sister, and he inhaled from her clothing the mingled scents of charcoal smoke and perfume. James came in with Lizzie, the pair of them laughing at some private joke, and Lizzie caught Gavin's eye and fell silent, and while James sat on the floor close to his mother's legs, his sister slumped in an armchair with one leg thrown lazily over the upholstered arm. Lorne Mowler looked in, glanced around the room and backed into a corner, sliding down the wall with his knees raised. The next-door neighbours, Jane and Patrick, had made a late appearance, and wandered in with their four year-old daughter Arabella, an attractive child who clutched a ketchup-oozing hot dog in both hands and smiled coyly beneath a cloud of blonde ringlets. Jane sat in the second armchair while Patrick squatted at her feet with Arabella on his lap.

"We could have the noise down a bit, perhaps," Vivienne said, flinching at the gunfire ricocheting off the furniture.

Maria stabbed the air with the handset, looking wearily indignant.

"My neighbours," Vivienne told Gavin, nodding at the armchair. "Arabella was a long time coming. They're trying for a little brother for her."

Gavin smiled sympathetically. Whenever he heard that a couple were 'trying for a child', he was put in mind of a coconut shy. Lob the shot high enough and hard enough, you'll knock one off, if you're lucky. Trying for a child. Sex become mechanical. Passion sublimated to methodology. How far away, he wondered, was the time when morality turned full circle, and the use of sex for procreation finally came to be regarded as a more anti-social habit than its indulgence as a vehicle for pure pleasure.

"I've seen this before," James said, yawning. "I know how it ends."

"So don't watch the end then," Lizzie retorted, swinging her dangling leg to and fro.

Maria was massaging Gavin's thigh with her fingertips. In the darkened room, the flickering light from the TV screen was beginning to hurt his eyes.

Little Arabella fell asleep, her mouth gaping open like a pink flower. Her parents scooped her up, made their apologies and crept soundlessly to the door.

"I can make popcorn," Vivienne offered, "if anybody wants it."

Lorne Mowler waved a languid hand to decline.

"Not long to go now," Maria said.

Lizzie stared at her. "Till what?"

"Till the film ends."

"I know what happens in a minute," said James.

"You tell us, you're a dead man," Lizzie told him.

The room was full of sleepy people. Conversation was snuffed out by tiredness. Dramatic music swelled from the set as the film ran into its closing sequences.

Vivienne reached across Gavin and pushed her sister's hand from his leg. "Stop mucking about," she said.

As the credits rolled up the screen, Vivienne jumped up and switched on the light. Everyone stirred into new positions, blinking out of bleary eyes.

"That's it," Maria said, patting Gavin's thigh again, "you can run me home."

They met Vivienne in the hall. "Take care," she said. "I'll wait up for you, Gavin."

He peered back through the doorway, catching Lizzie's eye. She waved a limp hand, unsmiling. James had shifted on to the settee and promptly fallen asleep. Lorne was crouching in front of the DVD player, extracting the disk. His grey cords were stretched tight by his thigh muscles. He had lean but powerful legs, and Gavin couldn't help but wonder if they had ever been wrapped around Vivienne's neck. No, anyway, this wouldn't do, not now.

Maria's hand was on his bottom. "Come on, it's late."

Traffic was light, and they were at the house in ten minutes. He found a parking space outside and sat there with the engine idling.

Maria picked up her bag from the floor. "Terrible cliché," she said, "but would you like to come in for coffee?"

Gavin studied her face in the street-light shadows. She was a good-looking woman, he thought. He imagined what she would look like without her glasses.

"Just for a few minutes," he said, turning off the engine.

She had left the porch light on. As she slotted her key in the lock, she hunched herself up and kissed him on the side of the mouth.

It was warm inside. She went from room to room, turning on the lights. She took off her coat and draped it over the banister rail. Gavin waited awkwardly in the hall, unsure where to go.

"It'll have to be instant, if that's all right," she said. "I don't want to start the machine now."

"Of course. That's fine."

"Go in there." She indicated the front room. "Draw the curtains for me."

When she came in with two mugs of coffee, he was sitting on the settee. She put the mugs on the floor, raised a finger and went back to the hall. The telephone was on a small mahogany table with a chair beside it. He clearly saw her lift off the receiver and place it next to the phone.

"Why did you do that?" Gavin asked.

"I should have thought that was obvious," she replied. She came in and backed against the door, closing it behind her.

No amount of coffee could lubricate Gavin's parched mouth. Over and around the caffeine, he could taste his own heart, wedged against his tongue.

Maria was kneeling in front of him. He leaned back and gazed at her face, upon which a thin but confident smile hung like a beckoning light. His eyes never strayed from hers as he felt her fingers deftly unfastening the buckle of his belt.

"This time," she murmured, "we won't be disturbed."

16

JANET LAKE had done this almost every night for twenty-seven years. In her nightclothes, on her way to bed, she had paused in the doorway of Gavin's room, rested one hand on the door-post and, with a breath lightly restrained yet not suspended, gazed in silent awe upon the sleeping form of her only child, the bedclothes gently rising and falling as he travelled serenely in his dreams.

Nearly ten thousand times she had performed this small, intensely comforting ritual. Now, tonight, it was no longer a comfort to her; it was quietly unbearable. As she searched for Gavin's pillow-shrouded face in the darkness, her vision was obscured by a veil of tears. Ten thousand times but, after this, no more. At the foot of the bed loomed the lumpish shadows of the boxes and suitcases containing her son's clothes, his books and music and a few framed photographs of people he must love and leave. She pulled the door until a couple of inches of dark space remained, then turned on to the landing. In her room, she sat on the edge of the bed with her hands in her lap. She would not sleep tonight. In her head, in her heart, was too much memory, too much longing.

Gavin had found the van company on the internet. *Man on the Move*, they called themselves. They arrived on time at 8am, two men in green overalls driving a yellow van. The men were Charlie and Les. Charlie had body odour, probably from wearing the same overalls to do strenuous work day after day. Les was black, his sudden smile a gleaming gash, like the sun coming out.

Janet hovered in the hall, watching the men load the van. She leaned against the wall with her arms folded, an attitude that said, 'That's it, the end of it, there's nothing I can do about it.'

"Best follow me," Gavin told the movers. "Just let me say goodbye here. Five minutes."

She made him coffee while he sat at the kitchen table. Even the resigned arch of her back seemed a kind of indictment. This was the right thing to do, he told himself, yet there was no pleasure in it. He felt like a deserter, as though his *graduation* was an act of betrayal.

Her hand crept towards his and tickled the backs of his fingers. "Now you take care," she said, and he could tell from the way she spoke levelly through half-gritted teeth that she was struggling to hold back tears. "You look after yourself. Don't give everything to her."

"What? What do you mean?"

"You know what I mean. You give too much of yourself."

"Marriage is about sharing," he said, with a shrug. "It's a balancing act."

"Hmm. You mind you don't fall to your death," she said, and at last a single tear rolled down her cheek.

He patted her hand, wondering if this might seem a patronising gesture. "Don't be daft, Mum."

"Believe me, Gavin, I'm wise, not daft. I see things coming."

"Yeah? What things are they, then?"

"Don't be flippant about it. I'm looking out for you, but I can't do it for ever." She took a tissue from her pocket and blew her nose. "I can't do it if you're not here, if I don't know what's happening to you."

"Mum, this is no big deal, really. You know I can't stay here indefinitely."

"Why? Why is that, Gavin? Is there a law against it?"

"Yes, I suppose there is, in a way. Call it the law of natural development."

"Oh, right. Or is it the law of diminishing returns - for me, anyway?"

"Now you're beginning to sound bitter, Mum," he said, sighing. "In any case, you don't have to stay here yourself. You could move."

"Move? Move where?"

"Anywhere you wanted. You could go down to Dorset, stay with Amanda for a while."

Her immediate response was a small explosion of scornful laughter. "Oh yes. Your sister'd love that. Me under her feet all day."

"You wouldn't be. She's out at work."

She was shaking her head, smiling sadly. "Men always think these things are so simple. That way they avoid confronting the truth. Your father was just the same."

"Mum, I'm just trying to make you see this as - as a new beginning, rather than the end of something. Is that so bad?"

"Drink your coffee," she said, scowling at him irritably. "Those men are waiting. They've got work to do. They'll be charging you extra."

He stood up, pushed his chair neatly under the table and kissed his mother on her dry cheek. "I'll ring you this evening," he said.

"Ring me tomorrow, when I've got used to the idea of you not being here. It's when I wake up in the dark, you see."

"You could take a sleeping pill, perhaps."

"You trying to kill me off?"

"No, Mum, I'm only - "

"Go on with you, I'm not serious. Look after that woman of yours." Her hand rested lightly in the small of his back, propelling him forwards. "And don't forget to come and see me - both of you."

Outside, he waved to Charlie and Les in the van cab, more in apology than recognition, and slid into his car. A thunderous diesel rattle, a cloud of blue smoke, and the van was on his tail, huge in his mirrors, while in the nearside door mirror Janet Lake appeared for a fleeting moment, one hand in the air, her frail frame eccentrically dwarfed by parallax.

"I have to do this, Mum," he said, under his breath. "You told me I'd be left behind - remember? It's for the best."

He had gone nearly a mile before the tears cleared from his misted vision. It would be good to stop and blow his nose, but Charlie and Les were right behind, so he carried on, controlling his speed so as not to outrun the heavier vehicle. As he checked the nearside mirror, he could still see her standing there, a blemish in his mind's eye, her vital stature, such a force in his life, somehow diminishing as her image grew smaller and receded into the distance, into the past.

Supposing she was right. Was he in love with Vivienne, or was he in love with the notion of being in love with her? For that matter, how sure could he be of her love for him? Her acceptance could so easily be a mere convenience, a non-committal experiment with something different. His mother's words of warning came back to him. 'Right now you can rely on her kisses and cuddles. But in forty years' time, can you be sure she'll still want to wash your underpants? That's what marriage is all about, Gavin. It's about not caring when you're both just soiled goods, tolerating each other in stagnant silence.'

Vivienne came out to meet him as he parked the car. Perhaps she had been watching from the window. He approached her for a welcoming kiss, and she turned her cheek towards him and murmured "Mmm" as his lips touched.

"It's good to be here," he said.

"It's good to have you with me. It'll be good for all of us."

She helped him bring in the cargo from the back seat and the boot. The sun was warm on his back as he bent to lift a box, a suitcase, a plastic sack. The kitchen smelled of baking. They dropped his stuff in the hall. When Vivienne bent down to lower a box carefully to the floor, a gap revealing several inches of bare flesh opened up between her wool top and the belt of her jeans, and the scarlet loop of the waistband of her knickers eased itself into the light. Nervously, he placed the pads of his fingertips on the pale skin, and it was smooth and cool as marble.

Upstairs, he unpacked the larger of two suitcases and hung his suits, shirts and trousers where Vivienne had made space for them at one end of the fitted wardrobe. The rest of his baggage he pushed against the wall, under the window. It made the neat bedroom look untidy, but he would attend to it later.

He sat on the end of the bed, gazing around the room. This whole situation seemed so unreal. For months he had pursued Vivienne Drexler, courting her affections with discreet determination, and now he was about to share the most private room in her life, unpacking his clothes amid the airy aroma of her perfume, wondering on which side of the bed she would invite him to sleep. He had slept with her before, of course; but that seemed irrelevant now, a trivial detail in the awesome tapestry of this relationship. Folding back the duvet, he slid one hand along the sheet, kneading the mattress with his fingers, feeling its contours yield and spring back against his palm. My place, he thought, *my place.*

When he imagined sleeping with her now, tonight, all the other nights, the idea somehow embarrassed him. The other times, there had been the adrenalin-fuelled distraction of sex, unfettered and uncomplicated, to protect him from any kind of spatial awareness of what was happening. It was as if they had crawled together into a vacuum, a dark enclosure where nothing else existed, where nothing but the silent, softly-glossy juxtaposition of their bodies had any form or consequence. Now, those constrained dimensions were about to change, to evolve into a design more complex and multi-faceted than any he had known before. Vivienne's body, he began to realise, would no longer be the ultimate objective he craved; it would become something dependable and symbolic around which an infinitely more volatile world revolved.

She had crept along the landing and was standing in the doorway. A floorboard creaked as she moved, and he looked up in surprise.

"Hi. Didn't see you." He stretched his arms above his head and kicked aimlessly at a box of books. "Making your room look like a squat."

"Our room," she said.

"Yes. Of course."

"You looked thoughtful, far away." She came in and sat next to him. "You're not sorry, are you?"

"Sorry? What about?"

"Being here. Moving in. It's a big step."

"One giant leap for mankind," he pronounced, feigning an American accent.

She took his hand and held it warmly. He couldn't think of anything to say. His stomach twisted and gurgled, a sound like the bath water running away. As she wrapped his hand more firmly in hers, he could feel a tension travelling down his arm, transmitting messages to the pores in his skin, until the stickiness of perspiration bloomed there, sealing flesh to flesh, and in that instant his mind lurched back through snapshots of the past, recalling that evening on the dance floor when he had felt his palm moisten against the hardness of her spine as the music crashed around them.

"We could have some lunch," she suggested. "I've some home-made soup in the fridge - leek and potato. With garlic bread, perhaps."

"I'd like that."

"I can help you with your things later, if you like. You know, find a place for them."

"Yes. I know they're in the way, only I - "

"Gavin, it's all right, really. You mustn't be - apologetic about things, about any of this. This is your home as well as mine, remember. And I'll be your wife, and Lizzie will be your daughter - okay, your stepdaughter - and James will be your stepson, and Maria will be your sister-in-law. So we're all in this together, see. I don't want you to feel like you're a guest here."

"I know, you're right. Only at first I sort of feel like a tolerated intruder. I have to work my way beyond that."

"Pretty damned quick, you do." She kissed his neck. "Come on, let's eat."

The soup was thick and rich and bulging with earthy flavours. The warm liquid slid down like a grainy linctus, warming his heart.

"There's more if you want it," Vivienne told him. "Otherwise I'll keep some for Lizzie. She'll be back later."

"Where is she?"

"Not sure. Gone out with Daniel, probably shopping."

"I see." He dipped a chunk of garlic bread into the soup and drew in the mingled flavours. "Are they - I mean, how long has she known him?"

"Daniel? Oh, about two years, I suppose. They were at college together."

"He's all right, is he - for her?"

"Seems a nice enough young man. Mother's a theatrical agent, father's a doctor. Daniel's a mate, that's all."

"Do you think they'll stay together - make a go of it?"

"How d'you mean, make a go of it?"

"Well, is there a future for them?"

Vivienne put her spoon down on the edge of her plate, next to the soup bowl, and stared at him. "A future? Gavin, hasn't she told you?"

"Told me what? She hasn't told me anything about him."

"Oh, right, I see." She shook her head, a wan smile creeping across her face. "Gavin, he's - you know - batting for the other side."

"What?"

"He's gay, Gavin. Daniel's gay."

With his spoon suspended in mid-air, Gavin allowed this information to slide down, cooling the soup. "He's - oh, I never realised. I never thought."

"Well, you wouldn't, not if she's never mentioned it."

"I did think she was a bit reticent about him - about their relationship."

"Oh, there's no relationship, Gavin. They're friends, that's all. He's just someone she likes to go around with."

"So they - they don't sleep together?"

"Heavens! I hope not!" She put a hand to her mouth, stifling laughter. "I can't imagine what they'd do. A virgin in bed with a homosexual. An unproductive alliance, I think."

"She's not - " Gavin bit his tongue. "Are you sure about that?"

"About Lizzie? Well, perhaps not exactly, but nothing serious, you know. Kids today, they fool around, don't they?"

Gavin made no reply. *They fool around, don't they?* Was that what he was doing with Vivienne's daughter - fooling around? Which of them, then, was the bigger fool? Surely, the one with the most to lose, the one with the biggest stake in the game. He imagined Lizzie in bed with Daniel, the two of them lying quietly on their backs, side by side, holding hands, gazing vacantly at the ceiling. *Look, that brown patch there could be Madagascar. Yes, what's the capital of Madagascar, Daniel, eh? I don't know, it's a long name, only I can't quite remember, Lizzie. Do you want to do anything? Not really, Dan, let's just lie here for ever and hope for inspiration to strike.*

"Shall I get you some more?" Vivienne asked.

"More what?"

"More soup, of course. What's the matter with you?"

"Sorry. I was just thinking."

"Hmm. Too much of that can be hazardous to your health." She picked up his plate and bowl. "Finished?"

"Thank you. I loved it. Can I help you wash up?"

"We put them in the dishwasher. You'll have to get used to the system around here."

Gavin nodded absently. The system. Well, he'd had a system, of kinds, locked away in his head, a scheme whereby he would help Lizzie to salve the pain of being upstaged by her mother in his affections by encouraging her towards a closer, more permanent relationship with Daniel. He would remind her of the quality of what she already had. Now, with Vivienne's revelation, that scheme lay in ruins, divested of its motive power. Until today he had allowed himself the luxury of an ambivalent attitude towards Daniel, perceiving him as someone whose influence might compromise Lizzie's capacity to feel for him, for Gavin, the love he secretly sought from her, but who at the same time could protect him from the intensity of that emotion as he worked to consolidate his position within the family. It was with curiously mixed feelings of relief and despondency that he turned to face the frustration of these ambitions.

One by one, he heaved the boxes on to the bed so that he had no need to scrabble about on the floor to unpack them. He always felt vulnerable on all fours. It was impossible, from that position, to defend yourself or attack an assailant. At school one day, he had crouched on one knee in a shaded area of the playground close to the bicycle sheds, to tie a trailing shoelace. A boy from an upper form, perhaps a year older, had approached him from behind and sat heavily on his arched back. The boy was too solidly built for Gavin to move him or stand up. The boy's name, he recalled, was Thomas Heckmanns. The minutes passed. Thomas Heckmanns was in no hurry. Gavin could feel him moving slowly backwards and forwards, legs akimbo, along the line of his victim's spine.

"Get off me, Heckmanns. You're breaking my back."

"Shut it up, Laker. I haff to finish."

"Stop it, you dirty German!"

"Is all right, Laker. No need to make noise."

"My name's Lake. You're hurting me."

"Soon will be over, soon...soon..."

Then the windblown yelps of running, jumping, tumbling boys rang clear in counterpoint against the chuffing of Heckmanns' breath, as the big boy closed his eyes and, within the crumpled confines of his polyester trousers, committed a small and viscous atrocity astride Gavin's rucked-up blazer.

Momentarily mired in memories, he didn't hear her come in behind him. "You've finally landed on our planet, then."

He dropped a bundle of underwear on the bed and spun round. "Lizzie! It's good to see you."

"You too. Do I get a kiss?"

"Always. You shouldn't even have to ask." He tilted his head and kissed her on the corner of the mouth, his lips just brushing hers. "Hi Lizzie."

She was staring at him, not blinking. "That was very decorous. Is that all I get now?"

"Umm. By 'now', you mean...?"

"Well, now I'm about to be relegated to the rather subservient role of your stepdaughter."

Gavin flinched, fumbling for an answer. "Are you - what's brought this on? I rather hoped you might be pleased to be my stepdaughter. That would make me feel good."

"I think we're talking love versus possession, aren't we?"

"No, we aren't. Come here." Clasping both her narrow shoulders, he leaned into her and folded his lips densely around Lizzie's mouth, exploring its warm wetness with a darting tongue. "Mmm. Better?"

"Better."

He sat on the bed and reached for her hand. "Been out with Daniel?"

"Yes. I bought these great new boots. Daniel got some CDs and a birthday present for his mum. Then we ended up in Starbucks with huge cappuccinos and I had this massive hunk of carob and banana gateau. Took me half an hour to eat it."

"I'm glad. That you had a good time, I mean."

"Right. Got lipstick on your face, by the way."

He grinned, wiping ineffectually at his cheek with his fingers. "Sounds like you and Daniel get on well together."

She shrugged. "He can be moody. But mostly he's a laugh. With Daniel, there's no pressure, see. It's just a friendship thing."

"Yeah, I get it. You - er - you never told me he was..."

"It's okay, you can say it. He's gay. It's no big deal."

"I didn't say it was. I was just a bit surprised, that's all. I never thought."

"Never thought what? Never thought we weren't just lying around, bonking each other?"

"No, that's not how I saw it, actually. To tell you the truth, I think it's rather nice that you - that you're good for each other."

"Now you're beginning to sound patronising." She freed her hand and shook the dark cloud of her hair. "Daniel's a gentle person. I like that. It's why I like you, remember."

"Is that the only reason?"

"Don't be daft. I like lots about you. I like your kindness. I like the way you know how to reassure people and respect them. When they behave irrationally, you can calm them down, remind them of their self-worth." She paused, head lowered, rubbing the carpet with her toe. "I like the way you wouldn't give up on my mother, even when she was unfair to you."

"Oh, right. So I must be quite a reasonable bloke, then."

She punched him lightly, playfully on the nose, a tap with the tight little shell of her fist. "You'll do."

He patted the space beside him. "Sit with me."

"Just for a minute," she said, settling down on to the package-strewn mattress and jiggling closer to him. "Lots of stuff, by the looks of it."

"Not really. Flotsam and jetsam of a life."

She was sitting on her hands, gazing pensively at the door. "Funny, I was thinking."

"About what exactly?"

"How things turn out. All those years I spent in the other house, lying in bed each night, queasy with apprehension in case my dad came in and tried to climb in with me or touch me; and now, here I am, half hoping that when I go to bed my dad - that's you, by the way - will be there, and perhaps he'll come in and give me a cuddle." She hunched her shoulders and sighed. "Just do what Daniel can't, I suppose."

Gavin sat quietly and thought about this confession. He thought about strength and weakness, honesty and deception, progress and regression. There were burdens of conscience to be managed between them: he with his guilty secrets; Lizzie with her unstable obsession. No matter how finely forged the links drawing together two human beings, could there ever be utter and complete truth and openness and honesty? Were such pure and absolute qualities prescribed within the chemistry of the human condition? Or were lies and deceit and self-interest simply what life was all about?

"We can work this out, you know, Lizzie," he said. "You and me."

"Can we?"

"We have to."

"That's not an answer. It's a cry of despair."

"Melodramatic, Lizzie."

"Yeah, well." She stood up and faced him with her back to the door. "Gavin, I've got some notes to write up for work. I need to go on-line for a while." A smile sparked across her face, a tremor of electricity. "Hey, they bought me a laptop, a Toshiba, wireless access and everything. Aren't I lucky?"

Gavin gazed at her solemnly. "No, Lizzie, I don't think you're lucky. You're funny and clever and sexy and beautiful. So you'll make your own luck, you'll get what you deserve. I only hope I deserve you."

"Oh Gavin, that's nice," she said softly, hanging her head. "Look, I gotta go."

"I know. Wait just a moment."

"What?"

"Hold out your hand."

"Jeez, you're not going to smack me, are you?"

"No - just this."

And he took her hand and drew the extended fingers very carefully into his mouth and she let him slide them on to his tongue so he could caress them, bathe them in his juices.

"That's nice," she said. "That always makes me go sort of woozy. Does it make you go woozy?"

"It does all sorts of things. Everywhere."

"That's good."

"I hope I meet him one day, Lizzie."

"What? Who?"

"Daniel, of course."

"Oh, him. Right. I guess you will, if you stick around."

"I'll stick around, then."

"Yes. My hand's all wet."

"Goodnight, Lizzie."

It took him another hour to make some semblance of order in the room. He upended the cases in the corner, flattened the cardboard boxes and pushed them under the bed. They could go down to the shed in the morning. At least, now, the room looked like a bedroom again. He straightened the duvet and plumped up the pillows.

Vivienne made hot chocolate and a large pile of warm buttered toast.

"You're good to me," he said.

"I've hardly started." She picked up a round tray and put a plate of toast on it next to a Mickey Mouse mug of chocolate. "You can take this up, please, for Lizzie."

"If you want. She's doing her project work."

"That's all right. Go on. You need to get to know her."

He carried the tray gingerly up the stairs, waited and tapped on the closed door to Lizzie's room.

"Hello!" she called.

He clicked open the door and peeped in. She was sitting upright in bed with just a pink T-shirt on, her legs folded tightly in front of her, bare knees jutting out either side of the open laptop perched below her tummy. From beneath the amber shade of a bedside lamp, a delicate fan of pinkish light spread across the bedclothes.

"Hi. Mum said to bring you this."

"Okay. Thanks. You can leave it at the end of the bed."

"Don't knock it over."

"I won't." She pecked at the keyboard, frowning.

Gavin lowered the tray carefully on to the flattened duvet and stood back. "You look lovely," he said.

"Do I?" Her eyes remained fixed on the screen.

"Can I kiss you goodnight?"

She hesitated, one hand in the air. "No, Gavin. Don't. You'll only make things worse."

He nodded. "I understand."

"Really?"

"Really."

"Goodnight - Dad."

Pulling the door shut behind him, he stepped back on to the landing and, glancing through the open doorway to the master bedroom, glimpsed the lights of the city winking in the darkness beyond the window. Downstairs, his supper snack was getting cold, but still he turned into the darkened room and stood in quiet reflection before the glittering nightscape. His mother was alone in the dark, somewhere out there over the clustered buildings on the horizon. Tonight she would cry herself to sleep, because everything changes, moves on and becomes something else and cannot be recovered. Everything, in time, becomes a loss.

So he stood at the window and watched the distant lights. In the morning they would all be gone, absorbed into the fabric of a new dawn, a face washed clean under a steely sky. He asked if he, too, could present a new face to his world. Was there time for him to re-invent himself?

Am I capable of change?

First, I must escape from myself.

17

Summer

THEY had arrived late, after a ferry crossing delayed by an unexplained accident in which a crewman had mysteriously fallen overboard before departure and vanished beneath the turbid waters of the harbour. Men in yellow jackets hurried to and fro along the jetty, shouting anxiously to one another, while over the promenade railings hung small knots of bystanders, watching the brown froth slapping against the hull of the ship and the rainbow oil streaks trailing like coloured scarves on the swell. All eyes were on the heaving water, but the fallen man did not appear.

With commendable promptness, divers arrived in a port authority van. Wordlessly, they lowered their visors and slipped down into the murk. After a few minutes, two dark forms broke the surface, bearing between them the inert body of the drowned seaman, his face blanched white with shock, long hair dark and gummy as seaweed.

Vivienne stared, hollow-eyed, at the divers with their grim treasure. "I hope this is not some kind of omen," she said.

"Freak accident," Gavin assured her. "Don't worry about it."

"Hard not to. That poor man, he's probably done the same job, day in, day out, for twenty years, and today he gets up as usual, kisses his wife goodbye and goes jauntily off to work. Then he trips on a rope and he's dead. Makes your blood run cold, doesn't it?"

Gavin hugged her close against him. "We'll be away soon."

A chill breeze sprang up as the ferry nosed out into the firth, the engine juddering fussily against the tide. Dressed for the sheltered warmth of the town, they sat below decks and gazed at the roiling water through salt-smeared windows. Seagulls, grey-uniformed outriders, cruised beside the vessel at funnel height, as though escorting them to the island.

The hotel occupied an imposing position on a high bluff overlooking the bay. As the ferry docked, its reversing propellers churning the grey-green water into crests of hissing foam, Gavin looked up the cliff from the deck rail and saw the downstairs lights glowing tawny yellow in the gathering dusk, sleepily searching the gloom like old, jaundiced eyes.

Hooked over a wooden post at the head of the gangplank, a plastic bucket bore a hastily scrawled, taped notice: 'Please give what you can for Hughie, who lost his life today'. Gavin rummaged in his pocket and dropped a handful of loose change into the bucket. His mind spooled back through the afternoon, to the slow brown convulsion of the harbour water as it pitched against the shore, and Hughie slipping and falling, heart lurching, the steel-cold smack of the sea on his face as he rolled over blind in a world without light, his lungs ballooning to engulf him before they finally exploded amid the red mist screeching in his brain.

The room was spacious, sombrely elegant, with tall windows and a high ceiling from which hung an ornate chandelier. A large four-poster, elaborately draped in Black Watch tartan, was so positioned that the occupants could lean back against the headboard and look out through the open curtains to the bay and the hills beyond. On the window sill stood a glass vase of freesias, their sweet perfume hanging in the air like incense.

Before Gavin had thought to close the door, a concierge tapped on it lightly, and they turned together to see him proffering an ice bucket containing a bottle of champagne.

"For us?"

"Compliments of the West Isles Hotel, Mr Lake. Our congratulations to you both. Enjoy your stay with us. We wish you a memorable honeymoon."

"Thank you. That's very kind." He took the freezing bucket and passed it to Vivienne.

"Not at all, sir. Our pleasure."

Gavin closed the door and rubbed his hands together to dry them.

"A tip, perhaps, would have been nice," Vivienne observed.

"Hmm. Maybe. I expect we'll see him again."

Though the main window was a few inches open, it was warm in the room, and Gavin slid the heavy frame up until a grey rectangle, dotted with the amber sparks of harbour lights, hung like a dim painting between the curtains. Scattered voices drifted up from the street, and when the evening breeze wafted in, it carried the smells of fish and diesel oil and decaying seaweed. Gavin took a wooden chair and sat by the window, breathing deeply. The mingled smells were friendly, reassuring, redolent of quiet work and the uncomplicated traffic of ordinary people who had made their peace with the sea.

She came up behind him and rested her chin on his shoulder, making him flinch. "Love you," she whispered.

"That's good," he said, not taking his eyes off the scene outside.

"Only, the thing is..."

"What is it? What's the matter?"

Standing back, she placed her hands on both his shoulders and kneaded the hard flesh. "It's just - I'm very tired. I think I'll rest for a while. Gavin, do you mind if we don't - you know. Not tonight."

He turned to look at her. "You look - grey," he said.

"Thanks."

"I'm being sympathetic, not critical."

"I know." She stepped away from the window. "That man. I can't get him out of my head - how he looked when they brought him up. His eyes, they were rolled back cold like a dead fish."

"Not a good way to start your honeymoon."

"I'm not thinking of me, Gavin. I'm thinking of him."

He crossed to the bed and pulled back the duvet. "Come on, lie down. Try to sleep."

"They'll be serving dinner," she said, unhappily.

"I'm not hungry. I might go out for a walk, get some air."

Vivienne kicked off her shoes and lay down, unfastening the front of her trousers. "Don't be long," she murmured. "Be careful."

He walked for half an hour. The long day had stressed him, and he shoved his hands in his pockets and shambled slowly along the waterfront, past the pale facades of all the coloured houses, their different hues bleached to greys and whites by the street lamps and the thick stain of the encroaching night. There were hoarse shouts from men tinkering on moored boats that bobbed with the swell, the thin rasp of their voices carried from afar on the breeze creasing the inky water.

Where the shops and houses ran out at the curve of the bay, he stopped to lean on a stone wall, facing the sea. He thought about today and the day before, and about Hughie, rescued too late from the terrible soundless darkness, a man who lived with the ocean in his heart and loved it until it killed him. Then he thought of Vivienne, his wife - *my wife...my wife...*and he spoke the words to himself, hardly believing it, even now, moving his lips behind his hand - who lay in a quiet room waiting only for him, for his appreciation, his exploration and delectation, maybe not tonight, but soon and often and again for ever, until the unbelievable became believable.

As for the day before, he thought of it and tried at once to dismiss it, in case, now that it was too late to change anything, there was possibly something he had not said or done that should have been made a part of the occasion. A short, simple wedding: that was what she had told him she wanted. Vivienne, to his relief and perverse delight, had seized upon the opportunity to make of the event a small, rebellious statement, the importance of which seemed almost to undermine the romantic significance of the ceremony.

"Just tell me what you'd like," he had encouraged her.

"I'd like it all to be over," she said, "so we can get on with our lives."

"Do I detect the merest hint of negativity?"

"You asked me. I told you. A wedding that costs a few pounds and takes twenty minutes. About the same as a Chinese take-away. No crap, no hysteria."

"What about the family - our families?"

She turned down the corners of her mouth until the pink bubbles gleamed. "They'll come, of course. But it's our day, our way. There's no drunken imbeciles prancing around in top hats, no simpering women balancing alien spacecraft on their heads, no shallow prayers, no-one mouthing platitudes or puking on their shoes. It'll be a wedding, Gavin, not a pantomime."

"And that's really what you want?"

"Emphatically. But."

"But what?"

156

"There's you. It's your wedding, too. You should have your say."
"Absolutely. And you know what I say?"
"Surprise me."
"Thank God."
"For what?"
"For common sense. For economy of scale. For selfishness. For a world in perspective. For dignity."
She had kissed him then and patted his hair, the nearest she came to being playful. "I love you."
"Sometimes I wonder why."
"For making me feel important. For showing me that I matter."
Maria and Lizzie, he thought about them, too. Throughout the registrar's delivery, Maria had gazed at Gavin, smiling and nodding, and her stance might almost have been taken for benevolence, except that there was another recognition there, one that said, 'I am content now because I have proved my point, I have uncovered your weakness.'
No smiles, though, from Lizzie, who had fixed him with a peeved, questioning stare, an expression that challenged not his reason or justification for entering into this marriage, but rather her own lack of forethought in so assiduously encouraging it, shying too late from the flames of a pyrrhic victory.
At his back, around a wooden bench set into an alcove in the wall, he heard a sudden commotion, the skittering giggles of young girls, and he turned to see three of them, maybe fourteen years old and scruffily dressed, jostling one another for space on the seat. The girls' mud-spattered bikes lay capsized against the stonework. He was about to resume his trance-like study of the bay, when one of the kids, her voice unexpectedly gruff, shouted, "You got the time, mister?"
Gavin looked at his watch and told her.
The group huddled together, bumping heads in another gale of giggles. "You want ta sit wi' us?" one of them called.
"No thanks, I'm fine here," he replied, waving the offer aside.
The first girl was bouncing up and down, snapping the seal on a bottle of orange. "You waitin' for a gurrl?"
"I - uh - not exactly."
"Wass that mean? We're gurrls."
The kid next to her, the only one in a skirt, nudged the girl with the drink and stuck out her chin, grinning impishly. "You want ta see ma fanny?"
Gavin leaned his back on the wall and allowed them what he hoped was a withering smile, while the trio subsided into paroxysms of whooping laughter.
"Thank you, but I don't think that'll be necessary," he said.
The skirted girl bobbed her head, eyes flashing in the dark. "Oh thenk you, but I don't think thet will be necessary," she intoned, mimicking Gavin's English accent, and they all squealed hysterically one more.

The third girl, who had not spoken up to now, leaned towards him, jabbing a forefinger at her friend. "So wass wrong wi' her fanny?"

Gavin swallowed and licked his lips. "I'm sure she has a very nice fanny," he said, glad of the darkness that concealed the colouring in his face, "but I don't need to see it. Anyway, it's too dark."

The first girl paused between swigs of her orange. "Tha's okay, I've a light on ma bike."

Amid fresh giggles, Gavin turned back to face the boats lurching on the black water, their metal masts clanking in ghostly counterpoint to the soft shuffle of the waves. His lips curled as he imagined the scene. A grown man shining a bicycle lamp up a schoolgirl's skirt. Blue lights spearing the darkness. A rough hand pressing the top of his head as they bundled him into the back of the police car. As they sped away, the muffled cries of the onlookers: 'Ya bleddy pervert!'

"Take care on your bikes, girls! I'm going back to my wife. We were only married yesterday." This he announced with some pride, though he knew it made him vulnerable.

The juice-drinker wiped her mouth with her sleeve and tipped the bottle at him as if offering a toast. "Oh, on yer honeymoon, then. You'll be wantin' ta get back all right. No telly for you the night."

The one in the skirt, little finger up her nose, peered at him critically. "Aye, ye can tell a newly-wed. There's that look."

The other two chorused in shrill voices, "Ah, it sticks out a mile!"

"Goodnight, girls," he called over his shoulder as he passed them, not looking back.

She was asleep when he entered the room. The bedside lamp was lit on his side of the bed. He stood by the door for a moment, listening to the slow, steady sibilance of her breathing. Quietly, so as not to wake her, he undressed, pulled on a pair of pyjama bottoms, slid into bed beside her and put out the light. He lay on his back, trying not to touch her, keeping his leg away from hers. His eyes roamed among the hatcheted shadows on the wall, cutting swathes between the shapes, imagining the black blocks of buildings and the lighted avenues between, bisected by blurred, angled spars, vague as streaks of smoke, that might be interconnecting bridges. He began to lose his way in the maze of dark images, then he felt himself falling through space, sinking serenely into sleep.

It was raining when he awoke. Through the open window, the earthy, electric smell of wet rocks and puddled pavements drifted into the room. A car cruised by, tyres hissing on the streaming tarmac.

Vivienne stirred and rolled into him, fists balled under her chin. "What's the time?" she mumbled.

He peered at the bedside clock through filmy eyes. "Ten to six."

"Mmm. Wha' time's breakfast?"

"Whenever. Eight o'clock." He turned over to face her. "You all right?"

"Think so. Tell you later."

He lifted the duvet to cover her shoulders, and he saw that her left breast had slipped from her nightdress and lay over her folded arm, a pale gourd crowned with the dark thimble of her nipple. For a few seconds he gazed at her there, feeling himself stiffen. His fingers trembled slightly as he began to stroke the cool, soft skin, working his fingertips back towards her armpit, feeling a quick rush of pleasure as her breast lolled against his wrist.

Vivienne squirmed into the mattress, pulling back. "Don't. I don't want to be groped."

"I'm not - groping you. I'm only touching. You're my wife."

"Exactly. I'm not your rubber doll."

He lay on his back, subsiding, wide awake, breathing deeply, listening to the rain on the window and the mew of gulls over the harbour.

They breakfasted at eight-thirty and were back upstairs soon after nine. The rain had abated to a thin, warm drizzle that seeped from the wraiths of low cloud drifting inland across the pewter-coloured water. The bay seemed to simmer under the cloud-banks like a great steaming cauldron.

"What would you like to do this morning?" Gavin asked.

"I'd like to go for a walk, but not in this," she replied, nodding at the window. "If it's all the same to you, I think I'll read my book in the lounge for an hour. Perhaps it'll have stopped by then."

"Right. I might go out, call in at the tourist centre."

"Yes. Bring back some postcards. And some midge repellent from the chemist."

He kissed her softly on the cheek. She reached up and touched his face. "I'm sorry," she said.

"Sorry? What for?"

"Last night. This morning. This hasn't started well."

"Oh. Day one, Vivienne. There's plenty of time."

She smiled, shaking her head slightly, as if in bemused wonderment. "What a strange man you are."

"Strange? How?"

"So - so calm and reasonable. So understanding. You make me nervous, sometimes."

"Vivienne, please. Why should you be nervous?"

"It's as if I have to justify you to myself."

"Well, you don't. Do you love me?"

"Yes, I do."

"Well then. I love you. That's an end of it. No doubts or recriminations."

"It's all so simple, isn't it? For you."

He stood and stared at her for a moment. He felt sure he would make love to her tonight. Exactly that. Not have sex; make love. The calm, quiet oasis of being peaceful and warm inside somebody else. Something secure, almost foetal.

"I am a simple man," he said. "I simply love you."

The misty drizzle stained his face as he stepped outside, a cold sweat that blurred his vision and prickled in his hair. He thought he might buy a hat.

In a gift and souvenir shop, the window display dimly visible through moisture-pearled glass, he found a chunky baseball cap in Royal Stewart tartan. It was a perfect fit. He studied himself in a tall mirror, jostled by backpackers. The cap was a little gaudy, perhaps, but it felt right, and it would do the job. He came out wearing it, and once he realised that nobody was smirking at him, as they would have done down south, he felt pleased with himself and gently gratified.

At the tourist office he bought postcards and picked up some leaflets on local attractions. The woman who served him directed him to the pharmacy, where he chose the most expensive insect repellent they had.

Yes, he thought, he would make love to her tonight. Probably they would go to bed early and lie there with the curtains drawn back, naked in the daylight. He imagined the evening's glimmer, a silvery gloss on their entwined bodies, their backs iridescent as sealskin. It would be worth the waiting.

Here they came again, the cheeky girls from last night, racing along the pavement on their grubby bikes, scattering pedestrians. Gavin smiled to himself as he stepped into the gutter to let them pass. This time, though, there seemed to be four of them, the last one trailing behind and, surprisingly, wearing a cycle helmet over a thick nest of dark hair. He raised a friendly hand as the three kids flew by, but they were going too fast to notice him, and he carried on walking, shaking his head, eyes trained on the approaching straggler, somehow reminiscent of someone he'd seen before, something in the eyes, the hair perhaps, but surely not, not here...

The helmeted girl braked her bike hard, head dipping almost to the handlebars, and skidded in a graunching arc to stop in front of him, blocking his path.

Gavin recoiled in shock, staring at her.

The girl, panting for breath, blew a curl of hair away from one eyebrow.

He stood rooted to the spot, gaping in disbelief. This was impossible, unthinkable. This couldn't be.

The girl on the bike sat back on the saddle, fiddling with her helmet strap. "Looks like I've surprised you," she said. "But then, you always said I was amazing."

Gavin's mouth opened and closed wordlessly, emitting as much sound as a goldfish. He was still standing in the road, and a passing van hooted at him, making him jump.

"So. You gonna say something? Hoo, you've gone a funny colour, Daddy." She reached for his hand and, as if helping an old man, hauled him up on to the kerb. "You'll get run over."

He watched as she calmly looped the helmet over the handlebars and shook her head in a vain attempt to disentangle her hair. "Lizzie, what on earth are you doing here?"

"Riding a bike, mostly."

"What I mean is - how did you get here, for God's sake?"

"For my sake, for your sake maybe, but not for his sake. Believe me, he had nothing to do with it."

"Lizzie!"

"Six hundred miles, Gavin. My bum ain't half sore."

"Lizzie, will you please just - "

"All right, all right. I was on the same boat as you. I hired the bike." She dismounted and stood close to him. "Here, what about that bloke falling in the water?"

"Yeah, I know," he muttered, absently. "Lizzie, I need you to tell me what's going on here. Please."

"Umm. Well, I think there's some kind of regatta this afternoon, and highland games in the park one day, it might be on - "

"Lizzie," he continued, speaking with his eyes closed, "you know perfectly well what I mean. Stop messing me about. This is serious, and you know it."

They were blocking the pavement now, people milling around them, spilling into the road, some almost tripping over their own feet. Gavin leaned into Lizzie and pecked her on the cheek. Her face was smooth and tacky with perspiration. There was some kind of madness happening here, he thought.

"Walk with me," she said. "Stay by me."

Steering the bike with one hand, the other tousling her hair, she walked with him beside the harbour railings. After about fifty yards he glanced across at her and saw that she was crying, tears coursing down her cheeks.

He took the bike from her and propped it against the railings. "Lizzie, what is it? What's this all about?"

The tears were coming so fast, she couldn't speak for a while, just stood and stared at him through flooded eyes. "It's all about you," she managed, finally.

"But why, Lizzie? I thought we'd been through all this."

"No. I don't know." She pulled a tissue from her pocket and wiped her eyes. "Where did you get that bloody awful hat?"

"I just bought it."

"Oh. I hope you didn't let anyone see you paying for it."

He grinned, grateful for a moment's respite. "Dear Lizzie. It'll all work out, you know. Just give it time."

She sniffed loudly and almost choked. "Not with a hat like that, it won't. Anyway, where is she?"

"Who?"

"Mum, of course. Your wife. Mrs Vivienne Lake. Why isn't she with you?"

"She's back at the hotel, waiting for the rain to stop."

"Huh. It's only a bit of drizzle."

"Yes. It's raining on your face, Lizzie."

"No, it's raining inside me, Gavin. My face is where it comes out. Do you like my face, Gavin? Do you want to kiss it?"

"Lizzie, please."

"Do you like her more than me, Gavin?"

"Lizzie, don't."

"You know, if I thought you liked her, really liked her, more than me, if I thought that - "

"Lizzie, will you stop this?"

She hung her head, pouting in a mock sulk. "Are you telling me off, Daddy?"

"No, I'm not telling you off," he said, wearily. "And don't call me Daddy."

"Why not? That's who you are, isn't it? My guardian and protector. A shadowy figure in the corner of my life."

"Come on, Lizzie. That's not what either of us wants."

"Isn't it? I don't know what you want any more," she sighed.

Gavin moved towards her and, with a lightly curled hand, ran the backs of his fingers gently down her cheek. "Tell me why you're here, Lizzie. Tell me what you've come to do."

"To rescue you, of course."

"Rescue me? From what?"

"From yourself. Before it's too late. You're making a big mistake, Gavin, probably the biggest mistake of your life. That mistake could be your life."

The rain was falling harder now, borne in on a breeze that furrowed the grey water into sheets of corrugated iron, here and there a disconsolate seagull riding the swell like a marker buoy. The wind whipped into Gavin's eyes, spinning a salt spume against his face.

"If your fears have any foundation," he said, fiddling with the collar of Lizzie's jacket, "then it's too late. The deed is done, and the damage with it."

The tiniest glimmer of a smile tickled her face. "So you agree with me?"

"I said 'if'. I understand your point of view, that's all I'm saying."

"God, that hat is just so dreadful." She shivered and stuffed her hands in her pockets. "I'm cold. Push my bike for me."

"Where are we going?"

"Top of the street. Buy me a coffee. There's a café on the corner. The menu's not much, but it's somewhere to sit in the warm."

He gripped the centre-bolt of the handlebars in his fist as they walked, his free arm thrown around Lizzie's shoulders. A minute later, without warning, she whisked the tartan cap from his head and flung it over the kelp-strewn rocks into the sea.

"Lizzie! What did you do that for?"

The cap bobbed on the eddying tide until the backwash mashed it flat and it sank like a red crab into a foaming hollow.

Lizzie yelped and punched the sky. "Because I'm amazing!" she cried.

162

18

THEY found a table in the window. The café smelled of damp coats and cheap coffee, and the inside of the glass was pebbled with condensing moisture, obscuring the view to the bay. Gavin pulled a handful of napkins from the dispenser on the table and mopped at the whorls of wetness, clearing a smeary porthole through which they could look out and see the bustling street and the harbour beyond the sea wall.

He pushed the typewritten menu, wedged in its red plastic stand, towards her with one finger. "Do you want something to eat?"

Listlessly, Lizzie picked up the menu and studied it for what seemed a long time. As if distracted, she paused, still holding the card in front of her face, and peered about in apparent irritation. "Why do the Scots do this?" she asked.

"Do what?"

"This," she snapped, flapping her hands. "Downgrade everything. They could have a perfect little bistro here - a lick of paint, jazzy tablecloths, a few pictures on the wall, a potted plant or two; it wouldn't cost much and it would make all the difference. Course, they'd have to change the menu."

"You mean, do a printed one?"

"I was thinking more of one that had decent food on it." She leaned back and turned the menu over, squinting down her nose. "I'll have egg on toast and a cappuccino, lots of chocolate on the top."

An elderly waitress appeared with a pencil behind her ear and a tattered notepad dangling on a string from the waistband of her faded floral apron. The woman hovered beside them, crouched over like a vulture. Gavin had eaten a full breakfast, so he gave Lizzie's order and just asked for a coffee for himself.

"So where are you staying?" Gavin asked, when the waitress had gone.

"B and B just up the road from here. It's nothing smart, not like where you are, but it's clean and tidy and the lady's nice. I've even got a room overlooking the sea."

"That's good." He fiddled with the menu, picked it up, put it down again. "Lizzie..."

"What?"

"Lizzie, why - what is it you want me to do? What's on your mind?"

"How do you mean?"

"Well, why have you come all this way? What's it all for?"

"I've told you," she said, in a small, slightly timorous voice.

"Tell me again. Tell me so I understand."

"Perhaps you'll never understand," she said, with a shrug.

"Try me."

He waited, while Lizzie sat immobile, gazing at him mournfully. When finally she opened her mouth to speak, all that came out was a tiny squeak, the sound a kitten might make, and then she slowly shook her head as the tears came again, a steady cataract down her face.

A dark cloud of despair settled over him. "Oh Lizzie. Please don't."

The tears were trickling down to her chin and dripping on to the table. She let them come, searching his face out of glassy eyes. "Can't do this," she whimpered.

"Lizzie, please don't cry. I can't bear it."

"No. Neither can I. You've got to help me, Gavin."

"Then tell me how. Just tell me."

"I can't do it. I can't face it. It's too much for me."

He slid a hand across and touched her wrist. "Lizzie, listen. As things were before, you'd only ever have seen me on odd days, very rarely. But now, well, I'll be there for you, all the time, every day. See. You'll turn round, and I'll be there. We can be together, go places together, do things together. That has to be better, surely. We can make it something special, something we would never have had."

"I knew it," she said, stifling a deep, convulsive sob. "I knew you wouldn't understand."

"All right. Tell me what it is I'm missing. Tell me so I know."

"That stuff about - being in the same house. You see, that's not it. That'll only make it worse."

"Worse, how?"

"Seeing you with her, knowing you belong with her. I'll be like - an accessory."

"Lizzie, that's ridiculous. I think you're getting a neurosis about this."

"Oh right, so I'm neurotic now, am I? I'm just a silly, neurotic kid."

"No, that's not how I think of you at all. I don't think of you as a child at all."

"Can't be my dad then, can you?"

"Now you're playing tricks on me. At least let's be fair with each other." He ripped a sheaf of napkins from the dispenser and held them out to her. "Here, wipe your eyes."

Through the glimmer of her tears, some brighter sparks of mirth softened her face. "Did you say, 'Wipe your arse'?"

"Wipe your *eyes*!"

The stooped waitress returned and unloaded a plastic tray. Under Gavin's saucer she pushed a folded scrap of paper. "Pay at the till when you're done."

Lizzie sliced into her egg, watching the yolk flood on to the toast. "Nothing wrong with my arse, mate. I've got a lovely arse."

"I know," Gavin said quietly. "I've seen it."

"That's right, you have. See it again, if you like."

"Lizzie."

"You wanna look at my bum?"

"Lizzie!"

A woman at the next table stared sternly at Lizzie, only averting her eyes when Gavin glared at her.

He drank some coffee, wincing as the scalding liquid scorched his throat.

Lizzie giggled, trembling. "Sorry. Am I embarrassing you? Am I a liability?"

"No." He stroked her hand again, pawing at it with his fingertips. "I love you," he said.

"Do you? How?"

"What do you mean, how?"

"Do you love me as a daughter or as a woman?"

"That's a provocative question."

"Don't evade the issue."

"You know how I feel about you," he said, speaking behind his raised cup.

"Okay. Then tell her."

"What?"

"You heard me. Tell her."

"Tell who what?"

"Tell my mother - about us."

He shook his head, smiling, but the smile was only a frail shield for his alarm. "Come on, Lizzie. That would do nobody any good."

Even as he spoke the words, he realised that, somewhere in the depths of her confused imagination, Lizzie identified herself as the sole beneficiary of such a revelation. She might claim an altruistic motive - he anticipated a statement of that intent - but in truth she could bring herself to ask him for what amounted to a sacrificial gesture only because she believed that, by this device, he would be expelled from the marriage and rebound into her embrace. In that instant, the rationale behind Lizzie's request, as he interpreted it, was at least as distasteful as the confession itself would be.

She let her knife and fork clatter into the plate and pushed it aside with a sigh. "I don't want any more of that."

"Did you have breakfast?"

"Just cornflakes and orange juice. This man sitting opposite had kippers. Stank the room out." She shuddered. "I can't imagine eating a kipper."

"Well, there's not a lot else you can do with them."

She laughed. "You're funny. We'd make a great couple, you and me."

"Lizzie."

"Yeah, right. So are you going to do it, then?"

"Do what?"

"You know what. Tell her the truth. Don't let her go through life living a lie."

"Remember what she asked you after the cemetery. It'd be your lie as well as mine, Lizzie."

"Doesn't matter," she said sullenly. "I can handle it if you can."

He rested his head in his hands and searched her face. "Be honest with me. Please. Why do you want to do this? Why do you want to spoil it?"

"I don't see it as spoiling anything, just making it better, like a fresh start."

"A fresh start? Lizzie, this won't start anything; it'll finish it. We'll be ruined, both of us. She'll never trust either of us again. Can't you see that?"

She turned to gaze out of the window, the daylight mirrored in her glazed eyes. The clouds were breaking apart, a brittle sunshine spilling into the bay, spiking the water to crumpled tinfoil.

"I don't know which is the bigger hurt," she said, "the greater insult. Deceiving her with this lie, or wounding her with the truth. It's an impossible choice."

"Sleeping dogs, Lizzie. Cans of worms. This was a wild moment in the past. It's not important now. Not important enough for - this."

"Spare me the feeble excuses, Gavin. Blokes always say stuff like that. 'It was a mistake. I didn't know what I was doing. It doesn't mean anything.'" She picked up a balled napkin and began tearing it to pieces. "Well, I was there too, remember. I knew what I was doing, and so did you. And you know something? I loved every minute of it, and I'm not sorry about it, but now I've got to face the music and pay for it, because that's how life is, Gavin, that's how it works. I've got a conscience, Gavin, even if you haven't."

Without speaking, without attempting a response, he stared at her, watching her nervous, trembling fingers as they shredded the paper, seeing the way the light shone on the high, glossed ridge of her cheekbone, lifted by the clench of her jaw. In a moment of searing pain, he realised all over again how much he loved her.

"Can we go?" she asked, banging her knuckles on the table. "This place is getting to me."

He paid the bill and followed her outside. The sun seethed on the sea in silver slicks, a torrent of mercury, blinding them. Gavin was tense and uneasy, torn between an anxiety to return to the hotel before Vivienne's curiosity was aroused, and the deep, gnawing hunger that bonded him to this wilful girl.

"Where are we going?" he asked, hardly daring to speak the words.

"Depends. Are you in a hurry?"

"To go where?"

"I don't know. Back to her. Back to your loving wife."

"I suppose I ought to. She'll wonder where I am."

She unchained the bike from a nearby litter bin, her eyes darting over his face. "You don't say it with much conviction."

"Hmm. Actually I was hoping to avoid conviction. I was hoping to go for repentance."

She laughed, leaning over the handlebars to kiss him. "I love you," she said.

"But not in the right way, eh?"

"If I love you, I love you. Who's to say what's right and wrong about it?" She started walking, steering the bike carefully between the pedestrians. "Come on. I'll show you where I'm staying - just so's you know. It's not far."

The room was on the first floor, overlooking the road, where it narrowed to a neglected track after the last shop, and a steep grassy escarpment sloping down to the unnavigable shallows beyond the harbour. Gavin looked out from the open window and could see the caramel-coloured mud on the sea bed lit in shifting panels by the sun on the water. When he stood back, grazing his head on the window frame, the net curtains ballooned gently into the room on the brackish breeze.

Lizzie was sitting on the bed, long slim legs in blue jeans stretched out before her so that her weight pivoted on her heels. "You going to tell her about me?" she asked.

Turning, he saw her reflection in the dressing table mirror. They were surrounded by plastic, melamine and chipboard, apart - incongruously - from a mahogany wardrobe with inlaid panels either side of the mirrored door, presumably a relic from the days when the house was a private dwelling. Still, the room was bright, clean and well-aired, with fresh flowers in a vase on the chest of drawers and, beside it, a generously stocked refreshment tray.

"Tell her?" He frowned at her nervously. "You mean, about us?"

"No, me. Will you tell her you've seen me?"

"Oh. I don't know. Are you planning to come to the hotel?"

"That depends." She kicked off her trainers and bent to inspect her feet. One big toe protruded through a hole in her sock. "If you tell her I'm here, and then I don't come and see her, it'll look a bit strange - don't you think?"

"What, like you've come six hundred miles just to see me?"

"Yeah, well I have. That's the only reason. You're the only reason."

"Hmm. Perhaps it's better she doesn't see it that way."

"Faint heart, Gavin." She pulled off her socks and waggled her toes. "I'll try and come along later, keep you honest."

"Thanks. So I can tell her then? I mean, she'll wonder where I've been all this time."

"Do what you like," she said.

He looked around pleasantly. "Comfortable room. You sleep all right?"

"Okay. Gavin."

"What?"

"Shut the door, please."

He did as she asked.

"Slip the catch."

"What for?"

"Slip the catch."

Gavin locked the door and slowly turned to face her. The light seared the side of her face, making her skin look almost white. She wore no lipstick today, her lips plum-coloured, overlaid with grey.

He stood and stared at her.

"Come here," she said.

He moved nearer.

"Give me your hand."

He smiled. "Not the fingers again."

"I like your fingers," she said. "I need your fingers."

She parted her lips slightly and drew his hand towards her. When his fingertips were almost touching her chin, she stopped. "Down on your knees," she murmured.

Feeling more apprehensive than foolish, he knelt between Lizzie's splayed legs. Tugging his wrist, she dabbed his extended fingers against her lower lip, like a child trying to put on make-up. Then, with her free hand, she unfastened the top of her jeans and dragged them down, exposing her thighs.

"Lizzie, what are you doing?"

"What does it look like I'm doing?"

Gavin let his hand float in hers as she guided it down to her lap. He kept his eyes focused on her face, seeing the light shift as she tilted her head back, just the quick blue flash of her knickers teasing him, the heat rising in his brain, his throat threatening to lock tight in adrenalin-spiked shock.

She was moulding his hand in both her hands, encircling his fingers, worrying at them in a kind of frenzy. "Middle finger and forefinger," she said hoarsely, "that's all."

"Lizzie, I think - "

"Shut up! Come on now, let me."

Suddenly he felt himself floating in space, in her total control, and she was turning his hand over, easing it towards herself, a motion like a slow, inexorable suction, and he jolted when his two fingers sensed the tight, viscous wetness of her and something small and firm, a mobile flesh-bud, rolling against his finger-pads, and still, still he wasn't looking there.

"Lizzie, stop this."

"Too late, lover-boy."

"I am not your lover-boy, I am - "

"Shut up!"

He tried to withdraw from her, but she gripped his hand, pulling it in deeper.

"Lizzie, this is madness."

"Yes, I know."

"Lizzie!"

"Yes?"

"Oh, Lizzie."

"Yes."

"Is this what you really want?"

"Yes."

"Is this doing us any good, Lizzie?"

"Yes."

She gasped, wincing. "You need to cut your nails. You'll make me bleed."

"Yes?"

"Yes."

"Lizzie."

"Yes?"

"Should we be doing this?"

"Yes."

"Are you happy?"

"Yes."

"Lizzie, I - "

"Shush! Don't talk. You'll spoil it."

"Mmm. Okay."

"Wait till I've come."

"Lizzie."

"Be quiet."

"Okay. Is that good?"

"Yes."

He felt her heat travelling up his arm, the sweat pearling his brow, his shirt clinging to his back. Closing his eyes, he let her feed herself, measuring the pace, until she drove one rigid arm into the mattress, arched her back and whimpered like a small child ensnared in a bad dream.

"You all right?" he asked her, as she let go of his hand.

She nodded, biting her lip.

He got up and sat on the bed beside her. Lizzie sat quietly for a minute or so, then pulled up her jeans and stared straight ahead, meeting her reflection in the mirror. A babble of voices drifted up from the street, children laughing, an old man coughing, a dog yapping. Somewhere in the house, a door slammed, rattling the window frame.

"   I suppose one of us should say something," Gavin ventured.

"How about...?" Lizzie smiled and slapped his thigh. "Please wash your hands after using this facility."

He managed a snort of ironic laughter. "What am I going to do with you?"

"You've already done it."

"Yes, so I have," he said soberly. "Are you okay?"

"Yes. I feel good."

"I know. You felt good."

"What I mean is - "

"I know, I understand." He stood up and peered out of the window. A ferry was cruising slowly into the harbour, the funnel wreathed in grey smoke as the engines were throttled back. "I ought to be going," he said.

"Of course. Well, thanks."

"For what?"

"You know."

"Oh, that."

"No, Gavin, not just for that. Don't ever think that. This isn't only about sex, believe me."

"That's the trouble," he said, sighing. "I do believe you. If it was about sex and nothing more, it would all be much easier."

"Maybe." She stood up and kissed him. "You be careful."

"Why?"

"In case - she might smell me on you."

"Lizzie!"

"You never know." She kissed him again. "I'll come along later, I promise - when I've thought of something to say to her."

"If you've time, it would be good. It would be helpful."

"It's okay, I've plenty time."

"How long have you got?"

"What?"

"I mean - how long are you off for?"

Lizzie turned away and began unlocking the door. "Long as I like," she said.

"How come?"

"There. You can go now."

"Lizzie, please."

"I'm a free agent, Gavin. And I'm not on holiday."

"Lizzie?"

"What's the matter?"

"I think I should be asking you that. Lizzie, how can you not be on holiday?"

She faced him, standing close, not blinking. "Because I'm not working. I've resigned."

He screwed up his eyes incredulously. "You've done what? Oh my God, Lizzie! Have you gone completely mad?"

Lizzie ducked round him and sat down heavily on the bed, flapping her arms helplessly. "I suppose. Yes, if you must know, I am mad. I love you madly, Gavin, and there's nothing you or I can do about it."

"Lizzie, this is serious now. This is just sheer stupidity."

"Yeah, all right, I knew you'd be angry."

"Lizzie, you're throwing your life away. You had a good job, possibly a career, and now you tell me you've chucked it up on some ridiculous impulse and - "

"You are not some ridiculous impulse!" She lifted her hands upright beside her head in concentrated emphasis. "I love you, Gavin. By day and by night I think of you. I try to get you out of my head, but it's like you've moved in there and you won't go." Tears began running down her face, collecting at the corners of her quivering mouth. "I don't know what I'm going to do, Gavin. I need you with me, otherwise I can't make it."

For a while he held her against him, wrapped in his arms, and his heartbeat drummed upon her breast. His blood raced not from that closeness, nor as a consequence of affection, but because he was afraid. There was so much at stake here, and he could feel it all slipping away, beyond his control.

"I wish you could hold me like this all day," she said, her voice muffled in his shoulder.

"You know I can't do that, Lizzie."

"Can't or won't?"

"We've been through this before. I've tried to explain it to you."

"But we belong together. I know it."

"We'll be together, Lizzie, but not in the way you want. You must learn to live with that."

She pulled away from him and sat up straight. "I can show you," she said. "I can prove we were meant to share each other."

"What are you talking about?"

"There's something I have to tell you," she announced.

"Go on," he sighed, "I'm listening."

Lizzie picked up a sock from the floor and wiped her eyes with it. She peered at her face in the mirror. "I look a mess," she said.

"This whole thing's a mess," Gavin said, miserably.

She took a deep breath, still clutching the sock in her hands. "I had - when I was little I had a teddy bear. He didn't have a name, he was just called Teddy. He was my best friend. He slept with me and sat next to me when Mum read to me and when I had my meals. Anyway, one day, I don't know how she did it, Mum knocked some stuff over on the table and vinegar got spilt on Teddy's leg. Well, that was it; after that, he was Vinegar, that was his name. Funny, we never could get the smell out. He always had this sort of sour wine smell. Vinegar. No more Teddy. And you know, fifteen years later, I've still got him. One of his eyes has got lost and one ear's hanging off, and he does look a bit scruffy, but he's still Vinegar. Now I've started taking him to bed with me again, and I hold him tight and whisper to him, and I imagine I'm talking to you, and it just seems so - right, somehow. It just feels so good."

"Lizzie, I think you - "

"Don't. I haven't finished." Reaching behind her, she took her bag from the pillow and searched inside, producing a small notepad and a pen. "Here, take these."

"What for?"

"To write something, of course."

"Okay." He balanced the pad in the palm of his hand. "Now what?"

"You write his name in neat capitals."

"His name?"

"Vinegar. Go on, write it."

Gavin wrote VINEGAR on the pad. "Is this a game?" he asked.

"No, it's very serious. It's not a game." She dropped her bag on the floor. "Did you wash your hands?"

"No. Don't worry about it."

"Oh. Did you like it - what I made you do?"

"Lizzie, can we get on with it, please?"

"Right. Vinegar. Now you strike out the letters of your first name."

Gavin crossed the letters out.

"What are you left with?"

"ER."

"My point precisely."

"I don't get it."

"ER, Gavin. Elizabeth Rebecca. That's my name, see."

"Oh, Lizzie, no."

"All those years ago. Elizabeth Rebecca and Gavin. It was meant to happen, see. Vinegar." She pummelled the air with clenched fists. "Vinegar!"

"I love the story, Lizzie, but it's just a coincidence. It doesn't mean anything."

"Gavin, you're wrong. You are so wrong! It is not a coincidence. Don't you see? It makes everything crystal-clear. It couldn't be more clear."

He got up and went to the window, not wanting her to see that he was crying. There was a scalding sensation in his throat, making him choke, and his nose filled with the trickling sediment of his despair. As his shoulders heaved, it was impossible for him to conceal his distress, and he felt her come up behind him and fold one arm around his back.

"I'm sorry," she said.

"For what?"

"For this. For doing this to you."

"You couldn't help it. You can't blame someone for falling in love."

"It's just - there's so much we could have done together. You and me, we could have moved mountains."

"Melodramatic, Lizzie."

"Yeah, well. That doesn't make it a lie."

"Right. No more lies, Lizzie."

"Sure. Are you going to tell her, then?"

"About us?"

"About us."

"I'll tell her I saw you."

"That isn't what I meant."

He thought for a moment. "Lizzie, I have to go."

"I know. It's all right." She opened the door and waited. "I'm sorry about your hat, really."

"It's okay. I love you, Lizzie."

"It's no good, Gavin. It won't work. It's too late now."

He bent to kiss her mouth, and she hung against him and let him taste her tongue. "Goodbye," she murmured, as they broke apart.

"Not goodbye," he said, forcing a nervous smile that somehow excluded his eyes.

"Goodbye, Gavin. Give her my love."

"What about you? Will you be all right?"

Tears were tracking down her face again, silver stripes glistening in the light from the window. "I will be soon," she said. "Just always remember how much I loved you. Remember how amazing it was."

"Lizzie?"

"Go. Don't look back."

She closed the door quietly behind him.

He went slowly down the stairs and stood on the pavement under the window. When he raised a hand to wipe his tears away, he noticed the red on his fingers. Trembling, he carried the blood to his lips and closed his eyes and consumed her.

The salted metal tang that came from her lay on his tongue, and it was amazing.

19

VIVIENNE looked up from her book and flicked her wrist to check the time. "Well, well, well," she said, "the wanderer returns."

Gavin settled into the chair next to hers, a tight, sheepish grin on his face. "I sort of got waylaid."

She reached to the table for her Campari and lemonade, taking a sip and pausing to prise out the slice of lemon and nibble, grimacing, at the sodden strands.

"What's the book?" he asked, nodding at it.

"John Updike. I can get high on reality. Do you want a drink?"

"In a minute."

"Get me another Campari. Not so much ice this time."

Gavin crossed the lounge to the bar and waited for Vivienne's drink. Cautiously, he lifted his hand to his face and sniffed his fingers. Lizzie was still there, a scent of dark fruit, slightly oaky. He carried the glass back in his other hand.

"Thanks," she said, absently. "So what happened? You were gone ages."

He put a paper bag on the table. "I got your things, cards and cream."

"Right. Didn't you want one?"

"What?"

"A drink." She glanced at him. "You look tense. It might relax you."

"I'll have a beer. Not yet."

"Suit yourself." She shut the book and placed it on the floor. "I was beginning to think it was, you know, like that man who pops out for a paper and doesn't come back for five years."

His response was a short, nervous chuckle, entirely devoid of humour. He was thinking of Lizzie again, and now he was getting a hard-on.

"I met someone in the street," he said, and he heard his voice falter.

Vivienne's glass hovered halfway to her lips. "You met someone? What, someone you knew - here?"

"Yes. Actually, it was Lizzie."

She took a mouthful of her drink and lowered the glass to the table, wiping her mouth indecorously with the back of her hand. "Gavin, what are you talking about?"

"In the street when I went out. Lizzie was there."

"Gavin, Lizzie is in London. We're in Scotland."

"She - she'd hired a bike," he said, ambiguously.

"I see," said Vivienne, loftily. "She's cycled up the motorway at eighty miles an hour."

"Look, I know it sounds daft, but Lizzie is here, on the island. I've just been with her. I mean, we sat in a café and she showed me where she's staying." He tipped the postcards from the bag and thumbed through them mechanically. "I suppose it was meant to be a surprise," he added, unconvincingly.

"A surprise," she repeated slowly. "A surprise." She seemed to turn the words over on her tongue, as if testing their appropriateness. "I don't understand."

"Understand what?"

"Well, if she's come all this way to - to surprise us, then where is she? She can hardly surprise us by riding up and down the road on a bike."

"I did ask her to come over. She said she would."

"You make it sound as if she would only do so reluctantly. Gavin, don't you see how odd that is?"

"Well, that's Lizzie for you, eternally unpredictable."

"Unpredictable? If you ask me, it sounds a bit - voyeuristic. What's the matter with her? We're on our honeymoon, for God's sake."

"I don't think she's planning to come round and peer through the bedroom keyhole."

"So what is she planning? What's she doing here?" She fixed him with a penetrating glare. "Gavin, did you know she was coming?"

"No, absolutely not." Whenever Vivienne challenged him with an unfounded accusation, he felt an absurd sense of relief in denying it, as though in so doing he could salve his conscience over past misdemeanours. "I would never have agreed to such a thing."

Vivienne sighed and finished her drink. "Did she say when she might deign to visit us?"

"No. She wasn't specific."

"Well, we can't hang around for her. If she's that unpredictable, she might never turn up. Anyway, what does she want a bike for?"

"I don't know, Vivienne. She was - on a bike, that's all."

"This whole thing is preposterous," she said, clicking her tongue. She dragged her chair back and stood up. "Come on."

"What are we doing?"

"In case you've forgotten, Gavin, we're on our honeymoon. We're going out."

In brittle sunshine more typical of a winter's day, they walked to the distillery at the end of town, Gavin surreptitiously maintaining a watchful eye in case Lizzie should appear, but there was no sign of her. They entered the low, white-walled building only minutes before the next guided tour was due to begin, and in the lobby a small group of tourists in anoraks and hiking boots stood waiting in a huddle.

Through a doorway next to the toilets a young woman appeared, smiling uncertainly. She wore what Gavin assumed to be the company uniform - a sky blue blazer over a knee-length navy skirt with an inverted centre pleat - and she hugged a clipboard to her left breast. Calling the group forward, she asked them for their first names, which she wrote on a pad attached to the board.

"Sorry, but we have to do this now," she explained. "It's for Health and Safety purposes. In some of the areas we'll be entering there are potential hazards, so I shall be calling out your names at the end of the tour to ascertain that no-one has been left behind. Are ye right? Good. Well, my name is Mairie McLennan and I'm your guide this afternoon. I'd like to welcome you to the Royal Huntsman Distillery, and invite you now to follow me, please, as we commence our tour."

From one house or gallery to another and then the next, and across an open courtyard to a block of outbuildings accessed by a doorway low enough for the taller visitors to dip their heads upon Mairie's warning, the group shambled, muttering, in the guide's footsteps, hovering at intervals to wait for stragglers before craning forward to hear the girl's commentary above the grind and grumble of machinery.

Inside the warmest room, where treacle-coloured liquid sloshed and surged in huge open vats and the fetid air bloomed with the reek of bran mash, Mairie removed her blazer and draped it over her sun-tanned forearm. A thin crescent of sweat discoloured the armpit of her white blouse. Gavin's eyes travelled along her slender brown arms, recalling Lizzie's smooth, thin arms, her small, round, dark-tipped breasts and the tight scud of wiry hairs that began below her navel.

He scarcely felt Vivienne nudge his ribs as she leaned into him with a grin. "I hope you're taking all this in."

"Yes, I rather hope there'll be free samples at the end."

"I doubt it. We can buy some miniatures in the gift shop."

Their guide slipped her blazer back on as they filed into the main building. Gavin watched her from behind, taking pleasure in the way she flicked her hands over her shoulders to lift her hair lightly over her collar as the jacket settled there, a gesture of self-assured femininity. He reflected that he liked a woman to be feminine, but not subservient; to be self-confident but not overbearing. Ironically, it seemed to him that, if the women in his life presently met these criteria, their compliance came at no little emotional cost to himself.

The gift shop assistant dropped their purchases - single-malt Scotch miniatures in a presentation pack, a drum of shortbread, a box of heather soaps - into a plastic carrier bag and held it out to Vivienne on the theatrically extended peg of her forefinger. "There ye go. Thank you for visiting Royal Huntsman."

In the road, they stood blinking at the sudden sunlight. Gavin waited with his hands thrust in his pockets. "Where to next?" he asked.

"Let's walk back. We can go along the shoreline, look in all the rock-pools. I used to love that when I was little."

They strolled by the sea wall until they came to a gap where a flight of stone steps led down to a narrow strip of grey sand, strewn with seaweed. As he descended, Gavin looked over his shoulder for Lizzie, but there were few people about, no-one on a bike, no girls who even looked like her. He hoped he might see her, though he wasn't sure he wanted to. That's how it was with her. When he raised his hands and tented them, as if in prayer, over his nose, he could still catch the scent of her on his fingers.

Vivienne had moved ahead of him, and he hurried to catch up. He fell into step beside her, slipping one arm round her shoulders, until the sand ran out and they had to break apart to clamber over the dark, slippery rocks.

"Vivienne, did Lizzie used to have a bear called Vinegar?" he called to her.

She hesitated, one foot hovering over a tawny mass of weed. "Why are you asking me that, all of a sudden? It's apropos of what, exactly?"

"Nothing. No reason."

She dropped her toes into the weed and hopped quickly to the next rock. "Yes, she's still got him. He's sitting in the chair in her bedroom."

Away to the right, where the incoming tide spilled into a scum-fringed pool, something red, partly submerged, caught the sun. Vivienne stepped nimbly over polished stones and bent to fish the object out with two fingers.

"Be careful," Gavin warned, "the tide's coming in."

"It's a hat," Vivienne said. "Quite new, judging by the label."

Water surged around their feet.

"I expect the wind took it," Gavin said, peering over her shoulder.

Pinching the hat by the peak, she skimmed it away towards the wall. "Let it dry out in the sun," she said, "in case the owner's thick-skinned enough to be seen walking about in something so ghastly."

They came to a ramp sloping up to the road. Vivienne took Gavin's hand, pretending to tow him up to the pavement. Behind them, the sea was advancing steadily, hissing fiercely on the rocks.

"Why did you want to know about the bear?" Vivienne asked again.

"It was just something Lizzie said. It's not important."

"No. I wondered why you were asking, that's all."

"I just - I don't know."

As they drew near to the hotel, she squeezed his hand, sidling up to him. "They'll have cleaned the room now. We can go back and lie down for a while."

"You mean..."

She smiled. "If you want."

When he noticed them climbing the staircase, the desk clerk looked up and smiled at Gavin, nodding his head slowly in a sympathetic manner which seemed vaguely conspiratorial, as though he had appraised the situation and now bestowed his confidential blessing upon the newly-weds in the consummation of their ardour. Gavin returned the acknowledgment, feeling irrationally uncomfortable as he did so, lest the mere act of accompanying his wife to their room at this hour of the day should be viewed as an impropriety.

Upstairs, Gavin locked the door and, wordlessly, they began to undress. The afternoon sunshine fell in bright panels on the bed, and they lay down, face to face, on the warm duvet and slowly, gently caressed each other's bodies. This time Vivienne made no protest when

Gavin touched her breasts, nor when he reached down and stroked the insides of her thighs, where the skin was smooth and cool, her moistening warmth only apparent as he drew upwards and felt the taut muscle between her legs and the springy roughness of her hair on the back of his hand.

Vivienne sighed, fluttering her eyelids in quiet satisfaction as she sensed his probing finger slide inside her. Inching closer to him, she traced the backs of her fingers languidly down between Gavin's ribs to his stomach, smiling at the small, electric pulse that jolted his body when she touched below his navel.

He hesitated, searching her face for a change of heart, an altered response, when he felt her gasp and flinch.

"You all right?"

"Yes," she whispered, sucking breath between her teeth. "You need to cut your nails. You'll make me bleed."

"Sorry. Do you want me to - ?"

"No. It's okay. Carry on. It's nice."

Very soon he felt himself encircled in her hand, stiffening and throbbing in her grasp. For a few seconds he lay there, flexing his legs in pleasure, savouring the delight of her attention; and then he withdrew his finger from her and brushed her hand away, knowing that otherwise it would all be over too soon and, for the present at least, the quiet magic would be gone.

A low, comprehending chuckle escaped from Vivienne's lips, and she brought her hand to his face and tickled the side of his nose and his cheek. "I love you," she said.

Unthinking, almost instinctively, Gavin clamped her trailing fingers and drew them into his mouth, tasting the salt of her fingertips, the bitterness of her nails. She let him flick his tongue over her fingers for a brief moment, then she pulled away, raking her skin on his teeth.

"Why did you do that?" she asked him.

"Do what?"

"Lick my fingers like that. What made you do it?"

He looked into her eyes and saw a hardness gathering there, a change of light that unsettled him. "I don't know," he replied, "I just did it."

"You just did it?"

"I just - what's the matter?" He sat up, drawing his knees up to keep his balance. "What's wrong, Vivienne?"

She had rolled on to her back, her full breasts compressing and swinging sideways. "I'm not sure," she said, speaking to the ceiling, "but something is. Something's not right."

"With us, you mean?" He reached back and brushed her left nipple, but she knocked his hand away. "Vivienne?"

His erection had subsided and the remains of him dangled forlornly between his raised thighs, a small animal nestling in the folds of the duvet. There was a strange taste in his mouth, a dry acidity.

"She used to do that," she said, still not looking at him. "Lizzie. She was always sucking on people's fingers, or else putting her fingers in their mouths." She flung one arm over her face, the inside of her wrist resting on her forehead. "I suppose it was a baby thing, only - well, I've seen her do it since. After Jasper...I sucked her fingers then, I remember. I sucked her fingers while she cried."

"I see," he said. He looked down and saw the tiny blonde hairs speckling her armpit. "Well - what's that to do with you and me?"

"You've done it with her, haven't you?"

"Eh? What?"

"This fingers thing. She's made you do it."

"Not exactly. I mean, she didn't really."

"So that's a 'yes', then."

"I don't know what you want me to say, Vivienne. It's like you're deliberately putting me on a spot."

She hoisted herself upright and leaned towards him with her chin over her upraised knees. In the cleft between her thighs, a haze of pubic hair glowed like a golden nest where it caught the sunlight. "You're incredible," she said.

Gavin hung his head and gazed at himself, limply bedraggled on the bedclothes.

Vivienne prodded his shoulder, making him jump. "You sit there with that daft, vacant expression on your face, and expect me to believe you can't be sure whether my daughter's had her fingers in your mouth. Oh, come on, Gavin!"

"Why is it such a big deal?" he yelled. "Why are you so determined to - ?"

"Because I think you're lying to me!" She hugged her knees, and tears swam in her eyes. "No," she said quietly, "I know you're lying to me."

He slid off the bed and started to put his clothes on. As he fastened his shirt buttons, he noted the trembling in his hands, and he felt unsteady on his feet, as if the floor were uneven.

Vivienne watched him intently, her jaw set as if suppressing a quiet rage. For a while the only sound in the room came from the movement of traffic in the street below. Gavin perched on the edge of the bed, his back to Vivienne, and pulled on his shoes.

"So what now?" he muttered, so that she could hardly hear him.

"Well, if you can't even face me."

He swung round and looked at her. She was an attractive woman, he thought. Her face was unlined, proud but not arrogant, and the slight puffiness about her lips merely made them more tempting. The flesh on her upper arms was smooth and still contoured to the muscle, and her breasts, though lent some elasticity by their weight, remained firm and globular, agelessly defying gravity.

"That's better," she said.

"No it's not. Nothing's better."

She reached out, touching his arm. "Just tell me the truth, Gavin. That's all I ask. We're on our honeymoon, for God's sake."

"Why do you think I need reminding?"

"Because I'm not sure about your commitment. A lie's as good as a betrayal, Gavin." She shivered and eased herself off the bed. "Can you get my dressing gown from the bathroom, please?"

He went in and unhooked the robe from the door. A tube of KY jelly was on the shelf, the cap lying loose. She had been ready for him; now the opportunity was squandered.

Vivienne sighed and grunted as she looped the cord ends and tugged them tight. "Now, tell me again about Lizzie."

"What's there to tell?"

"Gavin, don't do this to me, please. You've just spent half the morning with her. She must have said something."

"We talked. She seemed upset. I tried to reassure her."

"You tried to reassure her. Is that a euphemism for something?"

He waited, offering no reply, lest he be condemned out of his own mouth. The vacuum, he understood, would achieve the same effect, in any case.

Vivienne sat on the bed with her ankles crossed, fiddling with the dressing gown cord. "An eloquent silence, Gavin. Mere words could hardly have said more."

Shaking his head, he spread his arms in a gesture of submission.

On the bedside table, the telephone rang, and Vivienne picked it up. She listened, nodded, said "Thanks, we'll be down," and replaced the receiver. "Front desk," she said. "Someone's left an envelope."

"An envelope?"

"Well, a letter, presumably."

"I'll go. You're not dressed."

"Not so fast. I haven't finished."

"It might be important," he said.

"This is important. This is our lives, Gavin."

He sat down next to her, his hands clasped in his lap. "I love you," he said.

"That part I believe. Now go on. Tell me the truth. You can't love me and lie to me at the same time."

"No. It's just - I don't know how to say it."

"It's easy. You don't have to invent anything. Just answer me. Think of how much you love me, and let the words come out on their own, and it'll be the truth. It'll be all right."

"Will it? Perhaps we can't make it all right any more. Perhaps it's too late."

"Why don't you let me be the judge of that?" She took his hand, moulding it in hers. "Gavin, why is Lizzie here?"

"I told you. It's a surprise."

"It certainly is. She's come six hundred miles and hasn't even bothered to see me. I'm surprised and disappointed."

"She'll come," he said. "She told me she'll come."

"This - that thing with the fingers. That's a very intimate thing, Gavin."

"Yes."

"So what else did you do that was intimate, hmm?"

"How do you mean?"

"Don't, Gavin. You're insulting my intelligence. You know perfectly well what I mean. But I'm generous, so I'll spell it out for you. Are you sleeping with my daughter? In fact, are you sleeping with *your* daughter?"

If he took heart, momentarily, from the construction of the question, feeling himself technically absolved, he knew also that his relief was morally valueless. That he had not actually slept with Lizzie could not exonerate him. This was no time for semantics.

"Only once," he said, studying the floor. "It was before we were married," he added, striving for mitigation.

"I see. Does that explain the knickers in the car?"

"No. She - we - told you the truth. It was after that."

Vivienne released his hand. Her eyes, unblinking, rested trance-like on her bare feet. "It's all beginning to make sense now. The trip to the cemetery, the meetings you had, her coming all the way up here with no attempt to see me."

"And the fingers," he added lamely.

"And the fingers." She forced a stilted laugh. "The fingers gave it away."

"Lizzie and her bloody fingers," he murmured.

"Were you with her today?" She turned to look at him. "Is that why you were gone so long?"

"I told you I was with her."

"I'm asking you if you were having sex with her. I'm asking you if your wife was waiting for you in our honeymoon hotel while you were fucking her daughter, that's what I need to know."

"You make it sound - so sordid."

"Do I? Well, forgive me, Gavin. How dreadfully insensitive of me."

"We ought to get that letter," he said, standing up.

"You haven't answered my question."

"We didn't - I didn't actually have sex with her today."

"Right. Do I detect a 'but' in there somewhere?"

"Don't make me describe it all, please, Vivienne. What's the point?"

Arching back her neck, she stretched her arms and legs before her, inhaling deeply. "The point," she repeated thoughtfully. "Yes, Gavin, that's a very good question. What is the point? What's the point of all this? What's the point of us? What are we doing here? What are we going to do with all this wreckage?"

"What do you want to do?" he asked her. "Now the damage is done."

"Ah yes. Now that our horse has galloped over the horizon, ought we to consider repairs to the stable door?"

"It depends, I suppose, if what's left is worth repairing."

"Or if we can get the horse back."

Powerfully, he wanted to go to her now and gather her up and hold her close enough to feel her heartbeat; but the courage was gone, maybe the hope as well. Surely the hope.

"I'm going to find that envelope," he said, reaching for the door-knob.

"Before you do..." She leaned forward, and her left breast slid from the wing of her dressing gown to hang enticingly in his view. "One last question, perhaps the most important thing I need to know."

"Of course." He gazed at her, trying not to look at her body, his eyes finally settling on her face, and in that instant he shrank within himself, seeing the hurt that had gathered like a mist in her eyes. "Anything. Just - anything. There must be something I can do to - "

"No, there isn't. That's beyond your capability." With one deft hand she scooped her loose breast back inside her gown. "Why, Gavin?" She lowered her head, almost as if in shame. "In God's name, why?"

"I suppose because I couldn't help myself. It was easier to give in than to resist. She's a beautiful girl, Vivienne. The temptation was stronger than the man."

Vivienne nodded, as though she had known this all along. "Well, I'll say this. I don't know whether to curse you for your weakness or commend you for your honesty."

Unable to meet her eyes again, he opened the door and stepped out.

"I'll come down when I'm dressed," he heard her call behind him.

He went slowly down the staircase and approached the immaculate, silver-haired man behind the reception desk.

"Good afternoon, Mr Lake."

"Hello, I believe someone's left something for me."

"Indeed, sir - a young lady. She wouldn't give her name." Turning, he took a white envelope from a pigeon-hole and handed it to Gavin. "There was no other message, sir."

"All right. Thanks."

Gavin sat at a nearby table and looked at the envelope. On the front, in a neatly scripted hand, it said 'Gavin and Mum'. He tore the flap open. Inside was a letter, written in ballpoint on four sheets of paper. His mouth hanging partly open, he unfolded the first sheet and began to read. As he finished each page, he let it drop into his lap as he straightened the next one and read on.

A blur of blue brushed the corner of his eye as she descended, wearing a new lightweight cotton trouser suit. She looked poised and serious.

He grabbed the fallen sheets and brandished them before her.

"Well?" she said.

"It's a letter from Lizzie."

"As I expected. Are you all right? You've gone quite pale."

He scrambled to his feet, crumpling the pages against his thigh as he knocked the chair aside. "Come with me, Vivienne."

"What? Where?"

"We've got to find her. For Christ's sake, we've got to find her!"

20

Lizzie's Letter

Dear Mum,
Dear Gavin,

I can't believe I'm doing this. I just can't believe it. If I can't believe the letter, I absolutely can't imagine or comprehend the events that follow it. I am so very sorry, for I know I am about to hurt you both terribly. Whatever pain I have inflicted on you before, it will be as nothing to the devastation I now foresee. So I'll say it again: I am more sorry than I can express in words. Sometimes there simply are no words. Sometimes there is nothing left but love and memories.

I love you both.

Gavin, I hope to God you did what I asked. Now you'll see why I was so insistent. I really don't want this letter to be a total shock to Mum, the means by which she first learns of our friendship and the course it's taken. That would be compounding the unkindness. I love you Gavin (again!), but if you've let me down on this request, you're a fool. And that would make two of us.

Mum, this was never an affair. Neither was it my intention to be malicious or deceitful, although I can see how you could be forgiven for viewing it that way. I simply love him, and there's not a lot more to it than that. If you're a perceptive, sensitive person, Gavin is the kind of man you can't be with for long without falling in love with him. I think that's the most wonderful attribute in all the world, don't you?

This is going to sound really corny, but I had to stop there for a while because I started crying and I couldn't see. Sorry about the smudge on the paper. It's got my DNA in it.

Oh, by the way, in case you're wondering, I'm not pregnant. I never was cut out to be a mum. Shit, I can't even look after myself!

So what's this all about? I can read your thoughts, see. Why doesn't she just come round and talk to us? Is she such a coward? Well, the thing is, I know if I come face to face with you now I'll crack up and my words'll all get tangled, and most of what I want to say won't be intelligible. We'd be three confused people.

Gavin's tried to sort me out by reminding me that he's my stepdad now and we can be together most days. Bless you, Gavin, but you're missing the point - which is, knowing you makes me greedy. It makes me want more from you than I can expect you to give. You see, it's not a father I'm looking for. I'm not trying to replace a family member. I want something - someone - in my life that's not been there before. I want it to be mine to keep, my special treasure, a light constantly burning in an empty room inside me.

Inside me. That's it. I remember you there, Gavin, and I can't settle for just the memory. To lie warm and peaceful with the man you love resting inside you - if there's a more glorious feeling, it must be in the next world. It must be in our dreams. So this letter is because I can't wait any longer for my dream to come true. It's to tell you that I'm going away.

Soon it will be autumn. I always think that's a sad time, with the leaves turning and falling. Funny, I remember walking in the park with James when he was little, and it was October and the leaves were crunching under our feet, and he looked up all squinty-eyed and said, "Look, Lizzie, it's all the trees are crying." Well, okay, I don't want to be like those weeping trees when the sad time comes. I'll be gone by then.

But I'll leave a light on for you both, a light to remember me by.

Don't you dare cry for me, it would make me too sad.

In all sincerity, I wish you both the most wonderful life together.

Say goodbye to James and Maria for me.

Whenever you think of me, that light will blink, and I'll know you're there. That's how it works, see.

I know these things. I'm amazing.

Love for ever,
Lizzie xxxx

21

HE WAITED. Vivienne sat on a low stone wall bordering the hotel driveway, reading the letter through bronze-tinted sunglasses. Gavin, standing a few paces in front of her, shifted awkwardly from one foot to the other. Every so often he glanced around, and after a minute or two he checked his watch.

"Must you do that?" she asked, without taking her eyes off the paper. "You're setting my teeth on edge."

"I just think we should get going," he said.

"Another minute won't make any difference."

"We don't know that. It might make all the difference, if she's about to - " He stopped short of articulating the unthinkable. "If she's in distress, I mean."

Vivienne withheld her comment while she read to the end of the letter, finally thrusting the pages towards him with a contemptuous sigh. "Here. Stick it in your pocket."

"Is that all you've got to say?" he asked her, folding the letter into a neat square.

She slid off the wall, dusting down the back of her trousers. "I don't know what she's ranting on about. Going away, she says. Where's she going to?"

"She's speaking metaphorically, surely. Going away, as in - giving up."

"Yes, I'm thinking of giving up myself." She took off her sunglasses and put them in her handbag. "She is away. She's here. Where else does she want to go?"

"You're being deliberately obtuse, Vivienne. At least try to read between the lines."

"Ah, right. Don't tell me...what is it they always say? It's a cry for help, that's it." She shook her head pityingly. "You're too soft, Gavin. She's got you dangling on a string."

He reached for her hand. "Please. I'm worried. Come with me to the guest house."

This time her sigh was more weary than cynical, edged with sympathy. "Go on then. What if she's not there?"

"At this stage, I don't know. Let's eliminate the first possibility."

She shrugged and nodded. "Let's go. Perhaps we'll see her at the roadside, the back of her hand pressed to her forehead." Freeing her hand from his grasp, she mimicked the scene, tilting back her head in a theatrical pose.

"Now you're just being cruel," he said.

"I know my daughter. But then, so do you, by all accounts. Good, was she?"

They turned on to the road and began striding along by the sea wall.

"What do you mean?" he said.

"I'm asking you if you found my daughter, now your daughter, good in bed."

"Don't, Vivienne, please. Don't start up again."

"Don't walk so fast. These aren't hiking shoes." She licked her lips, throwing him a sidelong glance. "Her long, tanned legs and slim hips. Her pert little breasts and victorious smile. Must have been quite deliciously exciting for you. Forbidden fruit, and all that."

"Vivienne - "

"Yeah, I know. Shut up. Blot it out. Anything but the truth."

They approached the guest house to find the front door standing open and a woman in a plastic apron energetically polishing the brass letter box. She wore bulky brown shoes with the laces undone, trailing on to the doorstep.

"Excuse me," Gavin called from the pathway, "are you the proprietor?"

"The what?" the woman snapped back, looking annoyed at the interruption.

"Are you the landlady here?"

"Aye, this is my house. I've lived here thirty years."

"Right. And you have a guest named Lizzie Drexler?"

She sighed, mopping her brow with the back of her wrist. "Lizzie who?"

"Drexler," Vivienne repeated.

The woman looked guardedly from Vivienne to Gavin and back again, wrinkling her nose doubtfully. "I've no-one in by that name."

"But you have," Gavin persisted, "or you did have. I was in her room earlier."

"Oh, were you now?"

"Yes. I think it was Room Three."

"Room Three, you say? Let me think now." She bunched up the polishing cloth and stuffed it in her apron pocket. "No, that's not the name she gave."

Gavin stepped towards her. "So you do have a young girl in that room?"

"Mebbe I do. What's it to you?"

Vivienne pushed past him, her face colouring. "Look, please, I'm her mother. I - we need to speak to her." She opened her handbag and pulled out a thin photo wallet, the one Gavin remembered from their first lunch-time in the pub. "This is her," she said, flipping the plastic sleeves.

"Oh, I'll need ma glasses to see pictures." She brushed her hands together to wipe them. "Wait here."

They hovered by the railings while the landlady disappeared into the darkness beyond the doorway.

"This is ridiculous," Vivienne said.

"We could be anybody," Gavin pointed out.

"You've been here before. Didn't she see you?"

"Obviously not."

"This is crazy. Still, I'd hoped my honeymoon would be unforgettable. That much has been achieved."

"Perhaps we should ask your name," Gavin said, when the woman re-appeared with her spectacles.

"What for? I didnae ask yours."

"I'm Gavin Lake. This is my wife, Vivienne. We're here on our honeymoon."

"Oh aye. The weather's not bad for you."

Vivienne offered the photograph once more. The woman balanced her glasses on the end of her nose and peered at it. "Aye, that's her, right enough. Nice looking lassie."

"So what name did she give you?" Gavin asked.

"Elizabeth Lake," came the reply.

"That's her - adopted name," Gavin confirmed, "though she's not actually adopted."

He felt Vivienne jostle him impatiently, mouthing something inaudible under her breath.

"So what is it you're wanting?" the woman asked.

"We're trying to find her," Vivienne said, replacing the photos in her bag.

"She's not here. They're all out just now."

Gavin swept a hand wearily across his brow. "Did she say where she was going?"

"No, she did not. Why should she? Am I her guardian now?"

"No, Missi-" He shook his head in frustration. "I'm sorry, I don't know your name."

"It's Janet. Janet Campbell."

"Mrs Campbell, do you - ?"

"Miss Campbell, if you please."

"I'm sorry."

"Nothing to be sorry about. You were saying."

"Do you mind if we look in Elizabeth's room?"

"Look in her room? What for?"

"In case there's some clue there as to where she's gone." He waited while Janet Campbell stared at him. "It's really very important."

"I see. Is she in some kind of trouble?"

"She will be when I get hold of her," Vivienne muttered darkly.

Miss Campbell leaned on the door and stood aside. "You'd best go on up," she said. "Mind you don't mess the room, I've tidied."

Gavin felt uneasy and oddly disorientated, finding himself back in the room, Vivienne at his side, where he had so recently touched Lizzie and been aroused by her feral warmth. He saw Vivienne staring at the bed, and wondered what she was thinking.

"Now we're here, what do you expect to find?" she asked him, petulantly.

"It's more a matter of hope than expectation," he replied.

Vivienne sat on the bed. "Let me read the letter again."

He handed her the crumpled sheets. Then he went to the wardrobe and opened it. Some of Lizzie's clothes were hanging inside, impregnated with the faint smell of her perfume. The discovery at once reassured and confused him. His first thought was that, having left her clothes behind, she plainly intended to return. But then he reasoned that this logic was not without flaw, for she might as well have abandoned her possessions in the knowledge that, according to her intentions, she would have no further need of them and could see them only as an encumbrance.

Closing the wardrobe door, he turned to Vivienne. "She's left her clothes," he said.

She nodded vaguely. "What do you think she means by 'devastation'?"

"Do you really want to know? Do you really need to ask?"

"'I'll be gone by then'. What does that mean? Gone where?" She let the letter hang loosely in her hands, her eyes roaming the carpet. "Gone abroad? Or gone - somewhere else?"

He came back and slid open the top drawer of the dressing table. "There's underwear in here," he said.

"What's that?"

"Her underwear."

"No, there, on top of that information thing."

He picked up the envelope Vivienne had seen. It was sealed, and Miss Campbell's name was written on the front. His fingers shook slightly as he tore the flap. Inside was a cheque and a note on a small square of paper. 'Dear Miss Campbell', the note read, 'I am sorry to leave without giving you proper notice. Here is a blank cheque. Please fill in the amount for two nights, although I have only stayed one. Sorry about this. Elizabeth Lake.' The cheque was made out to Miss J Campbell, dated and signed. There was no address on the back.

Gavin turned, handing the envelope to Vivienne. "She's gone," he said, "she's not coming back."

He stood with his hands on his hips, regarding her despondently. She was toying with the envelope, seeming to avoid his gaze.

"What happened this morning?" she asked. "Did you have an argument?"

"Not exactly. I told her off for giving up her job."

"You didn't say she'd done that."

"Well, now you know."

Vivienne nodded gloomily, but she didn't seem surprised. "Anything else?"

"We didn't part on the best of terms. She said goodbye, but it was rather cold - sort of quietly desperate, really."

"I see. And now she's run off and left her belongings behind. Very strange, even by Lizzie's standards." She held out the envelope. "You'd better give this to the lady. What else is in the drawer?"

"Nothing. Maybe under her things."

"Well, go on, Gavin. You can fumble under her knickers, it'll be like old times."

He ignored the sarcasm. "Just a tourist office wallet." He passed it to her without interest.

Vivienne sat back on the bed and thumbed through the wallet. "Postcards and leaflets," she said, more thinking aloud than informing him.

"Such as?"

"Usual stuff. Two postcards of the island at sunset; something about the distillery; free tickets to a rabbit farm; harbour tide tables; leaflet from the cycle place; another one from - "

"Say that again."

"The cycle hire?"

"No, before that."

She shuffled the contents again. "Summer 2005. North Inchmurchan. Harbour Tide Tables." Her face was a sullen mask of incomprehension. "Is that what you want?"

"What I want, Vivienne, is to know why she would want it. What does she want with tide tables?"

"Search me. For the next boat, I suppose."

"Oh, come on, Vivienne. If you want to get off the island, you need a list of ferry schedules, not tide tables."

"Hmm. You could be right." She peered closely at the small print on the leaflet. "Look, she's put biro rings on this."

He snatched the leaflet and stared at it. "High and low tides. Shit, she's marked the tides!"

She stood up, confusion and alarm mingling on her face. "You think she's going to do something reckless, don't you?"

"It'll be reckless negligence if we don't get down there." He slammed the drawer shut and grabbed her arm. "Come on, now!"

They clattered down the thinly-carpeted stairs, past Janet Campbell standing sentinel in the dining room doorway.

"Did you find what you were looking for?" she asked, peevishly.

Gavin yelled over his shoulder. "No. Yes. In a hurry."

The landlady raised one eyebrow. "Aye, so I see."

A mainland ferry had just docked as they reached the harbour, and people were crowding the concrete causeway, eddying to and fro as they spilled into the road. Backpackers jostled fishermen, while ruddy-faced ornithologists with binoculars strung round their necks wove a path through faltering convoys of luggage trolleys towed by overdressed tourists wearing bewildered frowns. Close enough for the rush of air to startle the stragglers, a converging phalanx of cars and trucks roared up the slope as men in fluorescent jackets summoned them from the echoing bowels of the vessel.

Vivienne waved her arms in frustration. "We'll never find her in this mob," she shouted.

Gavin threw out his arm in a gesticulating arc. "Go round. There's a wooden jetty past the ship."

She screwed up her eyes as if in disbelief. "It doesn't look safe. The steps are all broken."

"Then wait here while I go."

"No, I'm coming with you."

"I'll go first. Take my hand."

A yellow-clad docker bawled at them as they clambered along the narrow walkway in the looming shadow of the ship's hull, but they ignored him and moved on with their heads down, pausing occasionally to take a longer stride across a gash in the woodwork where a plank was missing. Vivienne flinched and shuddered as the scarred black hulk of the anchored ferry wallowed in the current, graunching against the wooden pilings with the motion of the tide.

"We shouldn't be here," she said, timorously. "I hate places like this."

Through the gaps in the planking, sunlight danced on the swell, spinning golden webs that sparkled like jewellery in the green water.

They cleared the ship's bow and stumbled on to the weed-slippery beams of a disused jetty. Here, away from the fumes of the ferry's engines, the air was clearer and there was more room to move, but the rotting wood beneath their feet was wet and treacherous with years of accumulated slime. Gavin knew that it was madness for them to be staggering about out here, the sea surging below them, but it was too late to turn back now, he had to follow his instincts, to be sure one way or the other whether Lizzie had found her way to this deserted place.

He felt Vivienne tug fiercely at his hand. "Please, Gavin, let's go back. I'm scared. She's not here."

"We've not looked properly. I just feel this is - what she meant to do."

"If a big wave comes in, we'll be washed away." She cast around, hunched with fear at the sight of the open water either side of them, heaving and sucking at the barnacled timbers. "Gavin, it must be forty feet deep down there."

"We won't stay here a moment longer than we need. I just want to make sure. We've got to find her."

"Don't go any further out, please. While we're messing about here, she could be somewhere else, and we're wasting time."

He had let go of her hand to move ahead, and in the next instant he slipped on a metal plate obscured by weed, crashing to his hands and knees. For a few seconds he stayed there, kneeling on the splintered beams, staring down into the oil-green folds of the waves.

She was at his side, one hand on his back, clutching at his shirt. "It's all right. I won't let you go."

"This is crazy," he whispered, gulping for breath.

The wind rose, buffeting their ears.

"I'm sorry," he said, rising gingerly to his feet, "I shouldn't have brought you here. It's too dangerous. I'm being unfair."

190

"So what would you have me do? Wait back on the pavement, not knowing where you'd gone, not knowing if you'd fallen in and drowned? You think I care so little?"

"The wind's getting up," he said. "We could be blown off."

An aquamarine wave, trailing a dazzling mane of foam, tore into a thick stanchion ahead of them, showering salt spray over their feet. The old jetty trembled, as though sharing their trepidation, and the salt tang hanging in their nostrils seemed almost to presage the sea's discontent with its allotted place in the scheme of things, as if it might at any moment burst its unseen bonds and invade the air above.

Gavin stepped ahead of her again, his eyes following every spray-darkened angle and interstice of the crumbling woodwork. The wind roared in his ears, making a billowing flag of his hair.

"Go away! It's not safe. Just go!"

Vivienne stood twenty feet behind him, supporting herself against a broken wooden upright.

"What did you say?" he called to her.

"I can't hear you?" she cried.

"You shouted something."

"No. Come back!"

He turned and let the wind urge him towards her.

She held his collar, drawing his head down close to hers. "We have to go, Gavin. We can't stay here any longer. The sea's boiling."

"I wondered what you shouted, that's all. Before."

"Before? Before what?"

The cry came again. This time it was unmistakable. "Go away! It'll be too late!"

Vivienne clutched Gavin's arm, compressing the bone. "That wasn't me, Gavin. It wasn't me the first time."

"I know." He turned his head away, straining to hear any sound but the waves rushing beneath their feet.

"Why can't we see her, Gavin? I don't understand."

"Look for some steps." He had to shout now, for the wind was catching his voice and tossing it out over the sea. "She's got to be under us, under these beams."

"Gavin, she can't be. She'd be in the sea."

"I'm telling you - look!" He pointed off to the right, the one part of the staging they hadn't explored. "There's a gap there."

He took her hand and led her slowly across the broadest beams he could find, until they reached the other side of the jetty, where a rusting handrail, slick with spray, curved down to the first footing of a flight of storm-shattered steps. Vivienne let go of his hand and grabbed the rail. Her stomach ballooned with fear as she looked down and saw the sea churning below. When she turned back to speak to Gavin, he was crouching above the top step, craning his neck into the howling void beneath. The sea smashed past, plastering his face with salt foam. He could feel the whole frail structure shaking under the tide's relentless percussion. His misted eyes searched a dim green cavern where an avalanche thundered, hissing and spitting as it collided with weed-wrapped pillars.

"Gavin, come back! It's not worth it!"

But it was worth it. Yes. There, glowing in the gloom like a bright flower, he saw it. On the broken remains of a metal platform, perhaps ten feet above the water, a scarlet blob hovering in the murk.

"I can see her!" he yelled, lifting his head above the step, his eyes level with Vivienne's ankles. "I can see her red hat!"

A prism-shaped roller-coaster of jade-coloured water swept under the jetty, and Gavin watched, open-mouthed, as Lizzie scrambled from her seat on the platform and stood up on tiptoe, locking her arms around an upright, to let the huge wave pass. The water slapped angrily at her legs and roared on towards the shore.

At his back, Vivienne shouted hoarsely, but her words were lost in the tumult. He saw the broad beam, a pitted iron girder, which Lizzie must have used to climb across to her precarious perch, and he dragged himself on to it. He sat there, gathering his breath, eyes flicking desperately between the bedraggled girl, now seated once more on the metal plate, and the torrent rushing beneath his dangling feet.

She turned and looked at him, her neck thrust forward, stark white in the dim light. "Go back! You're mad! You'll fall off!"

"It's not me who's mad, Lizzie!"

He shuffled himself further along the bar, inching towards her. Lizzie stared at him, her mouth opening and closing, no sound emerging.

Something dug into his back, and he shuddered.

"Mum! Don't!"

Over his shoulder, he saw that Vivienne had slid on to the girder behind him, supporting herself like a pillion rider on a motorbike. Out of the corner of his mouth, hardly wanting to move in case he unbalanced both of them, he snarled at her in a frenzy of terror. "Go away! You'll get us killed!"

She leaned into him, yelling in his ear. "It's the only way, Gavin. I'm not going back till she does."

He swallowed, tasting the fear in his mouth, a sour paste that thickened his tongue. "Hold me," he said, "I'm going forward."

Lizzie sat motionless, staring out to sea through a tangle of ironwork and flailing weed. Gavin followed her gaze, out beyond the end of the jetty, where a patch of sunlight cast a luminous pool on the water. Another swollen wave rode in, quieter, less violent than the one which had threatened Lizzie on her perch, its silken green folds dappled with shafts of sunshine spilling down through the wooden spars above. The wind fluttered against their faces, sucked at their breath, then fell away to a whimper.

"The tide's turning," Gavin said, but Vivienne didn't hear him. They were close to Lizzie now, near enough to see the anxiety etched on her face and the salt-grit crusting her eyelids.

He steadied himself, both hands on the flat top of the girder, and called across to her. "Lizzie, what the hell do you think you're doing?"

"I'm sitting on this bit of tin."

"Don't piss me about!"

Vivienne grumbled in his ear, her chin working against his shoulder. "I can't believe this kid. What does she do for an encore? She's got us all stuck under the pier within inches of our lives, for Christ's sake!"

Lizzie removed her hat, mopped her face with it and put it on again. "If you could see yourselves," she said, shaking her head, "like two monkeys on a stick. You look ridiculous."

"No, Lizzie," Vivienne countered, "it's you who's ridiculous. Now I want you to climb off that thing and we can all go back and get dry before we catch pneumonia."

Lizzie swung her legs back and forth, staring sullenly at the roiling water under her feet. "Did you read my letter?"

"Of course we read your letter," Gavin answered. "That's why we're here."

"I meant it, you know. What I said." She pulled her hat off again and waited, waving it in front of her face, sensing the wind. "Here - catch!"

Gavin flung out one arm and caught the hat, gasping as he teetered on the brink of losing his balance.

"Very good, I'm impressed!" She clapped her hands in mock congratulation, and the slaps seemed to echo under the dripping rafters. "Does it still smell of me, Gavin?"

"I'm sure it does, Lizzie. But I want more than just your hat. Come back, please."

"You don't want me. I'll just be excess baggage. Now you've used me, I'm disposable."

"I never used you, Lizzie. Maybe it was the other way around, maybe you tried to be - "

"No! That's a lie! You're making me into something cheap. How can you do that?" She hoisted herself up, standing with her head almost touching the beams above. Turning to face him, she let out a low moan of helpless rage. "Can't do it, Gavin. Can't take it any more."

"Lizzie!"

Vivienne's piercing shriek drilled deep into his eardrum, as he saw Lizzie's body topple forward and plunge head-first into the water.

"Oh my God!" Vivienne gasped.

Gavin gripped the girder until his knuckles whitened, while Vivienne's hands, clenching and unclenching, rocked his shoulders. "Can she swim?" he shouted.

"Yes."

He stared at the water for a few seconds, a frozen instant that felt like hours. "I'm going in after her. Go back to the steps. Try and attract someone's attention."

"No, wait. She might - "

"What do you mean, wait? She's bloody killing herself!"

193

"I said wait!" She hugged him, her cheek sealed against his. "At school..."

"What?"

"Ninety seconds," she said, quietly. "She could swim underwater and hold her breath for ninety seconds."

"So what are we supposed to do? Sit here like lemons, waiting for her to pop up and surprise us? What if she doesn't do that, Vivienne? What if she stays down?" He wrestled himself free of her embrace. "Now you wait for me and I'll go in and - "

"No! Look!"

And her pointing finger tracked the outline of a shape looming below the surface, a dark ball rolling over, thrashing in a whirlpool of froth and bubbles. A blue-clad leg broke into the light, smacking the swell, and then with extraordinary swiftness, as if propelled from beneath, Lizzie's head burst through the green surge, her hair a livid black tangle, writhing like Medusa.

They stared at her, stunned into terrified silence.

Lizzie swept her hands through her hair, treading water. One arm flailed towards Gavin. "Pull me!"

"I can't, not here. Can you make it to the steps?"

She sneezed and spat in the water. "Think so."

A couple of sweeping overarm strokes, one final gliding kick, and she was clutching the wooden supports at the bottom of the steps, her back heaving as she fought for breath. Her head was in the sun, and water poured from her face.

Vivienne was first to reach her. "Come on," she said, coaxing her gently, "let's get you up in the warm. You go up ahead, and take your time. Gavin and I will catch you if you slip."

After the dank, menacing gloom of the weed-strewn vault beneath, the old weatherbeaten timbers on the top of the jetty, warmed by the strengthening sun, seemed strangely harmless, less forbidding than before. The wind had subsided to a feathery sigh, redolent of diesel oil and bird lime.

Gavin stood back while Vivienne made Lizzie sit down on the beams and knelt in front of her. Instantly, a pool of water spread around them, dripping through the gaps to the sea below. Lizzie looked pale and her teeth were chattering.

"We need to get you back to the hotel," Vivienne said, "get you out of these wet clothes."

Lizzie nodded, her eyes slack, unfocused.

"Let me look at you, love." She pulled up Lizzie's sleeves, turning her bared arms over, then leaning forward to inspect her neck and scalp. "Well, I can't see any injuries."

"I'm okay, Mum, really."

"What about your legs?"

"They're all right."

"You must be frozen."

"I'm cold. I'll be all right."

"You're sure now?"

"Yes. I saw a big fish down there. I mean, really big. I think it could have been a baby shark."

"So long as you're not hurt."

"You shouldn't do this. You shouldn't be nice to me." Tears welled in her eyes. "I'm - I'm such a mess."

"Never mind all that. We'll get it sorted. We're both here for you."

"I know."

When Gavin saw Vivienne reaching behind her, he began to step forward, believing that she beckoned him and expected his participation; but before he could move to her side, her arm swung back in a flashing arc, striking the side of Lizzie's face in a blow that resounded over the rasp of the waves.

He leapt at her in horror, but she caught the sudden movement in the corner of her eye, and lashed out, thumping him in the stomach. He bent over, gasping for breath. Doubled up in shock and pain, he saw Vivienne smash a second punch, left-handed, into Lizzie's other cheek, splitting the side of her lip.

She was on her feet now, rocking crazily, flapping her arms in front of her as though she no longer knew what to do with them. "You bitch!" she screamed, "You fucking bitch!"

Gavin staggered towards her, his eyes on Lizzie's huddled body, but she spun round, pushing him away with ferocious strength.

"Have you gone mad?" he yelled.

Vivienne towered over her cowering daughter. "You vile, selfish, mean-minded, cruel, heartless bitch!"

"Mum! Don't! You don't know what you're doing!"

"Oh believe me, Lizzie, I know exactly what I'm doing! I'm doing what I should have done a long time ago."

"I love you, Mum."

"I love you too, Lizzie." She was crying now, shaking her head wildly. "But I'll never forgive you for this - never."

A bead of blood trickled down Lizzie's chin, and Gavin sank to his knees before her, pulling a handkerchief from his pocket. Tilting her head with his fingers under her jaw, he carefully wiped away the blood and dried her eyes. A red weal flared beneath her left eye. The swelling on her right cheekbone looked ugly, the puffed flesh scored diagonally where Vivienne's wedding ring had cut it.

"No need for this," he snarled over his shoulder. Vivienne's shadow loomed across them. "You're a spiteful woman."

"I'm your wife, Gavin. Don't refer to me as a woman, like I'm a pile of clothing."

He took Lizzie's hand. "Can you stand up?"

She nodded. He put one arm around her as she rose unsteadily to her feet. Vivienne hung back, scowling, sucking her bruised knuckles.

"Walk with me," he said, and he hugged her tightly to his side, relishing the feel of her weight against him. "Come on, we'll run you a hot bath, make you a hot drink. We'll all go back to the hotel, and you can rest in a warm bed."

She stumbled along close beside him. "Can I go in your big bed?"

"Yes."

"Can I have a hot water bottle?"

"The hotel will have one."

"Will you be with me?"

"Course. We both will."

"Can I curl up in the middle, and you lie either side of me?"

He stopped, keeping one hand on Lizzie's arm, and waited for Vivienne to catch them up. "Well - I don't know, Lizzie. We'll have to see about that."

"Where's Mum?"

"She's right behind us. It's all right."

"No it's not. Do you think she hates me?"

"Of course she doesn't hate you. She loves you, she said so."

"Then why did she say those other things? She said such bad things, Gavin."

"Because you scared her. She was frightened of losing you. Sometimes, when people we love frighten us, that's a kind of hurt, and it makes us angry. That's all."

"That's all?"

"That's all."

"Have you still got my hat?"

"It's in my pocket. Do you want it?"

She shook her head, gazing ahead of her. Her right eye was half closed, sunk inside the lumpy swelling on her cheekbone. "He never cuddled me, you know, my dad."

"Maybe that's as well. What would it have done for your security?"

"When you're a child, security's just a sub-conscious thing," she said, with a shrug. "Like death."

"I don't think we should talk about death," he said.

She stopped and pointed. "My bike."

"What?"

"I had my bike. There. I chained it to that post, see."

Vivienne came up to join them. Her eyes were red from crying, and she twisted a tissue in her hands. She stood and waited, managing to look at neither of them.

Gavin asked himself what had been achieved here. If a life had been saved, there was surely a price to be paid in collateral damage. After Lizzie's letter and her antics under the jetty, Vivienne could be forgiven for losing faith in her daughter. Both before and after the incident, Gavin had seen in Vivienne something that unnerved him, a streak of resentment edged with malice, a festering aberration that sought to undermine the foundations of love. Vivienne would henceforth trust neither of them; the letter had seen to that. And what of Lizzie? Lizzie hung on his arm now, and if she trusted him, as a father or as a friend, the bond was effectively valueless, unencashable, because Gavin knew in the deepest recesses of his heart that he could not trust himself in her company. When so much trust had been squandered, all that remained were the sad fragments of too many small deaths.

They waited while Lizzie unlocked the bike. Grunting, she swung her leg over and dragged herself upright, standing with her feet flat on the ground, the frame balanced between her thighs.

"What are you doing?" Gavin asked her.

"What's it look like?"

"You can't ride it now," he said. "Push it and walk with us."

"It's easier if I ride it."

"I think you're crazy."

"Yeah, we established that a long time ago."

"Let her do what she wants," Vivienne interjected. "Don't let's have an argument."

He glanced at her quickly. "Who's arguing?"

Lizzie was peering around, searching the ground. "Someone's nicked my helmet."

"Then walk with us, it's safer," he urged her.

"It was over the handlebars. Thieving bastards!"

"We'll get you another one," he said. "At least they didn't take the bike."

She hoisted herself on to the saddle and flexed her arms against the hand-grips.

"Lizzie, please."

"What?"

He sighed. "Nothing. Forget it. Wait for us outside. Sit on the wall."

Dipping forward, she leaned into the pedals, rode a yard or two, braked and stopped. She turned and gave him a penetrating stare that seemed to knife through him. "I love you," she said, sternly.

He nodded and waved.

Vivienne took his hand and held it lightly as they climbed the slope towards the road. Growing smaller ahead of them, Lizzie was standing on the pedals, pumping hard as she worked against the incline, weaving artfully around strolling pedestrians. Gavin reached in his pocket and felt the red hat, teasing it between his fingers like a comforter.

It was that quiet, vaguely somnolent time in the afternoon, when lunch was over and people had gone indoors or returned to work. The waiting ferry would not depart until evening, and the next ship to arrive, steaming in from the outer islands, was an hour away. The street was practically deserted, as it so often was at this hour of the day. It was just a space filled with pellucid sunshine and the faint smell of fish.

So, in a way, no-one could have blamed Douglas Lachlan. Sometimes you don't get a chance not to do something. As though, perhaps, there's a script, and it's all been written down beforehand, and you just have to act it out, without knowing exactly what's going to happen.

Douglas was on time with his deliveries, so he wasn't going fast. He had just off-loaded gas bottles at the hotel and was coming down a side street, making for his next drop, the Royal Huntsman Distillery. He had two more deliveries after that, then he would have an empty lorry and could go home. He could have been doing thirty, no more. The junction where the side road turned on to the harbour front was more a bend than a corner, and there was an open view both ways, so he dabbed the brakes, checked that his exit was clear and accelerated along the promenade. The mainland ferry was in, and Douglas glanced at it, wondering idly who might be polluting the island peace today.

Gavin saw the blue cab roof slicing into view from behind a huddle of harbour offices. Then he saw the bike, Lizzie still standing on the pedals, head down, breasting the rise at the top of the ramp.

Vivienne yelped in shock as he squeezed her hand, his mouth agape.

Douglas Lachlan never even noticed the ferry ramp today, never thought about it. There was no-one around. It was a quiet afternoon. Soon he could go home. They were having fresh salmon for supper with buttered new potatoes.

A huge metal insect filled his windscreen, shattering the glass.

Gavin crammed a fist into his mouth and bit hard. Vivienne screamed.

The bike bounced into the road and spun sideways into the gutter, the back wheel rotating, the front buckled like a lariat freeze-framed in the air.

They met Douglas staggering from his cab, clawing his face. Chunks of glass glinted in his hair, studded his clothing.

She lay in the gutter beyond the mangled bike. Her face was pressed against a kerbstone, the pressure flattening her nose.

There was blood on Douglas' face. "Help me," he pleaded, his voice cracking. "Please help me."

Gavin knelt down and, taking Lizzie's head in both hands, gently eased her face away from the kerb. Her eyes were closed, but the bruises distorting her features appeared merely to be those inflicted by Vivienne on the jetty. His relief at the apparent absence of injury was short-lived, for as he drew back he saw the blood on his right hand, and knew that it had come from the back of her skull.

Vivienne crouched at his side, her fingers tousling Lizzie's hair.

A grey-haired man, yellow-jacketed, loomed over them. "I've rung for an ambulance." He reached down and touched Lizzie's cheek with grubby fingers. "Oh, you poor wee girl."

Between the bike and his lorry, Douglas sat on the kerb with his head in his hands, rocking slowly back and forwards. The man in yellow moved along and spoke to him. "I couldn't help it," Douglas said. "I didn't see her. I just didn't see her."

Gavin applied two fingers to the side of Lizzie's neck, and waited, averting his eyes. "Nothing," he murmured. He lifted her arm and placed the wrist over her thigh.

"We oughtn't to move her," said Vivienne.

"I'm not. I just want her to be - comfortable."

The man in the jacket was back. He stared at the crumpled body. "Wha's wrong with her leg?"

"Don't touch her," Vivienne said.

Gavin moved back. Blood stained his knees. He looked at Lizzie's folded left leg. It seemed to be hanging oddly, bowing away from her hip. With a shaking hand, he probed beneath her lower thigh, and he felt the warm, thick ooze of the blood that coursed out of her, already congealing in the gutter. There was a space there, a dark void, a ravaged emptiness.

A few feet away, Douglas Lachlan squealed in despair, his sorrow subsiding to a low moan.

A hand rested on Gavin's shoulder. The yellow wing of the man's jacket flapped in his face. "There's - uh - something you should see," he said, quietly.

Gavin looked up, squinting in the light. "What is it? I want to stay with my daughter."

"Needn't take long," the man said. He turned, beckoning Gavin over to the lorry. He pointed under the front wheels. "First I thought it was part of her bike. Now I'm not so sure."

Gavin crouched by the cab step, peering into the shadow. Wrapped in dark blue cloth lay a long rod, leaking oil. Stretching out his hand, he grasped the torn end of the cloth and pulled the object into the light. Then he let go.

Vivienne was weeping, stroking Lizzie's face. She looked up as Gavin approached. "Where's that ambulance?" she whimpered.

"Under the lorry, Vivienne."

"Mm? What?"

"Under the lorry cab. Lizzie's leg."

An irritable frown creased her face. "What are you talking about?"

"Put your hand under her leg." He turned away, tears clouding his vision. "You'll see what I'm talking about."

He walked over to the driver's side and sat next to him. Douglas was hunched over, one hand covering his eyes. "I couldn't avoid her," he said. "She came out of nowhere. She was amazing."

Gavin nodded. "I know. That's how I met her. She came flying out of nowhere."

The abandoned lorry shuddered at the roadside, standing askew where Douglas had left it. Black skid-marks imprinted the tarmac behind the rear wheels.

"Better switch your engine off," Gavin said, his voice a monotone drone.

"You can do it."

He lunged into the cab, turned the key and brought it back to the driver.

"And - who are you?" the man asked, shaking his head, dropping the key in his shirt pocket.

"I'm her stepfather."

Douglas lowered his hand and gazed at Gavin out of wide, tear-reddened eyes. "I am so sorry," he whispered. "I am so very sorry."

Gavin clutched at the man's shoulder, kneading the flesh.

"What will happen to me?" Douglas asked. "Will they lock me up, do you think?"

"I don't know. I can't think about that right now."

"I couldn't help it, you see." He was shielding his eyes again. The tears seeped through his fingers.

"I believe you. I understand."

"What's her name?"

"Lizzie."

"Lizzie. That's a nice name."

"Yes."

"Will they make her better, do you think?"

"I don't think so." He reached for Douglas' arm. "I have to go now. I should be with her."

"Of course. Thank you."

Vivienne had eased Lizzie's leg aside. The sun lay horribly white on the splintered stump of bone protruding from her hip. Creeping slowly along the gutter was a ruby-coloured chute of blood, dense as molten glass.

"Lights on the hill," Vivienne said, hardly moving her lips, eyes glazed like someone in a trance.

The scene seemed to recede from his vision then, as though he saw it through the wrong end of a telescope. As in a stylistically edited film - swift changes of focus, the sound cut down - he watched in the role of a bystanding extra, while the ambulance swung across his sight-line and a uniformed man and woman paced back and forth, gathering equipment, their gait purposeful but not urgent, for by now there was no urgency, no reason to infuse the situation with irrational drama. What they did would be clinical, quietly constructive, achingly respectful.

What struck him most poignantly, as he played the film over and over in his mind afterwards, was the lack of sound, a whispering, almost reverential silence. Then, too, he remembered the colours. He could see the cerulean blue of the sky and the silver of the sun on the sea. Overhead, persistent as vultures, the gulls wheeled, flaunting their snow-white breasts, opening their beaks with no noise. The paramedics' overalls were green and yellow flags waved in his face above the stark red river that stained his shoes and daubed his hands with darkening scars of resinous rust. He saw the brown-broth gush of the lorry driver's vomit, splattering the road, as they retrieved the grim trophy of Lizzie's leg and carried it solemnly to the ambulance. In his hands glowed the fierce scarlet of her woollen hat, and he pressed it to his face, inhaling her scent, and wept for her.

It was October and the leaves were crunching under our feet, and he looked up all squinty-eyed and said, "Look, Lizzie, it's all the trees are crying." Well, okay, I don't want to be like those weeping trees when the sad time comes. I'll be gone by then.

He kept the letter, of course. For a while, for a fortnight or more, he carried it with him, folded and warmly crumpled, in his pocket. It became a kind of poultice on the pain. Later, he transferred the paper-clipped pages to a flat cardboard box which he kept in the bottom of his chest of drawers, a box in which also nestled Lizzie's red hat. The hat would always smell of her, he was sure of that. The conditioner she used on her hair; the perfume she wore; the slow, accumulated impregnation of her perspiration: these intermingled aromas both saddened and aroused him. They *were* Lizzie. Sometimes, in the room alone, or even late at night, while Vivienne lay asleep, he would take out the box, slip off the lid and inhale her scent, a fruit-musk infusion, a cushion for the sharp edges of memory.

There was something else he remembered. From the platform of the ambulance, as he paused to speak to the lorry driver and the police officer accompanying him, he happened to glance up to the crest of the hill behind the town, the hill where Douglas Lachlan had glimpsed the harbour moments before his life changed for ever, and an evening breeze off the bay was threshing the leaves of the sycamores that stood in a green grove beside the road. In the flattened sunlight, the spangling foliage shone silver against the blue parchment of the sky, a million coins cascading. In the autumn, when the leaves were turning and the trees wept their golden rain, there would be a mist over the water, like a muslin shawl, and the dark shadows of distant boats hooting mournfully, riding with the grey whales of the mountains.

Along the fish-fumed street, the people would pass, smiling amiably out of short memories. The blood would be gone from the kerbside, the nuggets of glass swept away. The geography of death is transient and meaningless. Suddenly there is simply nothing there any more.

Gavin Lake knew that Lizzie was not gone from him, because he carried her spirit inside him, and he would not let her escape. He had invented his own geography.

It was a land of plenty.

It was amazing.

Printed in the United Kingdom
by Lightning Source UK Ltd.
114955UKS00001B/305

9 781846 853999